Deception

International bestselling author Lesley Pearse has lived a life as rich with incidents, setbacks and joys as any found in her novels.

Resourceful, determined and willing to have a go at almost anything, Lesley left home at sixteen. By the mid sixties she was living in London, sharing flats, partying hard and married to a trumpet player in a jazz-rock band. She has also worked as a nanny and Playboy bunny, and designed and made clothes to sell to boutiques.

It was only after having three daughters that Lesley began to write. The hardships, traumas, close friends and lovers from those early years were inspiration for her beloved novels. She published her first book at forty-nine and has not looked back since.

Lesley is still a party girl.

Find out more about Lesley and keep
Up to date with what she's been doing:

Follow her on Twitter
@LesleyPearse

Sign up for her newsletter
www.lesleypearse.com

Deception

LESLEY PEARSE

MICHAEL JOSEPH

PENGUIN MICHAEL JOSEPH

UK | USA | Canada | Ireland | Australia
India | New Zealand | South Africa

Penguin Michael Joseph is part of the Penguin Random House group of companies
whose addresses can be found at global.penguinrandomhouse.com

First published 2022
001

Copyright © Lesley Pearse, 2022

The moral right of the author has been asserted

Set in 15.5/18pt Garamond MT Std
Typeset by Jouve (UK), Milton Keynes
Printed and bound in Great Britain by Clays Ltd, Elcograf S.p.A.

The authorized representative in the EEA is Penguin Random House Ireland,
Morrison Chambers, 32 Nassau Street, Dublin D02 YH68

A CIP catalogue record for this book is available from the British Library

HARDBACK ISBN: 978–0–241–54493–8
TRADE PAPERBACK ISBN: 978–0–241–54494–5

www.greenpenguin.co.uk

I find it astounding that this is my thirtieth book. I was just finishing it as the war in Ukraine broke out, and I, horrified that Russia believes it has a right to wage war on a far smaller country and to create such terrible carnage and devastation. My heart goes out to all those millions of people who have been forced to flee their homes, to brave cold, hunger and terrible fear for both themselves and their loved ones. I pray that President Putin will comes to his senses, or find his heart and stop this madness and cruelty.

I would like to applaud all those who have given the refugees shelter, food and clothing; all the charities who have pulled out all the stops to help in any way they can. Also, all those who have given donations of money, often more than they can really afford. Bless you all.

I

Spring 2015

Alice Kent turned up the volume on her car radio as Eric Clapton, playing her favourite number, 'Layla', came on.

She was speeding down from Bristol to her mother's funeral in Totnes and she was late, delayed by wafflers at the meeting this morning. Now she'd have to go straight to the church in Dartington instead of meeting up with her family first. As that would give her enough time not to be late for the service, she relaxed a little and sang along with Eric.

Her mother, Sally Kent, had died of cancer ten days earlier. Alice had taken leave from work so she could nurse her mother for her last weeks and, sad as it was for her mother to die relatively young at seventy-five, Alice knew she was glad to go.

'I've had a good life,' she said one morning, as Alice was brushing her hair. 'A wonderful husband, the two best daughters any mother would want, and three grandchildren. But it's time for me to go now,

Alice. I don't like being in pain, or people taking care of me. I just want peace.'

As much as she was going to miss her mother, and she felt as if her heart was being pulled out, Alice understood it was for the best. She knew it had been agony for her once ebullient, active mother to lie in bed, and know she was never going to get any better. She just hoped her sister, Emily, and her father, Ralph, could see it that way.

Alice was thirty-five, tall, slender and dark-haired. She always thought of herself as single, rather than divorced: her marriage at twenty-one had been a travesty she didn't care to dwell on. Friends always remarked on her being so capable, and while she knew that was true, that she could handle anything thrown at her, she wasn't sure she wanted to be described as such. To her it suggested plodding, dull and unimaginative.

Now and again she analysed herself. Was her inability to fall head over heels in love an indication of dullness? There had been several lengthy relationships since she'd left her husband, but not once had she ever felt she could die for a man. Now she'd come to the conclusion she wasn't cut out for permanence, which was perhaps just as well as she could never say when exactly she'd be home.

She loved her small flat in Bristol's Clifton village, and she had many friends of both sexes. Mostly she felt she had everything a girl could want. But deep down she still hoped for the love affair that would turn her life upside-down.

As she came off the A38 at the Dartington and Totnes turn-off, she glanced into her mirror. There, almost hanging on to her bumper, she saw a black Jaguar with a male driver.

When people tailgated her she always wished she had a pop-up neon sign in the back window, saying, 'Get back, arsehole', to flash at them.

She slowed down, pulling as far to the left as she could to let him pass her. The road ahead soon became narrow and winding with many overhanging trees, and she wanted him gone instead of annoying her for the rest of the journey to the church. But he didn't pass her: he stayed right on her tail.

As she approached St Mary's she realized she had at least fifteen minutes before she needed to be there, so she drove on past, into Dartington, negotiated a roundabout at speed and pulled up on the forecourt of a shop.

Looking behind, she saw she'd lost him. He must have gone straight on into Totnes.

Rather pleased with herself, she drove slowly back to the church. The sun had come out on the drive down from Bristol, and it had been good to see lambs in the fields and primroses on some of the grass verges. It had seemed a very long winter, made worse by the knowledge that her mother was dying. But it was good that the sun chose to shine today, bringing back memories of Sunday school at St Mary's with Emily, the Christmas and Easter services with their parents.

In the last two years her mother and father had started to attend church every Sunday. She and Emily had wondered why – they had never seemed particularly religious before. Maybe it was because of the cancer: perhaps their mum had hoped that having a word with the Almighty each week would help.

There were at least twenty vehicles in the car park already, and a few people smiled at her, but Alice didn't stop to speak to anyone. She went straight up to the church to await the hearse and her family. Standing in the spring sunshine, looking out across fields, she felt at peace for the first time in weeks. She knew that the service, the hymns and the vicar speaking of her mother would make her cry, and it would be hard to watch her father and Emily grieving too, but she was focusing on her mother's last request: 'Be glad for me that it's almost over, Alice. I've had my life. Get on with your own now, and tell Ralph and Emily to do the same.'

The hearse approached, and the remaining people outside the church scuttled inside. The doors of the second car opened and her family spilled out.

Dad looked teary-eyed, as did Emily, whose three

children, Ruby, Jasmine and Toby, bounded up to Alice.

'We were worried about you,' Ruby said. Alice and Emily had recently nicknamed her Miss Sensible: although she was only ten she was motherly and very bossy.

'I was afraid if I came out to the house, you might have left already,' Alice said, taking the hands of Ruby and Jasmine to get them to follow the pall bearers into the church. She kissed her father, and left Mike, her brother-in-law, to go in with him, Toby and Emily.

The service was sad, but at the same time uplifting. Some of Sally's friends had decorated the church with an abundance of flowers, and it looked so pretty with sunlight streaming through the stained-glass windows. Each of the pew ends had a posy of spring flowers pinned to it, more like a wedding than a funeral.

The Reverend Henry Dawes had known Sally well and managed to bring a little humour into his eulogy by speaking of Sally's enthusiasm for jumble sales. He reminded them of when she'd put on an old lady's pink corset over her clothes, and a fancy but battered hat, then kept them on for the whole day.

Sally had chosen a poem to be read, and asked that Mike read it, as she knew that neither Ralph nor

Alice nor Emily would get through it without crying. It began:

Weep not for me though I have gone.
Grieve if you will, but not for long.

It was typical of their mother that she wanted them to celebrate her life rather than mourn. In fact, in the past she'd often joked that she wanted Queen's 'Killer Queen' played at her funeral. They'd laughed with her about it, but once they were planning the service it didn't seem right.

Alice glanced sideways at her father several times, but though his lower lip quivered, he was holding it together, as was Emily. The interment would be the testing time. Alice didn't like the idea of burials, but her mother had been saying for years that that was what she wanted, so it had to be done. Alice and Emily had dressed her themselves in the coral-coloured kaftan Sally had loved, and fixed two glittery hair slides in her platinum-blonde wig. Both daughters had wanted to keep her wig, but they knew that Sally would have been furious if they didn't put it on her, with full makeup and nail varnish that matched the kaftan. As she would have said, 'One has to keep up standards.'

She had looked beautiful in her simple white coffin but, then, she'd been a beauty as a young woman. Even age and cancer couldn't destroy that.

The interment was more painful than the service. Alice was all too aware of the horror on the grandchildren's faces when they saw the deep hole in the ground and realized that was where their beloved granny was bound.

For Alice it was the finality that was shocking. She'd never hear her mum's pealing laugh again, never feel the warmth of her hugs. They hadn't seen eye to eye very often – in fact they'd had some terrible rows – but they had loved one another.

It was only once the roses had been dropped into the grave, the last prayer said and people had started to move away that Alice noticed the tall, thin man with a deep tan. She knew instinctively he was the driver of the Jaguar earlier, although she'd only seen him in her rear-view mirror.

He was looking right at her too, and she nudged Emily to ask if she knew who he was.

'I've never seen him before,' Emily whispered back. 'But Mum knew all kinds of odd bods – she never gave up on flirting.'

Alice smiled. It was quite true: Sally had been a flirt, and could persuade men to do anything for her, from checking the tyre pressures on her car to carrying her shopping. She once said she couldn't understand why any woman would want to work for a living when she could marry a man who would keep her at home in style.

Alice was the regional manager of a group of hotels and worked long hours. She had immense responsibility but she rarely got any acknowledgement for all she did. Her male counterparts, however, were treated as if they could walk on water. Sometimes it even crossed her mind that a life like her mother's, just being the little woman at home, able to go out for girly lunches and shopping trips when she fancied them, might be very pleasant.

'Dad, do you know who that dark, thin man is?' she asked, nodding towards the man. 'He was driving right on my tail earlier today.'

'Never seen him before. Just one of your mother's admirers, I expect,' he said, with a faint smile. 'Go and ask him, Alice. You're allowed to do that at funerals, and if he is an admirer you'd better ask him back to the house.'

Alice approached the man. 'Hello . . . I wondered where you fitted into my mum's life.'

'We were friends years ago,' he said. 'I was down here on business last week and saw the obituary in the local paper. I just wanted to pay my respects and perhaps have a chat with you and your sister.'

'Come along to the house, then,' she said. 'We'd love to talk to you about our mum.'

'I feel that would be an imposition,' he said. 'But could you both meet me for lunch tomorrow at the Seven Stars?'

Alice took that to mean he was an old flame, and was being respectful to her father. 'I can come,' she said. 'I'm not sure Emily can, though. She has three children. What time?'

'Would one thirty be okay?'

'Fine, I'll see you there. I must go now, though. My father needs me.'

'How odd,' Emily remarked. They had been back at the house for nearly two hours and between pouring drinks, passing round food and chatting to people, Alice hadn't had a moment until now to tell her sister about the man in the churchyard.

'I forgot to ask his name,' Alice admitted. 'But do come, Em. I'm dying to know how he fits into Mum's past.'

'I can't. I've got loads of stuff to do, though I'm really intrigued. I was only thinking just now that there isn't one person here today from before her marriage to Dad. When I went through her address book to inform people, there wasn't anyone I didn't know – or, at least, no one I hadn't heard Mum mention.'

Alice frowned. Now she came to think of it, their mother had never talked about her life before she'd met their father. She would have been well over thirty when she married him – how odd she didn't mention those earlier years.

2

Alice, 2015

The following morning at eleven thirty, Alice opened the door to Emily. She had only just finished clearing up after the wake. Emily and her family had gone home at about ten, but Alice and Ralph had had a few more drinks and listened to music Sally had loved. Now Alice was intending to do a little shopping before she met the mysterious stranger.

'Have you changed your mind about coming with me to the lunch, Em?' She doubted that was the case as her sister was wearing an ancient baggy sweatshirt and torn jeans. Her hair didn't look brushed either: she'd just caught it up on top of her head with a clip. She'd always been a scruffy girl so it had been amazing to see her in a suit for the funeral.

'Do I look like I'm going out to lunch?' Emily laughed. 'I've got a zillion things to do, as I said yesterday. I only popped round to see if Dad wanted anything as I'm going to Morrisons. You can tell me about this chap later.'

Their father was coming down the stairs. He said

hello to Emily and added that he didn't need anything. 'There's enough leftovers to keep me going for
several days.'

'I'm meeting someone for lunch, Dad,' Alice
informed him. 'Is it all right if I leave my car on the
drive? Then I'll go straight back to Bristol.'

Ralph's best suit was back in the wardrobe, and
today he was ready for gardening in cords and a
much-darned old blue sweater. For a man of seventy
he looked good, especially considering what he'd
been through recently. Tall, fit, thick greying hair,
and the kind of rugged face anyone would love. She
was happy to see the gardening clothes: they meant
he had no intention of moping indoors while the sun
was shining.

'Aren't you going with Alice?' he asked Emily.

'No, I'm not. Too much to do at home.'

'I was so proud of you two yesterday,' he said, with
a smile. 'But as lovely as you both are, I'm welcoming
some time alone now. If anyone else asks me how
I'm holding up, I might scream! I'm off to potter in
the garden and enjoy the silence.'

Both girls knew he meant what he said. He was
what some people called a 'new man'. From an early
age they'd watched him pick up the reins when their
mum went off on cookery, pottery, yoga and goodness
knew what other courses. He could change a nappy,
soothe a squawking baby and cook remarkably good

meals, which was just as well because when Sally wanted to do something more than be a homemaker, she just disappeared.

Throughout her sickness he'd done practically all the chores, and never a word of complaint. He was also happy in his own company, often joking that he met a better class of person then.

'Okay, Dad,' Emily said, and planted a kiss on his cheek. 'If you start to feel like Billy No-mates, just shout and I'll come over – or come to us anytime.'

Ralph agreed and disappeared out of the back door. Emily hugged Alice tightly. 'Let me know how this lunch goes,' she said. 'And remember, no SGD.'

Alice laughed. SGD stood for Sadness, Guilt and Duty, the trio that often came along with the death of a relative. They had made a pact that they wouldn't give in to any of it.

'We both did our duty in the past weeks,' Emily reminded Alice. 'Mum was always good at burdening us with guilt, so I'm not wasting any more on her. Maybe a little sadness, though – at least for appearances' sake.'

Alice hugged her younger sister tightly. It was good that neither Emily nor their father was making out that Sally had been a saint: there had been times when all three had been astounded by her selfishness, callousness and her indomitable assurance that she was always right. When close relatives died people often tended to turn them into saints.

'You have fun with the handsome stranger,' Emily said, as she opened her car door. 'Just make sure you tell me all. It will be interesting to hear his memories of Mum. You know I never trusted her completely?'

'You didn't?' Alice was shocked.

'No. She avoided all leading questions. She fudged anything that happened before we were born. She told me she didn't even remember when she first came to Totnes, or why she had only one photo of her and Dad's wedding. Most women love to talk about their wedding, even if it wasn't all they'd hoped for. I think theirs must have been a quick register-office job. But why couldn't she admit that?'

'You're making something out of nothing, Em.' Alice laughed. 'Yes, it probably was a quick wedding with no trimmings. Perhaps she was pregnant with me, and back then people were funny about that. Although I've never seen their marriage certificate, have you?'

Emily shook her head. 'Finding Mum had lied about her age wasn't really a surprise, and I've got a feeling there might be a great many more.'

'Go on with you.' Alice sniggered. She had found it funny that their mother had knocked four years off her age. 'Once I turn forty, I'm going to lie about my age too. Give my love to the kids and tell them I'll be down again soon.'

She waved from the gate until Emily had driven away, then turned to look behind her at the spacious Georgian house, over two hundred years old, in the Bridgetown area of Totnes. Ralph had been born in it, and it had passed to him after the death of his parents. Apart from a new modern kitchen and an extra bathroom, it was virtually in its original state, attractive and quirky. As a young girl she had liked to curl up on one of the deep window seats at the front of the house to read and watch people going past. She knew her father would never go into sheltered housing: he was fiercely independent and deeply suspicious of all things that were supposed to help seniors.

Alice went back into the house and, through the French windows in the sitting room, she could see her father pulling out weeds from a border. Just the way he moved told her he was happy to be alone, with no more calls from upstairs to fetch this or that and no one asking him what he was doing. He'd had a hard time when Sally had become sick: she had treated him like a slave. Sometimes he looked dead on his feet, and she'd snap at him if he didn't get whatever she wanted quickly enough.

Alice made him some coffee and cut him a slice of chocolate cake a neighbour had made and took it outside to him. 'I'm going out now, Dad. I'll be back to collect my car, but I won't come in and disturb you. Put your feet up later, have a snooze. I'll ring you tomorrow to see how things are.' She put the coffee and cake on the table by the garden bench, then went over to hug him. 'Love you, Dad,' she said, into his neck, as they embraced. 'You look after yourself now and rest a bit. I'll come down again as soon as I can.'

He caught hold of her forearms. 'You've done more than enough for me recently. I can cope alone, Alice. I don't want you turning into a mother hen.'

Alice looked into his soft brown eyes and her heart melted. She knew she was lucky to have such a good father. He'd never let her down. He'd always been there at school open evenings, sports days, plays and concerts. He had always welcomed her friends, helped with homework, and didn't lecture her when she left her husband, despite the amount he'd spent on the wedding. In fact, he came up to Bristol when she moved into her flat, bringing his own camp bed with him, so he could help her decorate and build some shelves. He didn't believe in recriminations. In his view a little talk about a problem always solved it.

'There's as much chance of me being a mother hen as there is of me being a Hollywood actress.' She laughed. 'Now I must be off. There's a few shops I want to check out before lunch.'

*

Alice loved Totnes, but it wasn't until she moved to Bristol that she realized how much she liked the city's alternative vibe, the many wacky people who lived here, and the fascinating outlets that sold everything from handmade shoes in brilliant colours, to strange artwork and hippie-style clothes alongside quaintly old-fashioned shops that had been there for ever. The shops in Clifton were quirky too, but in a more sophisticated way. Alice felt that Totnes was a far more honest town.

She bought a framed print of a piece of cherry pie and custard for her kitchen, and an interesting patchwork jacket, which was half the price it would have been in Clifton. Then she made her way back down the hill to the Seven Stars.

The dark stranger was sitting at a table tucked into a corner. He rose to greet her and introduced himself as Angus Tweedy. 'I was remiss not to give you my name yesterday,' he said, as he shook her hand, 'but it was all a bit rushed.'

He got her a gin and tonic, and then they ordered food, a prawn salad for Alice, steak and kidney pie for Angus.

Alice noted he was well spoken, no discernible regional accent, and he was fastidious: he wore a fresh-looking pink and white striped shirt and a well-cut grey suit. His black shoes were highly polished, and looked expensive.

'I like to eat well at lunch,' he said. 'Much better for the digestion than overloading it in the evening. Your mother never ate much. I often thought that was why she was such a butterfly brain.'

'What do you mean by that?' Alice said indignantly.

'Oh, come now.' He laughed. 'I'm sure age hadn't changed her. She could flit from one subject to another, one theory to the next in the blink of any eye.'

Alice didn't want to admit it, but it was true. So many times she had tried to have a serious conversation with her mother, and she'd turn it into something else. It was also true she didn't eat much. But, then, she was vain and wanted to keep slim.

'Okay, maybe,' Alice said. 'So, tell me, Angus, what do you do for a living, or are you retired now?'

'I retired a year ago. I had a plant nursery. I specialized in exotic trees, tree ferns, olives and the like, but lifting heavy trees is a young man's game, so I sold my business. I thought I'd miss travelling to Italy and Spain for plants – I made a lot of friends in the trade – but I'm enjoying having no more anxiety and the freedom to do whatever when the mood takes me. I like fishing and long walks.'

The waitress brought their food, which looked very good.

'So where do you live?' Alice asked.

'In Wales, near Monmouth.'

Alice felt they'd pussyfooted around long enough. 'So why don't you get on with what you wanted to tell me? I assume you have an agenda.'

'Yes, I have,' he said gravely. 'Though I would've liked more time to get to know you before I charge into it.'

'Well, I'm sorry, Angus, but time is something I'm short of,' Alice said. 'I've got to get back to Bristol this afternoon. So fire away. As I don't know you, I doubt you can say anything to upset me.'

'I think I can. You see, you are my daughter.'

Alice froze with her glass halfway to her mouth. 'Don't be ridiculous,' she said sharply, after a few moments. 'What a very stupid thing to claim!'

'I wish I could say I was joking,' Angus said, 'but in 1980 I married your mother when you were on the way. Emily came two years later. The following year, I was convicted of bigamy and sentenced to seven years' imprisonment.'

For a moment or two Alice was too shocked by this bombshell to respond. The room seemed to spin and she felt cold, then hot. Surely this couldn't be true.

'You married our mum when you were already married?' she asked eventually, after the room had stopped moving, and her brain said she must have misheard what he'd said. 'Tell me you're joking. Though it's in very poor taste.'

'No joke, not for anyone,' he said dolefully. 'The absolute truth. But should you wish to look it up on the internet you will find at the time of my trial I had two daughters, Alice aged three, and Emily one, and had married Fleur Faraday three and a half years earlier, though her real name was Janet Masters. You are my daughters.'

'Our mother was never called Fleur,' Alice said. 'You've got your wires crossed.'

'She'd abandoned her real name, Janet Masters, by the time she was sixteen, in favour of Fleur Faraday. She became Helen Tweedy on our marriage. You and Emily were Tweedys, of course. As soon as I was arrested, even before I was convicted, she changed her name again to Sally Symonds. Later, after her marriage to Ralph Kent, she became Sally Kent, and he legally adopted you two so you are now Kents.'

The shock of what he had said faded and was replaced with confusion and anger. 'You bastard,' she hissed at him. 'Even if this is true, what sort of man would pick the day after my mother's funeral to tell me? What planet are you on? Did you imagine I'd fall at your feet and call you Daddy?'

She leaped up, making the table rock. 'I'm going. Don't even think of following me.'

'Sit down,' he said quietly. 'Why would I tell anyone something as shameful as being a bigamist if it wasn't true?'

'Because you're a sick bastard,' she snapped. But what he'd said, however strange, had the ring of truth, so she perched on the edge of her seat as if ready for flight. She didn't think she could eat a thing. 'Okay, we can check that out. But why would you come to Mum's funeral and try to see us, if it wasn't just to make mischief?'

'Make mischief? All I've done is told the truth. I doubt Fleur even told the man you call your father the truth about herself. She was the Queen of Lies. So plausible, too. But I didn't come here to try to destroy your image of your mother. I'm glad she found a good man to take care of you and Emily. But I felt you should know the truth.'

'Why tell us now?' Alice asked. 'Why not ten years ago, or keep quiet for ever? Are you hoping we might desert Ralph just when he needs us most? What sick game are you playing?'

At that he looked hurt and sad, but Alice didn't care.

'There is no game. I believe that you will both become better people from knowing the truth about me and your mother. I didn't attempt to tell you before because I knew she would go on the attack, hurt her husband and you two girls. That was what she always did when cornered. I admit I was a weak fool to marry two women.'

'So why the hell did you do it?' Alice interrupted.

20

'You seem intelligent enough. You must have known you could be found out.'

'I often ask myself that question, but Fleur was very forceful, and she wanted the security of marriage when she learned you were on the way. She knew I was married. I didn't deceive her. All her problems stemmed from lack of security when she was a small child.'

Silence fell. Alice picked up her knife and fork again because Angus was eating his lunch as calmly as if nothing shocking had been said. It was surreal. Like some sort of dream that didn't make sense. She began to eat.

'But what about your true wife?' she asked, after a few minutes. 'Didn't her feelings count? Did you have children together?'

'Yes, we have a son. I was a representative for a china and glass company back then, and I had to travel from Wales to London a lot, which was where I met Fleur. I didn't set out to be unfaithful to my wife, but Fleur flirted with me, and I was bewitched by her.'

'Bewitched!' Alice's scorn was like a laser, forcing Angus to look away. 'That's the sort of thing people claimed back in the Dark Ages. Are you saying our mother cast a spell on you?'

'That's just what it was like,' he said, voice trembling. 'I was several years younger than Fleur, a country boy

who had married his childhood sweetheart at seventeen. I wasn't worldly. Gwen, my wife, was the only woman I'd ever kissed until Fleur, let alone anything else. Looking back, I can't imagine why she made a play for me. I was a success at my job, I had a good salary, and people said I was handsome, but in the circles she moved in, there were far richer, more successful men than me. I suspect it was my naivety that was the attraction. She enjoyed watching me lose my head over her.'

There was a weird sense of logic in what he'd said. He was either as naive as he claimed, or a clever con man, but she felt it was the first. 'I can understand the affair,' Alice said, her tone icy. 'I know people can be swept up in the moment. It's the marrying bit I can't get my head around. So, you flitted between two women. Did Gwen know about Fleur?'

'She didn't find out until I was charged with bigamy,' he said, with a helpless shrug. 'I was away working so often it seemed entirely possible to keep both women. It worked too, at least until after Emily was born. Fleur never questioned me about Gwen – she seemed perfectly happy with the arrangement, me going back to Wales at the weekend. As for Gwen, her life was the same as it was before Fleur. I always loved Gwen, and that never changed, not then or now. I might seem a cruel, heartless man, but I was never that. If anyone was cruel, it was Fleur. She soon picked herself up after I was arrested. But perhaps she'd already met Ralph Kent.'

Out of loyalty to her mother Alice felt unable to admit that she knew her to have been malicious. If anyone had ever slighted her, even in the smallest way, she retaliated like a striking cobra. She and Emily had felt the full force of their mother's fury. She liked people to obey her, agree with her, and stand by her even when she was in the wrong. When Alice was at university, she asked once if she could go to a friend's for Christmas. Sally agreed, in a frigid voice, but she punished her afterwards by refusing to let her come home for the Easter holidays. It was only because Ralph had put his foot down that she was allowed to come home for the summer. Even then she barely spoke to Alice.

'So did Gwen throw you out?'

'No, she was terribly upset, of course, and embarrassed because it was in the papers. But she's old-school. She had promised in church for better or worse, so she stood by me. When I came out of prison, she said we must draw a line under it, and we're still together, happily so.'

'She sounds saintly,' Alice said, with a touch of sarcasm. 'That's more than you deserve.'

There were so many more questions she wanted answers to, but she needed to consider what line to take to get the most information out of him. Besides, she had to go back to Bristol, and to decide how much of this she was going to tell Emily. Mike and she were having a few difficulties in their marriage, and something like this might make the situation much worse.

Yet it wasn't just her and her sister who would be affected: Ralph would be devastated, and if Emily's children got wind of it, how would they deal with it?

'I think you've told me enough for one day, Angus,' she said. 'But give me your email address, and in due course I'll contact you again.'

They finished the meal in a strained silence. Alice had the feeling Angus had been expecting emotion, and probably thought she was a cold fish, but she had never been one for public displays of her feelings and, besides, she needed advice before she spoke to this man again.

It was a strained leave-taking. Alice politely shook Angus's hand, and he held on to hers for far longer than was necessary. He said he had booked a room in a hotel on the moors and intended to do some walking before he went back to Wales. It was only then that she got a really good look at his eyes. They were hazel, an almost identical colour to hers and Emily's, but the shape was different: theirs were slightly bulbous, his deep set, almost hooded. They shared his pronounced cheekbones too.

Yet whatever she thought of him as a man – 'weak' was the word in the forefront of her mind – his eyes were the type she associated with kindness. She also sensed he was truthful, without guile.

3

Janet, 1950

'I hate both of you,' Janet muttered to herself, as she cowered behind the lavatory in the backyard of Dale Street. 'I wish you'd been killed in the war.'

She knew the last remark was a bit stupid as she was only five when it had ended and couldn't remember it anyway. But she clearly recalled a day shortly before William Masters was due home on leave from sea. Mrs Lovett, who lived next door, was talking to another neighbour and Janet overheard what they were saying: 'There'll be hell to pay when William finds out about Janet. But Freda deserves all that's coming to her,' Mrs Lovett said.

When she asked her mother why there would be hell to pay, all she got was a shaking until she admitted where she'd heard it. Her mother's shakings were terrible, so fierce Janet thought her head might fall off, and always ended with a brain-rattling slap too.

Her memory of meeting her father, William Masters, for the first time a few days later was not a good one. The big man's face was all snarly, like a dog preparing to bite. She was sent out to play immediately and had to assume that the man she thought of as her daddy didn't like the look of her. He had been at sea when she was born and ever since.

Grown-ups who didn't like her were not unusual: her mother, Granny and the mad woman who shouted at all children when their ball hit her window were consistently grumpy. But there were others who could be nice one day, and nasty the next. She got the idea, though, that Daddy didn't even want her in the house and one evening Granny collected her while he was in the pub. She said Janet was to stay with her for a little while until the dust settled.

The 'little while' lasted two years and ended with Granny dying. Janet heard she'd had a heart attack while she was at school, but no one explained what that meant. Her teacher just told her she'd better go straight home to her mum.

By then she was seven and some things were clearer than they had been at the end of the war. She had learned that William Masters was not her father, and that her mother was what people called 'loose'. That meant she had made baby Janet with another man. That was why William Masters didn't like her. Perhaps, too, it was why he and her mother drank a lot. Going home really scared her: she knew it would be a lot worse than living with Granny.

Granny's house was messy and smelt of boiled fish

for the cat. But she made good dinners and cakes. Janet's clothes were always washed and ironed, her shoes cleaned, and on occasions, usually when Granny had been drinking, she was even affectionate.

The two-up-two-down house in Dale Street in Chatham, where her mother lived, might not smell of boiled fish, but it was dark, cold and unwelcoming. All the houses in Dale Street were much the same: two floors on their side, but across the street they were three floors and reached by steep steps. No one had a front garden, and as very little sunshine came into the long, narrow street, it had a gloomy, sinister appearance. This impression was enhanced by the gaps in the terrace where bombs had dropped during the war, now filled with weeds and rubbish.

Janet often explored the area on the outskirts of Chatham, where she saw lovely newer houses, with sparkling windows, fresh paint and gardens bright with flowers. She liked to pretend she lived in a particularly pretty bungalow that had a green-tiled roof, leaded window panes and a shiny red front door. It had two silver birch trees either side of the garden path. Beneath one of them sat a couple of pottery gnomes. She would chat to her imaginary friend Becky, and as she got to the gate of the house she'd say, 'I must go in now. Mummy will have tea ready, but I'll ask her if you can come next week.'

She imagined hot crumpets with strawberry jam, and fancy cakes on one of those two-tier cake stands, like they had in Patricia's Pantry down in the town. Not that she'd ever been inside the tea shop, but she always looked through the window. She also imagined Mummy wearing a pink twinset and pearls, and a checked pleated skirt. She would smell of lovely scent and would hug Janet as if she'd been gone for days, not just a few hours at school.

The truth was that her mother had rarely come to Granny's house to see her in the last two years, even though it was only a ten-minute walk away. She never hugged Janet, and smelt of cigarettes and fried food. Janet suspected that washed and ironed clothes or regular meals wouldn't be forthcoming from now on.

Yet the very worst thing of all about going home was Him. On the rare occasions she'd seen him in the last two years he'd made his feelings about her quite plain.

Clearly, he was furious that she now had to live in the same house: when her mother opened the front door, she told Janet to get up to the box room and stay there.

Within minutes he was ranting, his voice loud and harsh, and Janet shook in her shoes. 'Tell me why I should be expected to keep another man's kid? Fuck me, Freda, you've got some neck! Why didn't you get

29

rid of the little bastard? You must have known no man would be happy to come back from war and find his wife had been having it off with someone else.'

Freda responded in a loud but wheedling voice. 'I couldn't help it. I was lonely while you were away and really scared when they bombed the dockyard. He was kind to me, and I know I shouldn't have gone with him, but I couldn't help myself and it was only once.'

'Once, twice, a hundred times, what difference does that make? You were scared! Well, what about me on a minesweeper never knowing when the ship would be blown up or torpedoed? I was cold and wet most of the time and the only thing that kept me warm was the thought of you waiting for me when it was all over. Why didn't you get rid of it?'

Janet frowned. Did he mean kill her when she was a baby, or dump her on someone else's doorstep?

'I would've done, but I couldn't find anyone to do it. And don't tell me you didn't go with any girls while you were away. I had to go to the clinic because you gave me the clap when you come home.'

Before Janet could even ponder what the clap was, she heard a thud and a crash and guessed he'd hit her mum so hard she'd knocked something over.

'If you had the clap, you got it from some fancy man, not me,' he roared. Another thud and her mother screamed, then more thuds and screams until eventually she was silent.

He left, slamming the door behind him. Janet went cautiously downstairs and found her mother lying on the kitchen floor.

She had no idea what to do, but after sitting there for some time wondering if her mother was dead, like Granny, she went next door and got Mrs Lovett.

Mrs Lovett was a big woman, not so much fat, just wide and tall. She had five children and a wiry little husband who worked on the docks. Everyone in the street tended to run to her when they had a problem, be that childbirth or their old man had given them a battering. It was said she had a big heart: during the war she had taken in many people who'd been bombed out, or so Janet had heard.

'No, she's not dead, sweetheart,' she said, leaning over Freda. 'But if that man carries on this way, she'll soon be joining her ma in the grave.' She dragged Freda up onto a fireside chair and began dabbing the blood off her face. 'Have you had your tea, Janet?' she asked. On hearing that she hadn't, Mrs Lovett told her to go next door and ask Myrtle, her eldest, to give her a bowl of soup and some bread. 'I'll patch yer ma up and get her up to her bed. You come back when you've had some soup and I'll make up a bed for you.'

The soup was lovely, reminding Janet that Mrs

Lovett had always made nice food. She wished she could stay in her house, tucked in the bed between Susie, who was two, and four-year-old Alan. Myrtle, Fern and Rosemary shared the other bed. People who lived in Dale Street didn't have much space.

When she got back, her mother was in her bed, looking a bit better, though her eyes were so swollen Mrs Lovett said she couldn't see.

Janet's bed was a mattress on the floor in the box room. The blankets and sheets smelt of mould but, then, that was a smell Janet had known all her life. 'I know this hasn't been a welcome-home party, sweetheart,' Mrs Lovett said, bending down to kiss her. 'But I'll talk to yer ma when she's feeling a bit better and see if we can't find a way out of this. You'll need to get your things from your granny's house too. I'll ask my Myrtle to go with you tomorrow. But for now, you stay there, even if he comes home and starts shouting.'

Janet didn't need any warning. If she could have crawled under the floorboards to avoid him, she would have done. But with a tummy full of soup she fell asleep almost immediately.

As the years ticked by Janet grew used to hiding from the man who made her call him Master. Luckily, he was often away at sea for weeks on end, but when he was home, he laid into her so often with a stick that she grew almost used to it. When Freda wasn't clouting Janet, she made cruel remarks about her mousy hair and crooked teeth – anything, in fact, to make her miserable.

Janet's saving grace was that she was clever, almost always top of her class at St Michael's. She worked hard at lessons because she somehow knew it was one way of escaping the life she'd been born into.

She lay in bed at night considering what she needed. For the last three years Chatham Library had been her place of safety, and if she could have crawled into a cupboard and stayed there for ever, she would have done. She loved books as they had opened possibilities in her mind. One was to be an actress, but she was smart enough to understand that she couldn't walk into a theatre and ask to be cast just because she had once had a leading role in a school play. First, she needed a job that paid well enough for her to buy some nice clothes and somewhere else to live. More than that, though, she needed cunning to get what she wanted, and the ability to hold her own in better company than she got in Dale Street.

Better company turned up unexpectedly at school when Janet was ten.

Her name was Belinda Monroe, and her father was in the Royal Navy, as were so many fathers of children in the school. Most of the fathers were just ratings or able seamen in the navy or the merchant navy, as William Masters was. But Mr Monroe was an officer and St Michael's primary school was just a temporary measure for Belinda.

Janet took one look at Belinda's shiny hair, patent leather shoes, smocked dress and hand-knitted cardigan and knew the girl would be useful. The other children shunned her because of her posh voice and nice clothes, so it was easy to win her trust and befriend her. Janet had known her for just a week when Belinda invited her home for tea.

Her home was in Rochester Way, a detached pretty house with shutters on the windows and a lot of trees in the front garden, even nicer than her pretend bungalow. Inside was even better: it smelt of lavender polish and there were sparkling mirrors, soft rugs underfoot and all the paintwork was white.

Better still was Belinda's bedroom. It was like something out of a film. She had a white candlewick bedspread, a wall-to-wall pink carpet, and shelves full of books, games and dolls, which she quickly told Janet she was too old for. The view from the window was over the garden – it was spring, daffodils were everywhere and blossom was growing on the trees.

Mrs Monroe had wrinkled her nose a little when her daughter introduced her new friend, but Janet had expected that and set out to charm the posh woman, who wore a black and white sheath dress and had her nails painted scarlet. 'What a beautiful home you have,' she said. 'So many lovely trees in the garden too.'

The expected smile came, and Mrs Monroe told Janet they'd bought the house as her husband would be stationed in Chatham for some years. 'It's so good to be able to put down roots,' she said, 'to have our own things around us. Belinda has told me you've been very kind to her at school. Thank you for that.'

'Some of the other girls are jealous because she's pretty and has nice clothes,' Janet said. 'I think that's mean.'

Janet's reward was a poached egg on toast, then bread and butter and jam, and a selection of cakes. She had to control herself and not eat everything in sight, also to copy the ladylike way Belinda ate.

After tea they played Snakes and Ladders in Belinda's bedroom. Janet would have liked to play with the dolls, but as Belinda had said she didn't play with them any more, she didn't feel able even to ask to look at them.

Tea on Wednesday afternoons became a regular event, and Janet used the two-hour slot to take in as much information about the way nice people lived. Cleanliness was one thing, eating daintily at a properly laid table another, and there was no shouting. Mrs Monroe was a great reader too, and she played the piano. Belinda was learning to play too. Janet listened to the way they spoke, and over tea she asked Mrs Monroe if she'd had a job before her daughter was born, and what she hoped Belinda would be.

'I was a secretary,' she said, with a warm smile, 'and I met my husband at a dance in Dartmouth before the war, when he was at the naval college. My job was rather dull, just typing endless letters, so I'm hoping Belinda will go to university and maybe become something exciting, like a scientist, or doctor, or even a vet.'

'What would you like to do?' Belinda asked Janet.

'To be an actress,' she admitted. 'But I haven't got a clue how you go about it.'

'Janet's the cleverest in our class,' Belinda told her mother. 'I'm sure she could do anything she wanted to.'

'Well, not a ballet dancer or a concert pianist,' Janet said, with a grin.

'My grandmother was a wise old lady,' Mrs Monroe said, with a smile. 'She claimed that you can be anything you like if you're determined enough. I only ever wanted to be a wife and mother, but she used to say that if that's what I wanted, it was an equally important job.'

Belinda left St Michael's about two months later and was sent to a private school. Before she left, she told Janet she was to have private coaching so she'd pass her eleven-plus. 'Mum's got this thing about me going to university. She's always on at me to have ambition. But there isn't anything that jumps out at me and makes me want to do it.'

She didn't suggest they kept in touch, and Janet didn't ask as she guessed Belinda's parents had said it was time she made friends with someone on the same level as her.

Losing Belinda and the weekly joy of going to her beautiful house, made Janet feel sad. Her mother had made many sarcastic comments about her friendship with 'the posh girl', so she said nothing about missing Belinda as it was likely to spark a row.

Freda Masters drank far too much, which made her volatile. When her husband went off on a voyage to New Zealand life was a bit better for Janet, but though she escaped his clouts and insults, she still got them from her mother. Freda was lonely and as her husband wasn't sending money home, like he was supposed to, she spent most of the money she made from her two cleaning jobs on drink. Often there was nothing in the larder but stale bread. If it hadn't been for school dinners, Janet would have starved.

'If I wasn't stuck with you, I could have got a job as a stewardess on a ship,' she shouted at Janet, one evening. 'I'd be seeing the world instead of stuck in this crummy house without a penny to my name.'

Janet had no idea what stewardesses did, or what they looked like, but she was fairly certain they couldn't look as rough as her mother did. 'Take a good look at yourself,' William Masters had yelled once, holding her up to the mirror over the fireplace. 'You once turned heads, but now people would turn away, you look so ugly.'

That night Janet had felt sorry for Freda – no one deserved to be treated like that. She made a fuss of her, bathed her face and let her cry. But the next day Freda was as nasty as ever, and Janet vowed she'd never be kind to her again. Yet she still tried to win her love by cleaning up, taking the washing to the laundry room at the public baths, and making her cups of tea.

When a nurse on a routine visit to Janet's school found that she was very underweight and malnourished, Janet had no idea that the nurse had reported what she'd found. The first thing she knew of it was when a woman came to the door called Miss Cooling, who said she was a children's officer. She insisted on coming in to examine Janet herself.

'She ain't been eating because her posh friend left her school,' Freda claimed. 'I cook her food, but she don't eat it. I'm not good enough for her any more.'

Janet remained silent. She couldn't bring herself to say her mum was lying and the only hot food she ever got, apart from her school dinner, was a bag of chips, or if Mrs Lovett gave her a bowl of soup. 'I do miss my friend,' she admitted, thinking that was a far less dangerous thing to say.

The children's officer was not easily convinced. She went into the scullery and no doubt noted an absence of food in the larder, the amount of empty sherry bottles and general slovenliness. But all she said was that she'd be checking with the school nurse about Janet's weight, and she thought Freda should make more of an effort to cook nourishing meals. With that she left.

But she had barely got into her car when Freda rounded on Janet. 'What lies have you been telling at school?' she hissed at her, eyes narrowing with rage. 'Told them I go off to the pub, did you? Mooning over that posh kid and wishing you lived with them?'

Freda was so wound up she picked up the poker from the fireplace and hit Janet with that. Normally Janet tried hard not to scream when she was being punished, but the poker hurt ten times more than her mother's hands and she couldn't help but yell at the top of her voice.

Freda wouldn't or couldn't stop. She rained blows on Janet's back and head, then slashed at her legs and pushed her down onto an armchair to smash the poker across her knees. Janet felt a crack inside, and the pain was so intense she wished for death to stop it.

'Freda, stop that!'

It was Mrs Lovett. She'd come through the scullery door, which led onto a tiny yard both houses shared along with an outside lavatory.

'Put that poker down now, Freda,' Mrs Lovett said, coming closer, her arms out in front of her as if trying to head off an animal.

Janet's screaming turned to sobs, but she was in terrible pain all over, her knees being the worst.

The poker dropped to the floor and made Janet look up at her mother. 'What did I do to deserve that?' she sobbed out, unable to understand why her mother was standing, silent, wide-eyed and slack-mouthed, her arms hanging at her sides.

'She's not well, Janet, and I shall have to call an ambulance for you,' Mrs Lovett said. 'I won't be a moment. The phone box is only on the corner.'

'Don't leave me with her!' Janet pleaded, terrified she'd get more.

'She won't touch you again, sweetheart. If she does, it'll be prison for her.'

Mrs Lovett was true to her word. She was gone only a few minutes. Freda didn't move or speak, reminding Janet of the game of Statues: you had to freeze when the music stopped. Then she heard the ambulance bell.

4

Alice

Alice's head was whirling as she drove back to Bristol. Was Angus really her biological father? If he was telling the truth, why would he choose Sally's funeral to approach her and Emily? That was creepy and inappropriate.

She thanked Heaven that Emily had made other plans today. She was never one for thinking before she acted. She might have attacked Angus or, worse, insisted on marching the man home to tell his story to Ralph.

Ralph was the most honest and straightforward person she knew. There was no doubt in Alice's mind that he knew nothing of a bigamous marriage. As for adopting her and Emily, Sally must have spun him some yarn to get him to agree to it and promise never to tell them. No doubt it was a well-rehearsed story about them being in grave danger. For Ralph to be confronted with the truth about his beloved wife so soon after her death might well bring on a heart attack or stroke.

Then there was Gwen. Angus claimed his wife had drawn a line under his betrayal of her. How was she going to feel if she discovered he was now raking up events from more than thirty years ago? Alice knew that if it was her she'd be hopping mad. As for their son, what would it do to him?

Was Angus naive enough to imagine she and Emily would welcome him as another father? Or was this about revenge?

Alice drummed her fingers on the steering wheel in frustration. She wished she could put Angus out of her mind. She didn't want to see or speak to him again and certainly didn't intend to breathe a word of it to Ralph or Emily. But Angus had one thing she really wanted: the truth about her mother's background. As a young girl she'd once asked if she had grandparents, and her mother had said sharply, 'They died,' in a tone that invited no further questions.

As teenagers Alice and Emily had discussed their mother's reticence in talking about the past or her family. They came to the conclusion that there must have been a big fall-out and Sally left home when young, never to return. Perhaps her parents had died since. But the girls knew better than to question their mother. She was likely to clout them and say it was none of their business.

There was no mystery about Ralph's past. His father had been a fighter pilot in the RAF, shot down in the war when Ralph was just a baby. His mother had died of heart failure when he was in his early twenties, away at university, and Ralph had inherited their house in Totnes. A black-and-white wedding photograph of his parents hung in the hall, beside one of his mother with baby Ralph on her lap, and another of his father in his RAF uniform, looking very dashing.

Until his retirement a few years earlier, Ralph had been an accountant with a Paignton law firm called Prentice, White and Boyd. He often said he wished he'd studied law as it would have been a whole lot more interesting than rows of figures. But he was a relaxed, contented man, enjoying playing cricket in the summer, and acting as treasurer for two local charities.

Alice had never doubted Ralph's love for her and Emily. She'd felt it as a little girl when his big hand took hers if they were out for a walk or she climbed onto his lap to be read to. It was in the way his eyes lit up to see her or Emily and, as adults, in the help he offered so willingly, from plumbing in a washing-machine to painstakingly building shelves in their own homes.

Yes, he had chastised them sometimes – there had been heated arguments especially when they were teenagers, but he was quick to forgive, and always generous with his praise. Angus couldn't do anything to hurt Sally now, but he could devastate Ralph and possibly Emily. Neither of them deserved that.

'You must tread very carefully,' she warned herself aloud as she reached Gordano service station and the road into Clifton.

But what was she to say to Emily? She knew her sister would ring tonight for the lowdown on Angus.

In the days that followed the funeral Alice was so busy at work she barely had time to think about Angus Tweedy, let alone make any plans to check him out. She rang Emily and told her that Angus had been one of their mum's boyfriends long before she married Ralph. She said he was boring, talking about nothing except his work, and she wished she hadn't wasted her time having lunch with him.

Emily didn't question her but, then, why would she? No one would expect a man to admit to being a bigamist.

When Alice had a moment or two to reflect on Angus, and the many questions she had about her mother that she hoped he could answer, she also wondered why she felt the need to know anything. Surely she had all she needed: a sister who was also a real friend, and Ralph, who was the perfect father even if he wasn't biologically related to her. She had her own home and a job she loved. Why concern herself with her mother's past?

It wasn't like she had always been desperate to know family history. She was a here-and-now person normally. Her mother's death had skewed her.

People described Alice as dynamic, resourceful and a born leader. Everyone said that managing a group of hotels was the perfect job for her. She didn't go out of her way to tell them it wasn't glamorous, like they thought it was. Hiring staff was enjoyable, but firing them was horrible. She had some responsibility for accounts and advertising, but there was an assistant manager in each of the hotels, who checked the day-to-day routines, housekeeping, bars, restaurants, and kept a watchful eye on all his staff. Alice was the go-to person who kept all the balls in the air.

She had been at home looking after her mother for four weeks before she died and problems had arisen at the hotels during that period but hadn't been dealt with. Sorting them out, making phone calls and checking details took her mind off family matters, but she found a minute to ring Stuart McIntosh, a close friend. He had recently taken early retirement from the police, and she knew he'd give her sensible advice on what to do about Angus. Stuart was twenty-odd years older than her, but she valued his friendship and his integrity. They had met at a party six years ago, and she found him fascinating, a breath of fresh air: he had interesting opinions, believed in straight talking and, like her, he was divorced. He would

45

immediately understand why she was torn between wanting to reject Angus and using him as the key to unlock her mother's past. She wouldn't need to explain.

As she had expected, Stuart did grasp the situation, soothed some of her anxiety and suggested she come to see him on Saturday afternoon to talk more about it. He said that in the meantime he would use his old contacts to find out a bit more about the man. That was on Wednesday and it seemed for ever to Alice to wait for the weekend. She wished she could discuss it with Emily or even her father: they had always been her first choice of confidants. But this was explosive stuff and, like TNT, it needed handling carefully.

She woke early on Saturday morning, and was pleased to find that the spring weather was even warmer than it had been for the funeral. She nipped down to the supermarket in Clifton village and got some shopping, including a bottle of single malt whisky for Stuart.

Once she'd put away her purchases, she changed the thick black winter coat she'd worn daily since November for a cream leather jacket, jeans and a sweater and decided to walk to Stuart's. He had a first-floor flat in one of the grand old houses over-looking the Downs. He'd bought it when his marriage had broken up, around the time Alice had split with her husband. Stuart had day-dreamed of buying a boat he could live on and sailing to the Greek islands, but that hadn't happened.

He must have been looking out of the window because as she approached the front door, the intercom buzzed and the door opened.

'Hi, gorgeous,' he called down the stairs. 'Just what I needed to brighten the weekend. Come on up.'

Stuart was a Scot, though he'd lived so long in the West Country his accent was no more than a soft burr. He was old school: he called women 'sweetheart', 'darling' and 'gorgeous' and didn't see a tough childhood as an excuse for lawbreaking. He often said that he was a dinosaur because his views had no place in the modern police force.

But Alice knew that, along with being honest, he had a big heart, and she'd heard that many young people whom he'd nicked in their teens had a huge amount of respect for him. He had a big paunch, thinning white hair, and several chins, but his twinkling blue eyes, the ear-to-ear grin, and his welcoming hug showed genuine delight to see her.

His flat had been furnished with all the stuff his wife hadn't wanted: two chintzy sofas, a pastel Chinese carpet with a white fringe, dark polished-wood bookcases, and the pictures were bland watercolours.

Alice had teased him in the past that he'd never find a new lady to share his life as he'd brought his ex-wife's conservative personality to his flat. 'Chuck it all out and redecorate in your own style,' she'd urged him. 'This would make any woman think you had one foot in the grave.'

Stuart laughed. He agreed she might be right, but he'd never acted on her advice. She doubted he'd ever change anything now.

She had told him only the bare bones of what had happened down in Totnes. Yet as she sat in an arm-chair she smiled to see a file on the coffee-table marked 'Angus Tweedy'. 'You've made a start, then?' she said.

'I have indeed, but first things first. A gin and tonic? It's probably a bit early in the day for single malt.'

'It certainly is,' she agreed. 'Besides, that was for you, not to share.'

Once they were sitting with a drink, Stuart opened the file. 'First, I found that your mother was born in Dale Street, Chatham, in 1940 to Freda and William Masters. He was in the merchant navy.'

'So she really did lie about her age. And born in Chatham?' Alice was surprised by that. 'I had the idea she came from Sussex.'

Stuart shrugged. 'Don't think so. Anyway, Dale Street, Chatham, was an extremely poor area then. It isn't much better now.'

'Mum was a snob, so I suppose she didn't like to mention where she'd lived.'

'Maybe, but Angus Tweedy was telling you the truth about the bigamous marriage in 1980 and going to prison. That was in 1983. Until then he was a representative for a prestigious china and glass company, their top man. With his first wife in Wales and the second across the Severn in Bristol he might never have been outed.'

'How and why was he discovered?'

'I think your mother reported him.'

'Understandably. She must have been furious to find she'd been betrayed.'

Stuart's doubtful expression and his silence were worrying.

'What is it?' she asked.

He sighed. 'The last thing I want to do is add to your grief by being disrespectful about your mum, but certain things point to her as having been something of a schemer. First, all the changes of name. People often change a surname, after divorce, family disputes, and to avoid debts and suchlike. But not so much their Christian names. Sally, as you call her, started out as Janet Masters, then changed to Fleur Faraday. On marrying Angus she became Helen Tweedy. I think she changed it to Sally Symonds when she moved to Totnes. Finally becoming Sally Kent when she married Ralph.'

'It's not illegal to change your name,' Alice retorted. 'Two of them were through marriage.'

'Of course not, but put it together with her possibly reporting Angus and getting him arrested. If she did that, it smacks of deception. She'd clearly known the truth about him from day one, gone along with it happily, but maybe dobbed him in once he'd outlived his usefulness.'

'That's an awful thing to say, Stuart.' Alice was indignant, 'and if you haven't got proof it might not have been that way at all.'

'It wouldn't help you if I put a gentler slant on it. I'm being a policeman and presenting the evidence.' Stuart shrugged. 'A friend of Angus's, who was a witness for the defence at his trial, claimed Sally pressured him into marriage because she was pregnant, despite knowing he already had a wife. When he was arrested she immediately moved with you and your sister to Totnes, and put the house here in Bristol, which Angus had bought and put in her name, on the market. She didn't give any of the proceeds to Angus either. It looks pretty clear to me she'd already met Ralph Kent, or why pick Totnes of all places to move to? She had a few months in a rented flat, then married and moved in with Ralph.'

'Now just a minute, Stuart.' Alice's voice rose. 'Don't you dare suggest Ralph was in on this. He would never have countenanced anything underhand. Mum must have told him something totally convincing to get his support. Besides, they really loved one another. They were happy together and he was the best of fathers to Emily and me.'

'I'm sure they were happy together,' Stuart agreed. 'Living in a lovely house with Ralph taking care of her and her two little girls, she was living the dream at last. But going back several years, I can't understand why Sally would want to marry Angus knowing full well he already had a wife.'

'Maybe she panickcd if she was pregnant with me.'

Stuart gave a humourless laugh. 'Back before the war panic might have been understandable. A pregnant woman would have needed a husband for security. But in 1980 when you were born there was no longer any stigma in being an unmarried mother. She could also claim benefits from the state. And your mum was no spring chicken – she was in her late thirties. Hardly a dewy-eyed teenager.'

'Maybe she didn't like the idea of living on benefits,' Alice suggested.

'Come on, Alice! She did Angus up like a kipper, got him to buy a house, in her name, then married him bigamously knowing that was her get-out-of-jail-free card when she got tired of him or met someone better.'

'What are you saying, Stuart? Surely she couldn't have been that conniving,' Alice said angrily.

'I believe she was,' Stuart responded. 'Look at the evidence! Even if she hadn't known Angus was married when they first met, wouldn't she have questioned why he was away every weekend and why he put the house in her name? There's no record of her ever visiting him in prison. In fact, she dropped him and his name like a hot potato, moved away immediately, leaving an estate agent to sell the house. There were many mentions of her in the press, but no photographs, only of Angus. I'd hazard a guess that was partly because of her changed name, but also because she gave dirt on Angus to reporters, on the condition they didn't put in any pictures of her. You say Ralph would never have got involved if he knew she'd been married bigamously, so she clearly deceived him too.'

Alice was shocked and hurt by Stuart's opinion. She wanted to shout him down and convince him he was wrong but, deep down, she'd always known how devious her mother could be, and it was beginning to make some sort of sense.

'But she must have loved Angus. He was the father of her children,' she pointed out, desperately trying to find some reason or excuse. 'Maybe she needed a wedding to appease her parents.'

'I doubt that somehow. She changed her name like other women change winter coats. There appeared to be no family loyalty.'

'You mentioned the name Fleur Faraday. Angus said that was her name when he met her.'

'Yet she became Helen Tweedy on her marriage,' Stuart said, raising one eyebrow. 'I wonder what reason she gave him for changing from Fleur to Helen. She must have been up to something. It's that which makes me believe she plumped for Angus and had you two girls as an escape from the life she'd had prior to meeting him. He must have been very naive,' he said.

'He admitted he was, said she bewitched him. But what could have been so bad about her life before Angus? And why did he make a point of contacting us girls? What does he want of us?'

'Now that is the real mystery,' Stuart said thoughtfully. 'He surely couldn't imagine that two grown women would be looking for a second dad! Revenge, maybe, and he was too much of a coward to strike while your mum was alive. Yet what mileage did he hope to get out of it all these years later?'

'Maybe he's hooked on having secrets,' Alice suggested.

'At his age? He's late sixties. His wife Gwen is still in their home in Wales. He has a son, Ian, and four grandchildren. He started up a successful plant nursery when he came out of prison, so he's not just okay, he's done well for himself. But tell me, Alice, did Ralph ever make complaints about Sally?'

'Little whinges sometimes. She'd disappear with a friend, sometimes gone for days at a time without advance warning. She blew money on expensive clothes and shoes without ever consulting him. You were right, Stuart, she did call the shots. But can we backtrack to what she was doing before she met Angus?'

'She was an actress. She clearly thought the name Fleur Faraday had a more theatrical ring to it than Janet Masters.'

'Actress?' Alice's voice rose in shocked surprise.

Stuart chuckled. 'Well, it's clear from her later exploits that she had some talent for acting, but back in the sixties she joined a repertory company.'

'Wow! Fancy her not telling us girls that!'

'It would have been the time when farce or drawing-room comedies were very popular, and when even small towns had their own theatre. Repertory companies went from town to town performing plays, a new one each week quite often. Many now famous actors began that way, and honed their acting skills playing in seaside towns, like Ilfracombe, Bournemouth and Blackpool. But it was a hard life, seedy boarding houses, very low wages, and to learn a new part every week must have been very tough. Sadly there is very little on the internet about those companies, unless of course one of the cast became famous. Even then they don't mention the supporting cast in the production.'

'So how did you find out that's what she did?'

'There were a couple of lines in a newspaper when the bigamy thing came out. "Angus Tweedy said she was an actress when he met her." That was enough for me to trawl the internet. I was about to give up because I couldn't find anything, when I discovered Noël Coward's *Blithe Spirit* played at the Bristol Hippodrome during the 1960s. Because he was a famous and popular playwright there were pictures of the posters and flyers. A well-known actress called Genevieve Stratton played the lead, and Fleur Faraday was there in a supporting role, her name among others in very small letters. So I'm guessing she'd been with the same repertory company for a while.'

'How amazing,' Alice said. 'Why didn't she ever tell us that?'

'I'd imagine she was afraid to tell you her stage name in case you started poking around on the internet and found out about the bigamy.'

'I see,' Alice said. She needed time to process what she'd been told.

Stuart refilled her glass and waited.

'But she didn't meet Angus until many years later. What was she doing all that time? And when and where did she meet Angus?'

'I think you need to speak to him again if you want to know about how they got together, and his side of the story. Or you could just let it go, Alice.'

Alice pondered that for a moment. 'Letting it go

would be the sensible thing to do. But I want to know my mum better, or worse, whichever comes up.'

Stuart half smiled, his blue eyes twinkling. 'I expected as much. But in view of your mother's age, some of the people she was connected to might not be alive any more.'

'Well, Angus is, and so is Ralph. Though I've no intention of telling him anything you've told me.'

'Want a bit of advice from an old man?' he asked.

'Go on,' she said. 'And less of the "old man".'

'You should share this with Ralph. Not now while he's grieving, but he probably knows a great deal more than you think. He knew you weren't his children because he adopted you both, but never told anyone so. Why? Probably because Sally refused to let him. So, you aren't pulling the rug from beneath his feet, Alice. As long as you tell him that, in all the ways that count, he's your father, he'll be okay about it. It might even be a relief to unburden himself.'

'Maybe.' Alice sighed. 'What a tangled web!'

5

Janet

'Janet, if you can hear me, open your eyes.'

Janet heard the woman's voice as if from a long way off, and it wasn't one she recognized.

'You're in hospital, Janet. Open your eyes and look at me.'

Her eyes felt very heavy, but she forced herself to open them. A nurse in a striped uniform with a cap on her head was looking down at her and smiling. 'Good girl,' she said. 'Don't try to move as your leg is broken and the doctor had to operate on your knee as some of the bones were shattered.'

It was a little while before Janet was awake enough to know her leg was held in a strange wood and rope contraption. Later she was told it was called traction and it was to keep her leg in the right position to heal well. As she gradually woke fully, she felt terrible pain, but the nurse brought her medicine. In a short while the pain went, and she felt as if she was lying on a cloud.

She had no idea how long she was like that, being

spoon-fed and going to sleep again. She didn't know whether other patients were near her, or if people came to see her. Sometimes it was dark when she woke, sometimes daytime, but she gradually realized she was in a room on her own. The sleepiness wore off, and she could feel some pain in her leg, but it wasn't fierce pain any longer. The nurses propped her up with pillows and gave her books and comics to read.

That was when she was able to remember what her mother had done to her. She could still see her face contorted with hatred as she hit Janet over and over again with the poker. But after hearing the ambulance bell in the distance there was nothing. She certainly didn't remember being taken into the hospital.

A policeman came to see her, and she told him what she could. He said she was safe here in hospital, and her mother had been taken away to a special place. She wondered if he meant an asylum or prison but didn't like to ask. Meanwhile she was lapping up the sympathy and attention from the nurses. With three good meals a day, and extra milky drinks to build her up, she soon felt much better.

By the time she was moved into the children's ward, she was out of traction, but her leg was plastered right up her thigh. Now her black eyes and bruises had faded, she looked no different from the other children, who had an arm or leg in plaster.

She was torn about her mother. She wanted to save her from getting into trouble, yet hoped she'd never have to go back to her. Miss Cooling had asked her to describe happy times with her mother, but she couldn't think of any, not even one.

Her dreams now were about a new life where she wouldn't have to be ashamed of her worn-out clothes, her home or a mother who drank. The need to be in a safe place where she would never have to see William Masters again, to go to the seaside, the cinema, and have nice food was enough of a lure for her to admit to the policewoman who questioned her how awful he and her mother had been to her.

Later that same day Miss Cooling came to see her. Janet cried and told her how bad she felt. 'Will Mum go to prison?' she asked.

'I don't know.' Miss Cooling stroked Janet's hair back from her forehead and smiled down at her. 'In my opinion it's what she deserves but, sadly, my dear, children aren't protected by law as well as they should be. Parents think they have a right to beat their children, sometimes close to death, and quite often they get a bit of a lecture and go home to do it again.'

Janet looked at her in horror.

Miss Cooling took her hand to reassure her. 'No, my dear. Whatever the court decides to do with her, you will not go back to her. When you're ready to leave here, you'll be taken to a place of safety. I can't tell you where that will be yet.' She put her hand on her heart and took Janet's hand with the other. 'I promise you will never be sent back to your mother.'

After that day Miss Cooling came every few days and Janet looked forward to seeing her. She wasn't the preachy, stuffy kind of woman that people in Dale Street claimed social workers were. She told Janet she'd been a nurse before and during the war. 'That made me far more understanding of people's frailties,' she said. 'Shortage of money, bad housing and lack of education all work together to make life harder for people to bring up their children well. If I could be granted just one wish it would be for better education. That is the key to everything.'

She brought Janet books, jigsaws and an embroidery kit to make a tray cloth. 'It's all cross-stitch and easy,' she said. 'I thought it might make a nice present for Mrs Lovett. She's very concerned about you, and has been for a long time.'

Mrs Lovett had already sent a lovely card with a nice get-well-soon message. But Janet guessed she felt unable to visit. In Dale Street, calling the police about a neighbour was thought of as snitching. Visiting Janet would amount to the same thing.

'I'll do that. If you see her, will you tell her I hope to see her again one day? But what's going to happen to me?' she asked.

'You know, one of the best things about you, Janet,

is that you're very bright,' Miss Cooling said, with a warm smile. 'You already want to be taken into care because it will be better for you. Some children would still rather go home, whatever happened there.'

'Nowhere can be as bad as my home,' Janet said glumly. 'I just hope you aren't going to send me somewhere there are more bad people.'

'I know a lovely children's home called Summer Fields. It's near Aylesford, if you know where that is?'

'Yes, there's a paper mill and a friary there, and swans on the river. I went there once with my school.'

'It's a very pretty place. Summer Fields is a small home, ten to twelve children, and I think it will be just right for you. The local school is good too. But you're to stay here until your knee is mended enough for you to use crutches and until you've put on more weight.'

Janet was in no hurry to leave the hospital where she could read all day if she wanted to, where there was good food and nurses who made a fuss of her. It was like Paradise.

Nurse Swinton had been a hairdresser and she offered to wash and cut Janet's hair for her. 'It's straggly because you've never had it cut,' she explained. 'I suggest cutting it to your shoulders. That way it can still be plaited or put in bunches for school, but it will grow thicker and shinier.'

She washed it in the ward basin, and used shampoo too, which Janet had never known before. Her mother had always used carbolic soap on her hair. It stank, and if it got into her eyes it stung like mad.

'Well, there we are,' Nurse said, rubbing it vigorously with a towel. 'How does it feel?'

'Soft,' Janet said, as she touched it. Her hair had never felt like that before: it was always rough and tangled.

Nurse put the damp towel around her shoulders and pulled her scissors out of her pocket on her uniform. 'Now for the exciting bit!'

An hour later, after her hair was dry, Janet studied herself in a hand mirror. She couldn't believe how different she looked. Her hair was shiny, bouncier and more blonde than mouse. The bobbed cut suited her. She could never have imagined that a shampoo and cut could make her look so different.

'You've got to stop biting your nails now too,' Nurse said, lifting one of Janet's hands and wincing. 'It's like cannibalism biting bits off your own body. You're a pretty girl, Janet, but I don't think you've ever realized that.'

After lights out in the ward, Janet hugged those words to herself. Her mother and granny had told her she was plain, and sometimes, to be spiteful, they said she was ugly. But they were out of her life now, and she was going to forget the nasty things they'd said.

The day Janet arrived at Summer Fields it was hot and sunny. She took one look at the big white-painted house up a wide gravel drive and knew it was a good place. Roses grew round the central porch, the lawn at either side of the drive was a lush green, studded with daisies, and the garden was surrounded by trees.

Olive and Rob Duncan were the houseparents, and Janet took one look at their warm smiling faces and knew they were good people. There were five boys and, including Janet, seven girls. The boys ranged from four to eight, but the girls were a little older, from six to thirteen. Janet's bedroom slept four, with white metal beds and pink bedspreads. Each had a locker beside it for personal items. At one end of the room, cupboards and drawers held their clothes. Miss Cooling had bought Janet a smocked dress for best and two striped ones to wear to school. There were vests, knickers, socks, a couple of cardigans, two nighties, plimsolls and school sandals too, all packed into a small suitcase, with a new comb, a hairbrush, a toothbrush and a face flannel in a drawstring toilet bag.

Janet had never had anything new before: her clothes had come from jumble sales or been passed down by a neighbour. Often they were too big and made her look like a street urchin. When she was dressed in the new finery in the hospital ward, she was so excited she'd hobbled on her crutches to find Sister Jones to show her.

'You look beautiful, Janet,' she'd said, with a broad smile. 'Now just mind your manners, don't give anyone any cheek at the new home, and they'll love you.'

There was something magical about waking up at Summer Fields. Janet always seemed to wake before the others and she'd grab her crutches and go to the window to look out. The back garden had a big lawn, some swings and a see-saw, and the borders were bright with flowers. Beyond the trees and the fence at the end of the garden there were fields with black and white cows. With birds singing, insects buzzing, buttercups and daisies, she thought this was the best place in the world.

After breakfast the other children went to school, but she had to stay at home because of her crutches. Not that she minded: Mrs Wray, the cook, was always pleased if she came in to offer help, and she let Janet sit down to shell peas, or sometimes gave her a bit of pastry so she could roll out some jam tarts. Mrs Duncan was always glad of her company too: Janet would hobble out to watch her hanging washing on the line, or sorting clothes. Mr Duncan showed her the difference between flowers and weeds, and if she sat on the grass she could pull out a few weeds.

'As soon as that plaster is off your leg I'll have you weeding all the time,' he joked. He asked her once if she felt lonely without the other children around during the day.

She shook her head. 'I like the quiet, and pretending it's just me who lives here. I like to pretend that you and Mrs Duncan are my mum and dad.'

He didn't respond but she had the feeling he liked her saying it. But as lovely as it was being all alone during the day, it was better when the others came back from school.

After tea they usually went out into the back garden and played rounders, but as Janet couldn't run with crutches she'd sit on a bench and watch. Usually one or other of the children would join her, and they'd have a chat. They told her what they'd done that day at school, and talked about the teachers.

The plaster came off her leg just as the school summer holiday started, and it was good to have the company of the other children during the day.

She soon found that Jackie, Sandra and Wendy, her three roommates, were a bit dull. Now she could run about and climb trees, she wanted to play more imaginative games, like Pirates, but to her disappointment they couldn't seem to understand her rules. Back in Dale Street she'd invented the game, which involved pretending milk crates, in a pattern, were rocks, the rest sea, and the Pirates had to jump from one to another. If they stepped onto the pavement they were out. If no crates were available, they had to hop from one paving stone to another without touching a crack. There were no spare milk crates at Summer Fields so she had to use bean bags, skipping ropes and other items as rocks.

Someone had to be the captain and shout if any of the Pirates had fallen into the sea, but although her three roommates were good at hopping from one rock to another, when it was their turn to be the captain they couldn't seem to get it, or maybe they just didn't watch carefully enough. But even if they were useless at the game, she'd rather be sharing with them than be in the other room with Brenda. She was thirteen and very spiteful. She regularly reduced her two roommates, Pat and Ann, to tears.

Overall, the summer holiday was marvellous to Janet. The weather was good, and the children stayed out in the garden playing hide and seek, chase, making a den under the bushes at the bottom of the garden, hopscotch squares on the path, or swinging on the rope that hung from the big oak tree. On wet days they stayed in the playroom and looked at comics, books or did colouring. Janet liked Snakes and Ladders and she always had someone who wanted to play with her.

But Brenda was a fly in the ointment. She did her best to spoil most games. When Janet was organizing

Pirates she'd move the pretend rocks so they couldn't possibly jump from one to another. She'd snatch comics and run off with them, tipping the Snakes and Ladders board up as she went by, so they had to start the game again.

But what Janet despised most was how she humiliated the younger children. Little Philip often had toilet accidents. She called him 'Shit Pants' and 'Stinky Bum'. Janet was very glad she had no obvious defect, other than crooked teeth, as Brenda picked up on anything she could use. Jackie stuttered, Wendy had a lazy eye, Brian had a dark red birthmark on his right cheek, and hardly a day passed without Brenda saying something hurtful about these things. Even worse, whoever her victim was that day, she would shout out the reason he or she had been sent to Summer Fields in the first place.

Janet knew she must have either overheard staff discussing a child, or got into the Duncans' office to look at the files. It was fairly certain that she hadn't got her information from any of the children as it seemed to be an unwritten rule that they wouldn't talk about their past and background.

Janet had learned at an early age it was good practice to get some information on bullies to use against them. So, she watched Brenda carefully and observed that she buttered up the staff and told tales on the other children. Some of the children had occasional visitors, mostly relatives who brought them sweets. These sweets and other little presents always disappeared from their lockers, and Janet was certain that Brenda was the culprit.

One morning they were all out in the garden playing rounders. Sandra was fielding and caught the ball, so Brenda was out before she even reached first base.

Predictably Brenda was furious, rounding on Sandra with some ridiculous claim that Sandra had cheated. 'No wonder your mum left you outside Woolworth's in a pram,' she yelled at her. 'You must have been a horrible baby.'

The way Brenda had delivered that information made it seem likely it was the truth, and perhaps Sandra had even known she'd been abandoned because she burst into tears.

Sandra was nine, pretty with pure blonde hair and large blue eyes, but Janet had realized almost on their first meeting that she was sensitive and very nervous.

'That's it, cry like a baby,' Brenda taunted her. 'Was yer mum drunk and went off with a man too?'

'Don't be so horrible.' Janet squared up to the older girl. 'I bet your mum begged a social worker to take you away because she couldn't stand you.'

Brenda's face flushed angrily, and she lunged at Janet to hit her.

Janet had learned survival in Dale Street. All of the

kids there had to learn to fight their own corner at an early age and Janet was no exception. She jumped nimbly to the right and Brenda fell flat on her face. Janet leaped astride her back, catching her hands and holding them down. 'Not so tough now, are we?' she said.

All the other children had gathered around them, and Janet knew it would be only a matter of minutes before Mr or Mrs Duncan came out to intervene.

'You are a bully, a snitch and a thief,' Janet said. 'I know it's you who steals sweets.' She turned her head to Paul, one of the older boys. 'Run up and check her locker. If there's sweets, bring them down.' She returned her attention to Brenda. 'What gives you the right to be so nasty to other kids? We're all the same here. We've either got no mother, or a useless one.' She slapped Brenda round the head as hard as she could. 'You're a big, stupid lump. All you'll be good for is working in a factory when you leave here. And I bet you'll be up the spout with the first man who even looks at you. Chances are that baby will be taken from you. God knows you've shown you can't care for anyone.'

Paul came running out holding sweets in the bottom of his shirt. Hot on his heels was Mr Duncan.

'Let Brenda get up, Janet,' Mr Duncan called. 'What's this all about?'

Janet stood up and pointed to the sweets Paul had

dropped on the grass. 'She's a bully and a thief. She steals sweets from the other kids. And she says cruel things about all of them. You'd better watch out she's not stealing from you too. And she pokes into your files to find out about the rest of us.'

'That will do, Janet,' he said.

Janet liked Mr Duncan. They all did. Tall and well built, with a shock of untidy curly brown hair, he made Janet think of an oak tree, strong enough to take all winds and weathers and providing welcome shade to those who needed it. He played games, he comforted, advised, and took as much interest in each of them as if they were his own children.

Brenda was crying, but as she was three years older than Janet and much taller, no one would have taken her for a victim. Mr Duncan looked down at the sweets on the grass. At a rough guess there was about half a crown's worth. 'Where did you find these?' he asked Paul.

'In Brenda's locker drawer,' Paul said. 'And it's true what Janet said. She is a bully.'

'Fighting is no way to deal with situations like this,' Mr Duncan said to Janet. 'You should have come to me.'

'You wouldn't have believed me,' she responded, 'because she sucks up to you and Mrs Duncan. You don't hear the cruel things she says about some of us.

Today she told Sandra her mother abandoned her in her pram outside Woolworths.'

'Did you take these sweets?' He moved closer to Brenda and his expression was very cold. 'Don't even think of lying to me.'

'Yes,' she whimpered. 'But I never get given any sweets.'

'Neither do several other children here, but you have pocket money to buy your own. Now go to my office and wait there.'

She walked towards the house a little unsteadily.

Mr Duncan took Janet's hand and led her to a garden seat away from the others. 'As I said, fighting is never the answer. You're probably delighted with yourself for taking Brenda to task for bullying, and I expect she deserved your anger. But I don't want to see you trying to sort things out yourself again. That's what I'm here for. All you children have been through some very bad times, and at Summer Fields my wife and I are trying to help you forget them and learn to live as if the other children here are your brothers and sisters. Most families have squabbles from time to time, and it will be no different here. But after I've dealt with Brenda, you must make up with her. Don't shut her out or she'll become even more bitter than she is now. Can you do that for me?'

Janet looked into his dark brown eyes and felt the difference between him and William Masters.

Mr Duncan was kind, fair-minded and nobody's fool. She wished she'd had a father like him.

'Yes, sir,' she said.

With clenched teeth Janet apologized to Brenda, who was never destined to be a friend to her but after that day she was less nasty. Janet wondered what her story was. She thought it must be as sad as her own. Sandra clung to Janet now, and there was comfort in that. It was like having a little sister.

But even Brenda couldn't spoil her happiness at being sent to Summer Fields. She loved everything about it, the comfy clean beds, and wearing clothes that smelt of outdoors, not mould. They had good meals and hot baths. Mr Duncan made them all squeal when he chased them with the garden hose while he was watering the flowers, and Mrs Duncan gave lovely hugs.

Before Janet knew it the holidays were over, and she had to start at the school in the village. She needed some extra help with arithmetic: she was behind the rest of her class, because of the weeks she'd been in hospital, but also because at St Michael's they'd spent more time learning the catechism than they had conquering fractions and decimals. But she was good at English because she read so much.

The autumn term passed quickly, then Christmas was over, the best she'd ever had, and Easter, and before long she'd been in Summer Fields for a year. It was during the summer holidays of 1951 that Mrs Duncan took her to an orthodontist to have her teeth straightened. Janet had passed her eleven-plus and was due to start at Maidstone Grammar School for Girls in September, and Mrs Duncan said she would feel much more confident about the brace on her teeth if she had a few weeks to get used to it before she started at her new school.

At first, the brace was torture, and Janet didn't believe she'd ever get used to it or to being able to speak without hissing. But she'd been shown before and after pictures of other girls who had had their teeth straightened and the results were astounding. She resigned herself to it. It wasn't very long before she had forgotten it was even in her mouth.

Miss Cooling had come to see her just after she'd heard she'd been accepted at the grammar school. 'I'm so very proud of you, Janet,' she said, taking Janet's hand in hers affectionately. 'So many children who have had a bad start in life haven't got the strength of character to overcome it. The grammar school will be another test of your spirit and ability. If you do well and pass your O and A levels, you can go on to university and choose the career of your dreams. Have you considered what that will be?'

'I want to be an actress.'

Miss Cooling's face fell. 'That isn't an easy field to

get into. I know you played the lead once in your school play, but from what I know most actors come from rather grand backgrounds.'

'I can easily pretend to be quite grand,' Janet said airily. 'You just watch me.'

6

Alice

Alice was compelled to put her mother's past on the back burner for a couple of weeks because she was so busy at work. Most of the hotels under her supervision had a wedding at the weekends, and some were revamping bedrooms and the public rooms. All this involved strong organization, especially as weddings could be a potential minefield.

In May she managed a three-day break midweek and planned to go to London to meet the actress Genevieve Stratton. It seemed she was well known back in the sixties, with many parts in films, in Britain and in Hollywood. She now lived in Fulham.

When Alice rang her to ask if they could meet, Genevieve didn't remember a Fleur Faraday, but she appeared very keen to talk about her time in repertory and said that if Alice had some photographs of her mother, she was sure they would jog her memory.

The photographs were a problem: all the ones Alice owned were from the eighties onwards, but

Stuart had trawled through an online collection of old theatre flyers and found just one with Fleur and Genevieve in it.

Unless the photographer had touched up the picture before it was printed on the flyer, both women were gorgeous, Fleur a blonde bombshell, and Genevieve a dark-haired beauty. Alice was surprised to see that her mother had been quite so lovely when young. While people had always remarked on her good skin, her slim figure, and that she was unfailingly glamorous, she supposed few children viewed their mother as adults did.

On the train to London, Alice felt a trifle panicked. Genevieve had sounded as bright as a button, and spoke with faultless BBC diction, but she had to be eighty, so her memory and hearing might be failing.

'Cross that bridge when you come to it,' she murmured to herself. While googling the actress she found she had been in a film Alice had once hired from a video shop. It seemed weird now, with Netflix and smart TVs, that there had been shops full of films for hire. This one was called *The House on the Marsh*. Made in 1990, it was billed as a thriller, and Genevieve had played a rather sinister housekeeper.

Alice had loved the film, even though there were no big names in it. In fact, she'd recommended it to several people. Perhaps if she'd mentioned it to her parents, it might have provoked her mother to speak out about knowing the leading lady. But she didn't think her parents had ever hired a video.

As she was early, Alice stopped for coffee near Fulham Broadway tube station. She hadn't been to Fulham since she'd worked in London in her teens. It was an up-and-coming area then so she certainly couldn't afford to get a flat there. Now Fulham was completely gentrified, and when she looked in a couple of estate agents' windows for house prices, there was hardly anything for less than a million pounds.

Tournay Road was a smart Victorian terraced street of mainly three-storey houses, with evidence of further renovation work going on at several. Alice smiled at the number of plantation shutters that had been installed: once, gentrification had meant coaching lights at either side of the front door. She could bet most of the houses had a huge open-plan living space, and a bathroom for every bedroom.

Number twenty-nine was tidy, but it looked tired compared to its neighbours. She noted six bells: Genevieve hadn't got the whole house to herself.

Taking a deep breath to steady herself, she pressed the button marked 'Stratton'. She heard it buzz, which suggested it was the ground-floor flat. It seemed for ever before she heard the crackle of the intercom. 'Who is it?' a cultured voice asked.

'Alice Kent,' she replied, and there was a buzz from the front door.

Alice went into a somewhat dingy hallway. The door on her left opened.

'Do come in, Alice,' Genevieve said.

Alice had imagined the actress to be of statuesque build, but she was no more than five feet tall. Her face was deeply lined, and she was very thin, yet her commanding voice belonged to someone much bigger and younger.

'Please call me Genny,' she said, after Alice had thanked her for inviting her. 'And the pleasure is all mine. I'm terribly alone most of the time. All my old pals have either fallen off the stage of life or moved to nursing homes by the sea.'

Genny's flat was rather dark and musty and appeared to be two rooms knocked into one, every inch of it stuffed with objects that had to be memorabilia. Although the window was large it faced north and the room was made darker still by theatrically draped old cotton lace curtains. Through a doorway, she glimpsed a kitchen and sunshine from a window. She assumed the bedroom and bathroom were back there too.

The theatrical theme was everywhere: a red trunk for a coffee-table, framed photographs of actors and posters of shows. A few old string puppets hung beneath a high shelf that held porcelain heads wearing wigs or headdresses. In the window a round Victorian supper table was covered with a heavy chenille cloth, which made Alice think of fortune-tellers. She spotted a crystal ball among a collection of antique elbow-length gloves and close by a tray was laid out with flamboyant brooches and necklaces.

'All things I've worn in stage shows or films,' Genny said, waving her hand to a corner by the window where a dressmaker's dummy wore a racy-looking red and black satin dress. 'I wore that in a Western. I loved being a saloon girl – it was such fun.'

'Gosh,' was all Alice could say. 'There's so much to look at, and I'm sure every single thing has a story.'

It was scarily dusty. She doubted the room had been cleaned thoroughly in years.

'It certainly has. So many memories . . . but do sit. Shall we have a glass of sherry?'

Alice would have preferred tea or coffee, but she had a feeling Genny wanted sherry. 'That would be lovely. Thank you.' She sat down on an almost thread-bare chesterfield, the back of which was strewn with silk scarves.

'Have you lived here a long time?' she ventured, as Genny poured sherry into two glasses.

'Donkey's years,' she said. 'I bought the place when Fulham was working class and cheap. I can't believe how much houses cost here now. My tenants have all been here for years too. It's a house for waifs and strays.'

After she'd handed Alice her sherry and sat down on a chair opposite her, she began to tell a tale about one of her tenants, who was titled but down on her luck: she had married a real cad who spent all her money. It was fascinating, but Alice knew she'd be there all day if she didn't get the old lady back to the point of the visit, which she suspected Genny had forgotten.

'It's all very well being Lady Whatever, but it doesn't cut much ice when you need to live on a tight budget and have to apply for assistance. Poor woman, when she first came here she'd walk all the way to Fortnum's to buy tea and biscuits, which I suspect was all she lived on. I had to tell her about Tesco just down the road and suggest easy things to cook. She didn't have a clue about domestic matters – she'd been looked after by servants since birth.'

It was only when Genny went to pour herself another sherry that Alice took out of her bag the flyer for the play in Bristol that Genny starred in. 'I found this,' she said, holding it out to her. 'You're with Fleur, my mother.'

Genny took it, picked up some gold-rimmed glasses and studied it. 'Oh, yes . . . It's coming back to me now. Fleur was a very pretty girl, and this was in Bristol. I loved playing there,' she said, smiling at Alice. 'Such a delightful city. I took Fleur on a long walk to see all the sights. She was very taken with the suspension bridge and the Downs. She'd never been to Bristol before. She was a Londoner, I seem to remember.'

'Was she a good actress?' Alice asked. 'You see, until just a short while after she died, I never knew she'd been on the stage.'

'She was good in *Blithe Spirit* – the character of Elvira, a ghost who wants to disrupt the second marriage of her husband Charles, was ideal for her. She was, as I recall, a mischievous minx.'

Alice knew from the way Genny pursed her lips that she hadn't liked her mother. 'In what way?' she asked.

'I don't like to speak ill of the dead,' Genny said. 'However, I don't think you would have come to me unless you were puzzled by something about your mother. Is that so?'

Alice took a sip of her sherry and, although it was something she never drank, she enjoyed the instant hit of warmth. 'She never told my sister and me anything about her past. We didn't even know she was once called Fleur Faraday. It wasn't her real name.'

Genny smiled and reached out one tiny hand to touch Alice's forearm. 'Actresses who change their name are as common as wasps at a picnic,' she said. 'I was lucky, I suppose, that I was given a good stage name at birth. Poor Diana Dors. Imagine being called Diana Fluck.'

81

Alice laughed. She knew Genny was attempting to dissuade her from further questions, and it made her like the woman more to find she was protective.

'Tell me,' Genny said. 'What sort of mother was she to you?'

'Not exactly Mother of the Year, but I had a happy childhood. But whether she was a good mother or not isn't my issue with her, Genny. It's the lack of information about before I was born that concerns me. I know she was born in Chatham, but that's about it, not what her parents were like, if she had any siblings. Or how she came to end up in Devon.'

Genny frowned, as if she was struggling to remember. 'She didn't say much about her past. She wasn't the sort to do that. But I don't think she'd had a happy childhood,' she said finally. She glanced at Alice as if wanting to stop there but sighed as if she knew she was expected to carry on. 'My feelings were that she'd closed the door on her past, intending to reinvent herself. I felt she muscled in on those who might be useful to her. She certainly tried to befriend me.'

She got up to refill her glass and Alice sensed she shouldn't push this any further. So she asked Genny to tell her about Hollywood and flattered her by saying how much she'd liked *The House on the Marsh*.

'I enjoyed making that one,' Genny said, looking suddenly animated and younger. 'It was filmed in Norfolk, miles from anywhere. The old man who had owned the house had died, and his family were happy to take money from the film company and let us romp around in it. My God, it was cold, though. Terrible draughts, the boiler always giving up when you wanted a bath. We all drank a great deal to keep warm.'

There were several other racy stories and finally Alice felt brave enough to broach the subject of Fleur again. 'I think you didn't trust Fleur,' she said. 'Am I right?'

Genny had refilled her glass several times as she talked and maybe she'd forgotten that she'd moved away deliberately from the subject earlier. 'That's right. I didn't like the way she outmanoeuvred people.'

Alice didn't know what to make of that statement.

'It was traditional to have a party at the theatre after the final dress rehearsal. The local press would be there, and the cast would be in their costumes. We often carried on in character for the benefit of the reporters – if we entertained them well, they gave us better reviews. But Fleur didn't always play the game. She'd waft in wearing something sensational and, of course, she hogged the limelight, the press thinking she was a big star. She did it once when we were in Edinburgh. She had only a few lines in that play but arrived in a hired ball gown and convinced the journalists she was going to be the next big show-business name. They were all agog. But, as annoying as that was, we all made allowances for her because she was hungry for fame. The thing we really disliked, though, was the way she delighted in making a play for any man in the cast that one of us girls fancied. She didn't want those men. She did it just to show us she could get them if she felt like it.'

Alice had a sudden memory of her mother in a red sparkly frock, flirting shamelessly with a neighbour's husband at a Christmas party about ten years earlier. She and Emily had been embarrassed because their mother was so brazen. The man's wife was in the room, and she looked like she wanted to kill Sally. Alice knew her mother was doing it purely to show the woman that she could have him if she chose to, and Emily was upset by it. Alice had to convince her sister that their mother was drunk, and it didn't mean anything.

Oddly enough, at the funeral she'd heard another neighbour say, 'Well, at least we won't need to lock up our husbands any more.' Clearly Sally had behaved like that many times in the past.

Genny was on the verge of dropping off, her chin nearly on her chest. The endless sherries had taken their toll. Alice knew it was time she went.

'I'd better go. I've taken up enough of your time,' she said, getting to her feet. 'You've been marvellous. But, tell me, do you know anyone else from that time who might give me a new perspective?'

Genny yawned and rubbed her eyes. For a moment Alice thought she'd forgotten about her visitor. But then she smiled. 'She told me once about a friend who often turned up to the theatres to see her. I think she said she was an old school friend. I even remember Fleur laughing about the girl's name and it certainly was a weird one. Petula Goodwilly. I've often laughed about it myself.'

'Even worse than Diana Fluck.' Alice chuckled. 'If I was Petula, I'd have changed it.'

'At least people remember those with weird names. I knew an actress called Julia Caesar.'

Alice moved in the direction of the door but bent down and placed a card with her phone number on the red trunk. 'I'm sure you've had enough of me, so I'll be off. Thank you for talking to me, and if you think of anything else that might help, do ring me.'

'I've a feeling Fleur's agent was Diane Lombard. She'd be long dead now, but I'm certain her daughter Mira kept the agency on. It's a long shot but her mother knew everyone, and she may turn out to be a chip off the proverbial.'

'I'll check her out and drop you a line if anything good turns up.'

Somewhat disheartened, Alice walked back to the tube station. She had booked into a bed-and-breakfast in Chiswick and had arranged to have dinner tonight with an old friend, Louise, but she had hoped to find out something positive before that.

The sherry she'd drunk was making her head feel fuzzy, so she went into a café near the tube station and ordered a pot of tea and a prawn mayonnaise sandwich.

While she was waiting she googled Mira Lombard, not for one moment expecting to be successful. But, to her surprise, there she was, an attractive redhead. Daughter of the theatrical agent Diane Lombard, she had followed in her mother's footsteps and ran an agency for entertainers, singers, dancers, comedians and magicians. Her office was in Shepherd's Bush.

In less than an hour Alice was in Shepherd's Bush Road, standing at a door beside an off-licence and looking at a sign that read 'Lombard Entertainers. 1st floor'. She rang the bell and told the person who answered she wanted to see Mira Lombard about a friend of her mother's. She waited and waited. Then just as she was about to ring again, she heard a buzz and the door opened.

She had expected grubby starkness, but instead the carpet up the stairs was charcoal grey and the walls had two-tone grey wallpaper with dashes of silver, very designer chic.

The staircase led into a reception area, still all grey

but with a scarlet sofa and two marble-topped side tables.

'Miss Lombard wishes to know the name of your mother's friend,' said the receptionist, who had poker-straight, very shiny long black hair. Her lips looked pumped up with fillers and her lipstick was the exact colour of the sofa.

'Genevieve Stratton.'

The girl disappeared down the passage but returned almost immediately. 'Miss Lombard can give you ten minutes,' she said crisply.

Mira Lombard was no longer a redhead but had dyed her hair black – she looked as if she'd stuck her head up a chimney. In contrast her thin face was deathly pale. She wore winged glasses that were purple and worthy of Dame Edna Everage. Her suit was the same purple and she had a choker necklace of black beads. She was certainly theatrical-looking, but not glamorous, as she was on her website. In fact, she looked scary.

'You know Genny Stratton then?' she said, holding out a skinny hand to Alice. It felt as welcoming as a dead eel.

'I contacted her about my mother who died recently. I hadn't known she was an actress once, and it made me excited to know more,' Alice began. 'Genny said you were a baby back then, but she thought your mother might have mentioned Fleur Faraday to you.'

Mira nodded. 'Yes, she did, but I'm not sure you'd want to hear what she said.'

'Bad as that?' Alice said, and forced a smile.

'Mother had issues with her because she had a fling with my father. Well, Mother said she flung herself at him. She didn't say if the flinging had led to sex. Apparently, no man who had a few bob was safe from her.'

'I'm sorry to hear that,' Alice said, blushing furiously. 'I know so little about my mum . . . Maybe I ought to refrain from digging any further.'

'My mother once said it was a shame because she wasn't a bad actress. But Mother took what she'd done very personally, and I suspect she made sure Fleur got no more acting work.'

Alice didn't know how to reply to such a blunt explanation. She'd think about it and work out how she felt. 'Well, thank you for seeing me,' she said. 'There's no point in apologizing on behalf of my mum, any more than you'd apologize for yours.'

'I suspect mine was every bit as treacherous,' Mira said, and gave what passed for a smile. 'Hardly a day passes that I don't wish she'd given me up for adoption.'

'Really?'

'She was a witch,' Mira said. 'And that's not just my opinion. But, hey-ho, we don't get to choose our mothers. I'm grateful she left a healthy business for me to take over, and that I appear to have inherited her steel spine.'

Alice smiled, beginning to think this woman was nicer than she appeared. 'I don't suppose you knew a friend of my mother's, Petula Goodwilly? Such a ridiculous name.'

'I do indeed,' Mira said, and gave a real smile. 'She worked for me for a couple of years as a reception-ist – she was good too. Remembered the name of every client, extraordinarily efficient. I thought I'd go under without her. But the poor sap fell for some farmer and disappeared off to Sussex. She's Petula Parks now, and still sends me Christmas cards, always with a picture of their Georgian house in the snow. I think she hopes it makes me jealous. Which it does.'

Alice laughed, for that last remark showed Mira wasn't as nasty as she liked to pretend she was. 'Could you give me her address?' she ventured. 'I promise I won't tell her she's made you jealous.'

'She'll tell you stories that'll make your hair curl,' Mira said. She opened a desk drawer, rummaged a bit and drew out a card. 'You can believe about half of them. She rang me about a month ago and said she had dementia. She proved that wasn't true because she mentioned quite a few old clients and didn't get anything wrong.'

Alice took the card. It wasn't a standard Christmas card, but a print of an original and superb watercolour. The grey Georgian house, sheep standing by a fence in the snow, the leafless trees, and a leaden sky, were all so sombre, yet the pillar-box red front door brought the whole scene to life.

'I'd like a bigger version of that to hang on my wall,' Alice said.

'It was painted by Petula. She's a very talented artist,' Mira said. 'I always said it was a shame I didn't handle painters. Go and see her. You'll like her – even I did.'

As Alice rode back to Chiswick in a taxi, she studied the card more closely. It was a lovely picture, and as she gazed at Petula's classic copperplate handwriting inside, she felt a warm glow. She knew she would like her.

7

Janet, 1956

'Janet, I'm sorry, but you have to leave Summer Fields. We're only allowed to keep you here until you're sixteen,' Mrs Duncan said gently. 'The rule the Children's Department has made is that at sixteen you're old enough to fend for yourself.'

'But I wanted to stay on at school and do A levels,' Janet said, her eyes filling with tears. She had been so sure the Duncans would bend the rules for her. They had been thrilled when she got a place at Maidstone Grammar School for Girls and continued to be overjoyed as she had remained top of her class for the last five years. 'I can't stay at school if I've got to go and live in a bedsit or something. I was hoping I might even get to university too.'

'Janet, there are so many young children needing a home like Summer Fields. They can't fend for themselves, but you can.'

'So I just have to go?'

Olive Duncan felt an ache in her heart for Janet. Both she and her husband Rob had grown very fond of her over the five years she'd been with them. She was clever, hard-working at school, good with the younger children, and she'd grown into such a beautiful girl, with her blonde hair and expressive brown eyes. Knowing the awful home she'd come from they had expected trouble with her, but there had been none. She was grateful to live in such a good place, appreciative of their loving care. Now to be forced to sling her out without any kind of further guidance felt so very wrong.

When girls were sent out into the big, wide world with no supervision, advice or encouragement, all they could hope for was domestic work or a job as an office junior or shop assistant. She wasn't old enough yet to get into nursing training and would struggle to pay rent, buy food and clothes, and she'd be lonely. That would single her out as easy prey for manipulative men. Olive didn't know how many girls treated so badly ended up as unmarried mothers, but she was certain it was a huge proportion.

'We can get help for you in finding a room,' Olive said. 'Maybe some money towards bedding and household items. Once you've found a job you could enrol at night school to do your A levels. If you've done well enough in your O levels, which I'm sure you have, you could get into banking or something.'

'However you say it, I'll still be alone,' Janet said, her lips trembling and eyes filling with tears.

Olive put her arms around her. The girl was normally tough, rarely cried about anything and was so outwardly bold and confident that most thought she was hard-hearted. But this situation was different. If Janet had been going to college or university, she'd have been with girls of similar age who were also alone and the pastoral care would ensure they made friends. Olive cursed the Children's Department who imagined girls of sixteen were adults. They weren't: they were still children who needed protection.

'Let's see if I can just wangle you staying here at least until your exam results come through and you find a job,' Olive suggested. 'As you're so bright you could easily get an office job, and make friends with other girls working there.'

Janet was clearly horror-struck.

'Don't look like that,' Olive said. 'I know office work sounds boring, but I did it before I got married, and we had a lot of fun. I made so many friends there. But if you don't like the sound of that, what about a mother's help? You'd live in, and even if you did it just for a year and went to night school, you'd be safe in a good home.'

Janet lifted her head to look at Olive. 'That doesn't sound too bad. How would I go about finding a job like that?'

'*The Lady* is the best magazine for such positions,' Olive said, 'but we could look in the local paper too.

You might even get a place in a swanky part of London, or in Scotland or even abroad.'

Janet's face brightened. 'Maybe an actress with children would want some help. Imagine that! I could ask her how to get into acting.'

Olive laughed. For as long as she could remember Janet had been saying she wanted to be an actress. She hadn't encouraged that ambition, but neither had she shot it down in flames. Janet had had parts in all the school plays, and had the knack of rising above the other kids, getting herself noticed, but that wasn't evidence of acting talent. 'Well, don't bank on it,' she said. 'Most actresses don't have kids, and if they did, they'd be relying on their mum or a nanny to look after them. Acting doesn't pay well unless you hit the big-time.'

But Olive saw, from the sudden light in her eyes, Janet had already decided that was what she wanted to do. She was mercurial, down in the dumps for a little while, then flying high again on ideas and dreams. She guessed the girl was imagining living in a smart house in Kensington or Chelsea, strolling round the London parks pushing a big pram. Maybe she wouldn't get that, but Olive guessed it beat working as an office junior or waitress and living in a bedsitter.

Olive and Rob waved until Janet's train had left the platform at Chatham. Her resilience at the young age of sixteen had astounded them. The day after her chat with Olive she'd got a copy of *The Lady* and applied for three jobs. Her O level results came through just a week or two later and she'd passed eight subjects, including maths, English, French and science. Excellent results if she wanted to do A levels at night school.

'She'll land on her feet whatever she does,' Rob said, putting an arm around his wife as they walked out of the station. 'No one would ever guess she'd had a terrible childhood – she just bounces back from everything. I wouldn't mind betting she finds a way to get on the stage or screen too. Stop worrying about her.'

Olive smiled more brightly than she felt. But she wasn't as sure as Rob about this child. The scars from her early days were still there: she had just learned to hide them. She was off to work for a family in London's Belsize Park: they might not be as wonderful as they sounded. Janet had arrived back from her interview raving about Katy, the adorable two-year-old, and her equally lovable four-year-old sister Suzie. It seemed they had taken to her immediately, while Mr and Mrs Whitestone, who said she was to call them Roger and Mabel, also appeared smitten with Janet. Their home, a spacious Edwardian villa, was apparently lovely, and Janet had a room with her own bathroom, something she'd never imagined. Mabel said she could enrol locally at night school for her A levels, and they would pay her three pounds ten shillings a week all found.

Roger worked at the Stock Exchange and Mabel was a seamstress for a costume-hire company. Janet had told Olive excitedly that the costume company made clothes for films at Shepperton Studios, and for the London theatres. Her work room was in the basement of the house, and she wanted Janet to dissuade the little girls from coming down to see her during the day.

On the face of it, Olive thought it was the perfect job for Janet, at least for now. She liked children, and was good with them, she could cook adequately for children's lunches, and she was so enthralled by the theatre that Mabel would probably find her a first-class sounding board.

But to Olive it was just a bit too perfect. First she would have liked Janet to stay closer to her, so she had someone to run to with any problems. She also knew that any sixteen-year-old might take advantage of the couple's easy, bohemian ways. At Summer Fields they had firm rules, and all the children had to come home straight after school. They could go out to play or have tea with another child as long as there was a proper invitation from his or her mother. In the holidays they had to play in the garden: no roaming around the town with other children. Olive would take them to see a film at the cinema if she considered it suitable, and they sometimes went by train or bus to the seaside too.

Just recently Janet had been dawdling on the way home from school, which meant she was hanging around with someone. She'd also asked to go into town on Saturdays to meet school friends. Olive knew this was entirely normal for a teenage girl who wanted to spread her wings, but she took no chances with children in her care, and if she came across as too strict then so be it. She wondered if she ought to telephone the Whitestones and explain that they should lay down a few rules for Janet, or she might get sucked into bad company.

In the end Olive didn't say anything to them. She saw how excited Janet was to go to their home, and she didn't wish to make the couple suspicious of her. She had behaved perfectly at Summer Fields and there was no reason to suppose she'd go off the rails now.

She remembered when Brenda had had to leave Summer Fields a couple of years ago. She had got a live-in job as a chambermaid in a hotel in Rochester. She had been destined to fall into bad ways – she hadn't made any real friends at the home so there was little hope of her making any at the hotel. Olive could almost write the script for what would happen to her: a waiter would seduce her, then leave, and she'd probably find herself pregnant.

Maybe Janet sensed this too: she gave Brenda a little china dog as a keepsake, hugged her and said, 'Just be careful. Don't trust any men and don't get into trouble.'

Janet had always had the gift of saying the right thing to people. Brenda left Summer Fields with a smile on her face, thinking Janet cared about her. Olive was still expecting a call from Brenda saying she needed help.

Somehow Olive knew that Janet would never ring for help, forced at an early age to take care of herself. Rob had said she would always bounce back, whatever life threw at her.

Just a couple of days earlier Olive had watched as Janet took off the top of a boiled egg for one of the small boys and cut his toast into soldiers to dip them into the yolk. There was so much tenderness in her, real care for those smaller than herself. She just hoped Rob was right.

In early December Janet was at her night-school class in Chalk Farm, sitting next to a girl called Pamela. Since she'd started her course in September she and Pamela had always chatted in the fifteen-minute tea break. They didn't claim to be friends, the time they spent together wasn't sufficient for that, but this evening their teacher Miss Featherstone hadn't turned up and all sixteen students were chatting nineteen to the dozen. Pamela asked Janet where she went on Saturday nights. When she said she never went out in the evenings, except on Wednesdays when she came here, Pamela looked shocked.

Pamela worked for the post office as a telephonist, and she wanted to get a couple of A levels to gain promotion and earn more money. She didn't appear to think much of Janet's job: she said she couldn't think of anything worse than looking after someone's children.

Janet laughed at that. 'They're lovely kids and I'm very happy taking care of them. We go for walks on Hampstead Heath most days, but if it's raining we snuggle up on the sofa and I read to them. I keep their bedroom clean, wash and iron their clothes and make them lunch, but it's not hard work and it's not boring.'

'So you don't ever go to a dance or to the pictures with a boy?' Pamela asked.

Janet shook her head. She didn't want to admit she had no friends to go out with and never got a chance to speak to any boys, let alone get to know them well enough to be asked to the pictures.

'Have you ever had a boyfriend?' Pamela asked.

Again Janet shook her head. 'Have you?'

'Not a proper one. I sometimes go to the pictures with James from work, but he's a bit drippy. I go dancing in Camden Town with a couple of girls from work. I've met a couple of boys there that I danced with and liked. You should come with us one Saturday. Do you like dancing?'

'Yes, I do.' Janet had a happy flashback to evenings at Summer Fields when she and the other children would dance to Radio Luxembourg in the playroom. Bill Haley's 'Rock Around The Clock' was their favourite song, and as they'd seen 'jiving' on the television, all the older girls practised it endlessly. Sometimes the Duncans would come in too, and they taught them to waltz to slow songs.

'What about this Saturday, then?' Pamela suggested. 'Come to my house about seven. You know where I live in Haverstock Hill. I'm less than ten minutes from you.'

'Are you on the phone? Only my boss might have planned to go out that night.'

Mabel and Roger didn't go out often, but she had to ask them if she was allowed. She wasn't sure they would let her.

However, Mabel smiled warmly when she asked permission to go dancing with Pamela. 'Of course you can,' she agreed. 'I was getting worried that you didn't have any friends. At sixteen you should be with people of your own age sometimes. But mind you leave with Pamela. Camden Town can be a bit rough on a Saturday night. And be back here by twelve. Now what are you going to wear?'

Janet had saved her wages for three weeks when she'd first arrived at the end of August and bought a red dress with a scoop neck and a full circular skirt then added a net can-can petticoat to make the skirt of the dress stand out and swish about. Roger White-stone had teased her and said she looked like an extra for *Swan Lake*.

'My new red dress,' Janet said.

'Well, you'll stand out in that, I'm sure every boy will want to dance with you. But be careful, Janet. Young men can be very pushy. I'm sure you know what I mean.'

Janet did. She had overheard a social worker telling Mrs Duncan that Patsy, one of the girls who had been at Summer Fields, had got herself into trouble and she was trying to find a place for her in a home for unmarried mothers.

Janet might not know a great deal about dances, dating boys and such, but even as a six-year-old in Dale Street she'd seen and heard what could happen to girls and women who trusted men blindly. After all, wasn't she a product of her own mother's 'loose' behaviour? She often wondered what her father was like – she liked to think he was a tall blond gentleman, perhaps an officer in the Royal Navy, but common sense told her he was far more likely to be some randy stoker or docker who had plied her mother with so much drink she'd forgotten she was married.

So Janet had promised herself she would never fall for some sweet-talking charmer. She had plans: she was going to become an actress and make a name for herself. She had a profile of the man she would eventually marry in her head. He'd have a good income, preferably in one of the professions, he'd be kind and would show their children the love and care she'd never known. But that would come later.

Meanwhile she wanted to have fun and adventure before settling down. She knew, too, that she had to learn a great deal more about men and life than she knew now.

The dance wasn't quite what Janet had expected. It was in a big room over a large furniture shop and during the week ballet classes were held there. It had a good sprung floor, a big glitter ball in the centre, and the large mirrors and windows were swathed in gold material and some fairy lights. It seemed the barre for ballet was portable, taken out for Saturday night. At the end of the hall a bar was set up with soft drinks. The glasses were plastic.

The music was provided by a man with a greasy quiff who wore a Teddy-Boy red drape jacket. He had a portable record player on what looked like a tea trolley. As Janet moved closer she saw he had his records in small piles. Before Pamela pulled her away to get a drink, she saw one pile marked 'Irish', another

'Slow' and a third 'Jive'. It was the 'Irish' ones that puzzled her.

'Camden Town has a huge Irish population,' Pamela whispered. 'They love their patriotic and soppy songs.'

At first there were only about fourteen girls and five young men so the girls danced together and the men stayed by the bar, watching the girls. Janet felt a bit sorry for the men: she could tell they were manual workers – their hands were rough and calloused, but scrubbed clean. With their cheap, badly fitting suits, unable to stop running a finger round their over-starched shirt collars, they'd never be taken for anything but navvies or dockers.

She'd seen Irish men like them constantly back in Dale Street. On weekday mornings she'd heard the click of their steel-tipped boots as they'd walked to work in the docks. The same men went straight to a pub afterwards. Yet on Sunday morning they were always at Mass, all spruced up, their faces reddened from carbolic soap.

It was said they came to England to make money to send home to their families, but many a time she'd heard the neighbours saying they guessed more money went to the pub than back to Ireland. The men here at the dance were younger, she thought, no older than mid-twenties. Were they hoping to find love here? A nice English girl they could marry and settle down with?

The dance was fun. Janet and Pamela had plenty of partners, but only a couple of the men could jive well, and they were asked to dance more for the slow numbers. Several of the men pressed their bodies up against Janet, which made her stiffen and step back.

When the Irish records played the men sang along. Some even looked emotional, with damp eyes.

'There's no one who can love like an Irishman, so I've heard,' Pamela whispered to her during 'Forty Shades Of Green'.

A lad called Rory asked Janet if he could walk her home. He seemed nice, the only one she'd danced with who could do the waltz. He said in a few months his apprenticeship as an electrician would be up. He came from Cork, but his Irish accent was no more than a soft lilt, which suggested he'd been gently brought up. He had a freckled face, a sticking-out jaw and his teeth were bad but he had good manners, so she let him down kindly, saying she was staying the night with Pamela and that maybe she'd see him next week.

'So what did you think of the dance?' Pamela asked, as they got on the tube to Belsize Park.

'It was fun,' Janet said, not wishing to hurt her new friend by pointing out that it wasn't what she had hoped for.

'We could go to the Empire in Leicester Square next, if you like. That's a proper dance hall and hundreds of people go there. My mum likes me to go to Camden Town – she thinks it's safer, but she's Irish so maybe she hopes I'll fall for an Irish lad.'

They parted at Belsize Park tube station, and Janet stood for a moment, watching her new friend walk away. Pamela was the eldest of five children, and the way her family lived reminded Janet of Dale Street. She had only been asked into the dingy hall of the basement flat, but she was pretty sure there were no more than two bedrooms, and it smelt of damp. She could perfectly well understand why her friend wanted something more from life. Janet wanted to live like the Whitestones did. She wondered how Mabel had met Roger, and how, once you'd found the man with the right credentials, you managed to keep him.

8

Alice

The morning after Alice had met Mira, she set off for Victoria station to catch a train to Arundel to see Petula.

The previous evening she and her friend Louise had drunk too much wine at their get-together dinner in Chiswick but, as always, it had been fun. They'd met as twenty-one-year-olds, working and living in the same grand hotel in Bath. For a year they had shared a rather squalid room in the attic, freezing in winter, baking in summer, and were paid a pittance, but they compensated by whooping it up whenever their evenings off coincided. Later Louise had gone on to work for a catering company in London, Alice to another Bath hotel as assistant manager, and married Simon. Fast forward many years, Louise had her own catering company, which was incredibly successful, and Alice ran her group of hotels.

As always, on the rare occasions they met up, they reverted to eighteen-year-olds, giggling and drinking. They'd gone to a Chinese restaurant and were there till nearly twelve before Alice staggered back to her bed-and-breakfast and Louise to her husband.

On the train Alice glugged down a couple of paracetamol with her bottled water to ease her hangover. But excitement was already making her feel better and she hoped Petula would be as jolly as she'd sounded when she phoned her last night to ask if she could come to see her. She didn't mention her mother, thinking it might be better to approach that after she'd sounded out Petula.

'I'd be delighted to meet you,' she said. 'If Mira gave you my telephone number you are obviously a very special person. She's normally such a dragon that people run off for fear she'll breathe fire on them. Ring me once you're on the Arundel train and I'll come and pick you up.'

There were a few ladies waiting to meet the train, but Alice immediately knew which one was Petula. She was a statuesque woman, wearing a turquoise-embroidered long silk jacket and matching plain silk trousers beneath. Her fiery hair was held back with a yellow and turquoise chiffon scarf and even her shoes were covered with jewels. She had to be getting on for eighty, but she'd have passed for fifty.

Alice went straight up to her. 'Hello, Petula. I hope my radar isn't wrong and in fact you're someone else!'

She laughed. 'You've got the right one. But it was a

case of picking the odd one out! The other women look like little sparrows.'

'I love people who aren't afraid of colour,' Alice said. 'You look amazing.'

It was less than ten minutes to her house, and after insisting Alice was to call her Pet, she chatted the whole way about Mira. 'Her mother, Diane, was an absolute Tartar. If someone was dying of thirst, she'd have charged them for a glass of water. To her, everything and everyone had a price. I wouldn't have lasted with her for five minutes. But Mira is a partial chip off the old block. She pretends to be callous, and convinces most people, but she has a kind heart, and she appreciates real talent. Diane didn't. She saw her clients as a meal ticket.'

Pet went on to say that Jasper, her husband, would be joining them for lunch. 'I tried to put him off, he's got plenty of work to do on the farm, but he always wants to check out new friends. He can be such a bore too. I just hope he doesn't annoy you.'

Alice smiled. Many of her girlfriends had the same problem with their husbands.

It was a very beautiful house, with Georgian arched windows. The seats built into them had cushions that invited you to curl up on them and were upholstered in William Morris fabric. There was a sweeping walnut staircase with an intricately carved newel post. The fireplaces were huge and beautiful, but it was the use of vivid colours that Alice liked best. An enormous jade green sofa was strewn with cushions that were orange but with no uniformity in the fabrics. The lights were astounding, not just fabulous crystal chandeliers, but table lamps in yellow, turquoise and zebra stripes. Alice thought it was time she injected a bit of colour into her flat.

It was only after a delicious lunch of salmon and salad, that Alice felt able to speak about her mother. Jasper wasn't boring – in fact he was charming, frightfully upper class, with a shock of butter-coloured hair, and piercing blue eyes, but he did keep going on about his ewes and the market price for their meat.

After nearly a whole bottle of wine he'd quietened so Alice spoke out: 'I believe you knew Fleur Faraday,' she said to Pet.

'"Knew" in the biblical sense.' Jasper chortled. 'I think everyone did.'

Pet silenced him with a glare. 'Go away, Jasper,' she said. 'We grown-ups have things to talk about.'

She turned back to Alice once he'd left the room. 'I'm sorry about that. He does tend to let his mouth overtake his brain after a couple of glasses of wine. I love him dearly, but I do sometimes plan his funeral to cheer myself.'

Alice giggled. She really liked this woman and hoped they could become friends.

'Yes, she was a dear friend, or at least I thought of her as such. Not sure she valued me. Fleur was quite a force to be reckoned with,' Pet went on. 'What is your connection with her?'

'She was my mother.' At Pet's startled expression Alice realized she'd been too blunt. 'I'm sorry. Perhaps I should have told you on the phone before I got here. But please don't edit any recollections of her or your opinion of her because she's dead. Until her funeral I had absolutely no knowledge of her background.'

'Oh dear.' Pet gave a deep sigh.

Alice took that to mean she didn't know where to begin or was afraid of hurting her feelings. 'Just say it as it was. I only want the truth, and I promise I won't get upset if it's unpleasant. I believe you went to school with her.'

'That isn't so, but we'll come back to that. I think you and Mira have something in common. As I said earlier, Diane, her mother, was a witch. For a long time no one dared give their real opinion of her,' Pet said, 'but maybe you're truly like Mira and already know your mother's faults.'

'I didn't know my mother had been married bigamously until the day after her funeral, or that she'd been an actress. She never told my sister and me anything about her life prior to marrying Ralph. We believed he was our dad, but he isn't. She even lied about her age.'

Pet looked thoughtful. 'Well, I'm all for that. I intend to say I'm seventy for evermore,' she said, with a smile. 'Now I did hear about the bigamy. People were saying Fleur knew about his wife all along, but I didn't believe that. I mean, why would she knowingly marry an already married man?'

'That's the bit I can't get my head around,' Alice said. 'One school of thought is that she wanted something over him so she could get rid of him easily when she was tired of him. But that seems outrageously calculating, even by her standards. She did like to manipulate, and always to be the top dog. But could it really have been about getting a house from Angus, the man in question?'

'Let me put my cards on the table,' Pet said. 'I loved Fleur. She was funny, stimulating, great company, but she told a lot of lies, and she was driven by some demon. She never told me about her background, and I suspected, because of her silence, that it was grim. She wanted to be the centre of attention, and she mostly was. Woe betide anyone who outshone her. She'd go out with men and sucker them into buying her expensive clothes and jewellery. When I remonstrated with her, she laughed. "I don't see anything wrong in selling yourself. Let's face it, Pet, if a man is ugly, he's not going to get a beautiful girlfriend without buying her affection."'

'That's a bit cynical.' Alice laughed, not in the least offended. 'If the woman is famous in her own right, or rich, maybe she'd choose an ugly man because she knows he will always value her.'

'I dare say a few are like that, but Fleur wasn't rich or famous. She was beautiful, and maybe if she'd met up with a film producer who gave her the right role she might have gone places. But, as lovely as she was, in the theatre she was just another mediocre actress. Though I believe Diane, Mira's mother, thought she was good – at least until she got up to no good with her chap. But what is it you want to know, Alice?'

'Just to be able to see the entire woman, not just my mother.'

'I could tell you lots of stories about her, but I don't think any of them will satisfy you. To start with I didn't go to school with her. I was working at the Everyman cinema in Hampstead. My parents despaired – they hadn't aimed for me to show people to their seats and sell ice cream. I was changing the posters outside when Fleur spoke to me. She was carrying a suitcase and looked worn out. I sensed she'd run away from home, a job or a man. She was a teenager and this was the late fifties. As pretty and outwardly confident as she seemed, I thought she'd just come through something awful.'

'Like what?' Alice asked.

Pet shook her head. 'I never did get her to tell me. Not even after we became firm friends. But that day, when she broke down and cried, my heart went out to her. She said she needed a job and somewhere to stay. I've always been a bit of a sucker for lame dogs, and as it happened I knew Frankie James, the land-lady of a theatrical digs. She was always looking for help. And Frankie was a good, kind woman. By the way, your mum told me that day her name was Fleur Faraday. From the way she said it, I knew it wasn't real, just one she'd plucked out of the air in an instant.'

'Weren't you afraid of helping someone you knew nothing about?'

Pet fluffed up her hair while she thought about that. 'I was young then too, only three years older and impulsive. I just wanted to help her. Besides, I knew Frankie would take her in hand. She was used to people coming and going – it was a messy, noisy house and I thought she was very likely to winkle out of Fleur what had happened to her.'

'Did she?'

Pet smiled. 'You're every bit as persistent as Fleur was. You don't really look like her, it's the dark hair that throws me, but there is something, a directness. If Frankie found out Fleur's story, she didn't tell me. But, moving on, as it happened she and Fleur were a match made in Heaven. Fleur was a great little house-keeper. Somewhere along the line she'd learned to clean well, and to cook. Frankie loved her, so much so she used her influence to get Fleur some work in a repertory company.'

'So is that how she became an actress?'

Pet threw her head back and laughed. 'You're as

naive as your mum was. There's a bit more to acting than walking onto a stage and saying a few lines.'

'So how did it happen for her?'

'She had a knack of buttering up the right people. Well, men anyway. And Frankie introduced her to one or two who would push her forward. But, Alice, at that time many of the theatres up and down the country had travelling companies that put on a new play each week. Farces were particularly popular back then and they always called for a naive pretty maid, and it turned out that Fleur could do the wide-eyed innocent very well, so she was taken on.'

'Did she do the casting-couch routine for it?' Alice asked, with a snigger.

'I suspect so,' Pet said. 'She worried me in those early days. It was clear she was carrying something bad inside her. Frankie and I were her only friends – she had no family. She did tell me she'd been going to night school with a view to university, but she never said why she abandoned the idea. It was like she'd built a brick wall around her to hide her past. She never dropped her guard, not the odd little story from childhood, not mentioning a place she'd lived in. I wondered how anyone could do that.'

'Is Frankie still alive? Maybe she'd know more?'

'She died about ten years ago. She'd been in a nursing home before she had the stroke that killed her. I had kept in touch, just the odd letter and Christmas card. She sold the house in Hampstead and moved to a bungalow in Broadstairs – I went to see her there once, must have been fifteen years ago or more. She asked me about Fleur, but I couldn't tell her anything. It seemed she'd disappeared entirely. Like me, Frankie had heard about the bigamy. We even heard she had two children, but we didn't know where she was.'

'So if you were friends, why did she run from you? What went wrong? Why didn't she stay in touch? I mean, even if she was in trouble, surely she could count on you.'

Pet closed her eyes as if needing a moment to consider what she'd been asked. 'If only she had, Alice. I'd have loved to be involved with you and your sister, be an aunt to you both. It grieved me that she was able to forget what good friends we'd been. But Fleur was in the habit of dropping people once she'd got what she wanted from them. I'm not sure what she wanted from me, maybe just insight into how posh people live – she hung on with me longer than she did with anyone else. But shortly before she disappeared, if I turned up, she'd say she was meeting someone or had to go somewhere. I soon cottoned on that she'd lost interest in me, or she was up to something she knew I wouldn't approve of, so I backed away.'

'That's very sad,' Alice said, and she meant it. She could have done with an auntie like Pet while she was growing up.

Pet gave a brittle laugh. 'The strange thing is, I suspect if she'd known that by marrying Jasper I'd end up with this place, she'd have been inviting herself down. She met him several times at backstage parties, but although she played up to him, she wasn't interested enough to find out what he did or anything about his background. She slipped up there as his family are stinking rich.'

'Jasper implied she slept around. Did she?'

Pet sighed again. 'Yes, darling, she did. They said no man was safe with her, but that's an exaggeration. She only went for money and power.'

'Angus wasn't rich,' Alice pointed out.

'Nor was Barney, another man she was with for a time. As with Angus, I never met him either. So she slipped up with them. Maybe it was love. But, tell me, what is Angus like?'

'Well, now I know he's my real father that kind of puts a new slant on him. I'd say he's a decent man and hard-working, but weak. He said Mum had bewitched him!' Alice wanted to giggle every time she said that.

'I think a lot of men she ensnared would think that,' Pet said, with a wry smile. 'I can remember wishing I had the same effect on men.'

'But you got what you wanted without guile,' Alice pointed out. 'How many years have you been married? Did you have children?'

'Married for forty years, and two sons, both in

their mid-thirties. It was far better than any illustrious career. I gave up working for Mira when the first of the boys arrived – I'd been commuting to London three days a week, and there was no time for my art, or anything else. But although I'm very happy with my life, I miss Mira.'

'Any idea what my mum did after she stopped acting?'

For the first time Pet wasn't looking at Alice but began fiddling with her scarf and seemed ill at ease. 'Not really,' she said, after a moment's thought. 'Of course, rumours flew around – she was one of those people who are always talked about.'

'So what was said?'

'I don't want to tell you that.'

'We agreed we'd be honest.' Alice looked at Pet's face and saw anxiety written all over it. 'She was my mother and I need to know, however bad it is.'

'I don't think I can, Alice,' she said, her voice strained and weak. 'It's too shocking.'

'You can't say that and leave me wondering. For goodness' sake, tell me!'

There was a moment of utter silence while Alice waited to hear what Pet found so upsetting.

'God forgive me, Alice,' she said eventually. 'I was told she was running a brothel.'

9

Janet

Janet was putting on her make-up when Mabel knocked on her bedroom door. 'I don't want to spoil your evening, dear,' she said. Her anxious expression immediately told Janet that that was exactly what she was about to do. 'I've just had a phone call from my sister. Our mother is gravely ill and she says I must get to the hospital tonight. Roger is going to drive me to Surrey, but I have to ask you to stay here this evening with Katy and Suzie.'

'Of course I will,' Janet said, though her heart plummeted. She'd been looking forward all week to going to the Empire in Leicester Square. 'I'm so sorry to hear your mother is so ill. I can cope, however long you'll be away.'

'You're such a good girl,' Mabel said, and reached out to caress Janet's cheek with affection. 'The girls love you, as do Roger and I. He'll be back tonight, but I won't. I'll phone in the morning to see how the girls are and tell you when I'm coming back.'

'Don't worry about the girls. They'll be fine,' Janet

reassured her. 'Go now. I promise you I can manage until you get back.'

Mabel went along the landing to her room, and there was a muffled conversation between her and Roger. Then they went down the stairs, and Janet heard the front door open and close quietly behind them. The car started, and it was driven away into the night.

For a few moments Janet sat dejectedly on her bed, contemplating going out anyway. The girls never woke up at night and she'd be back before Roger came home. But then she remembered how often she'd been left alone at night and how scary it was, and reluctantly she made her way downstairs to phone Pamela.

For a whole year they'd been friends, going out almost every Saturday night. They'd met lads they fancied, some that scared them, a few they couldn't bear. They had made many great memories and had had a great deal of fun.

Next month they would be sitting their exams at night school. Janet was quietly confident she would do well, particularly in English, but Pamela was lagging behind. She didn't seem to care much about her prospects any more. She kept suggesting they got a flat together, not really understanding that her friend hadn't lost sight of her goal to go to university.

It was becoming increasingly obvious to Janet that

when she finally applied for a university place her friend-ship with Pamela was likely to end. The trouble was their bond was formed by going dancing. They had no other shared interests. Janet read a lot, everything from the classics to works on child psychology. While she still had the ambition to be an actress, she had begun to lean towards a career in psychiatry. Pamela had no ambition other than to get married. She had a long list of things she wanted in her husband, wealth being top of it, and imagined herself as an expensively dressed decoration on the arm of a successful man. She claimed she wanted to learn to cook well, and maybe take up ballet, but those aims were just to boost her desirability as a wife. While Janet found her friend's yearnings com-pletely understandable when her family home was so crowded, mucky and noisy, she felt Pamela shouldn't rely on a man to get her out of it.

As expected, Pamela was cross that Janet couldn't come out. 'I had my hair done today,' she said pee-vishly. 'I had it put up in a beehive, and now no one is going to see it.'

Janet apologized. 'I can't help it, Pam,' she said. 'It's the first time I've ever let you down. Can't you go with Karen?'

Karen lived in the flat upstairs to Pamela and was older than them.

'I suppose I'll have to,' Pamela said. 'I don't like her much, but it's better than missing a night out.'

Janet put the phone down, hurt by her friend's attitude, but she'd noticed before that Pamela had very little empathy.

She stood in the big hall looking around her. It was a lovely house. In summer the sun came in all day through French windows leading to a pretty garden. The kitchen was modern, straight out of a magazine, with some cupboards in pale pink, others in pale green. Janet had only ever seen a kitchen like it in American films. The sofas in the sitting room were orange, and the carpet was so thick it squidged around your feet. Her employers didn't go in for traditional pictures: they had huge, wild-coloured abstracts, which puzzled Janet a little. The dining room had dark red walls, and the children's large playroom was a riot of primary colours. It was an exciting house to live in, and not for the first time she felt so grateful to the couple for trusting her with their children and being prepared to share their home. Dale Street was a vague memory, and if it hadn't been for a moment of weakness, she might have forgotten it and all it stood for.

She had learned a few years ago from a social worker that her mother had not gone to prison for the attack on her daughter: all she had got was a fine, and she had stayed in the house in Dale Street. Janet had been shocked that the courts felt beating a child so badly wasn't serious enough for prison, but apparently William Masters came home every few months and Freda was admitted to hospital several times after his beatings. It seemed to Janet that perhaps the beatings from her husband amounted to a prison sentence.

She hadn't expected to hear from the social worker again, but eighteen months ago she had contacted her to say Freda wanted to see her. It was a good six months later, when Janet was in London, that in a moment of weakness she wrote to her mother. She imagined that when Freda heard she was happy, working in London and planning to sit exams to get her into university, her mother would feel exonerated and forget her.

But as soon as the badly written reply arrived she regretted making contact. Somehow the cheap lined paper, which smelt of cigarettes and mould, brought everything back: the humiliation, the hunger and cruelty. In that letter Freda said William Masters had died of a heart attack, and she had a chronic chest complaint. Maybe if she'd asked Janet personal questions, how she'd got on at school, the people she worked for, if she'd made friends and what career she had in mind, Janet might have felt her mother cared for her. But the letter was all about Freda — lack of money, ill health, neighbours who talked about her behind her back, the rundown state of her home.

Janet wrote one cold letter, pointing out that her

mother was getting what she deserved. She told her not to write again, but Freda did. Each letter was more self-pitying. But the worst thing was that her words brought Dale Street and everything that went with it back into Janet's head. She could smell the damp, feel the cold and hear her mother shrieking at her. She knew that when Freda was writing the letters she wasn't thinking of her little girl, or feeling sorry for what she'd done to her: she was just angry at how her own life had turned out.

Janet didn't tell Mabel or even Pamela about the letters. She just tore them up and buried them in the dustbin – she hadn't even opened the most recent ones. But ignoring them didn't stop her memories, or the feeling that maybe she belonged in a place like Dale Street.

At ten that evening Janet went into Katy and Suzie's bedroom to check on them before she went to bed herself. She stood for a minute or two looking at each of the girls, their eyelashes lying like small fans on their plump pink cheeks. She loved their adorable button noses, and smiled as she heard their little snuffling sounds. She wondered if her mother had ever looked at her like that, her heart welling with love. She couldn't imagine it.

You two will never doubt your parents loved you, she thought, and kissed each of them as she drew the covers over their shoulders and tucked them in. Katy had a night light like a fairy cottage, but Suzie's was like an aquarium, with fish on wires so they moved with the heat of the lamp. Their shadows were on the ceiling, and Suzie always fell asleep looking at them.

'Goodnight, sleep tight,' she whispered, then went off to her room further along the landing.

She awoke to hear Roger parking his car on the drive, glanced at her alarm clock and saw it was nearly two in the morning. She turned over and snuggled further down the bed, glad he was home as the house would feel more secure.

The bedroom door opening woke her. 'What's the matter?' she asked sleepily, thinking it was one of the girls.

'I thought you might like some company.'

Janet was suddenly wide awake. She'd heard from other girls at Summer Fields about what men wanted when they came into girls' bedrooms and if it had been anyone but Roger she would have screamed. But Roger was like a big teddy bear, who would get down on his hands and knees and let his girls ride on his back. He had a loud, jolly laugh. He was kind and funny. Not much to look at perhaps, small eyes, balding and a fat face, but he was just the father of the girls she took care of, and she'd never had any reason to see him in any other light.

'I – I – I –' she stammered '– I'm sleepy.'

She expected him to go, but instead he came in, shut the door behind him and sat on her bed. 'I just wanted to cuddle you,' he said, his voice low and wheedling. 'You're so pretty, I thought we could take this opportunity to get to know each other better.'

'It's not right for you to be in here,' she said desperately. She wanted to scream loudly to frighten him off but she was afraid to do that in case she'd misread his intentions and ended up alarming the children.

'It is right,' he said. 'I've seen the way you look at me.'

He moved then to lie on top of her, pinning her to the bed beneath the covers. She jerked her head away from his face, but he caught hold of her chin and began to kiss her. It was hideous, his tongue like a fat, slimy snake, and his breath smelling of drink and cigarettes. She tried to move her head away but he was holding it too tightly. All at once his free hand was pushing under the bedclothes and pulling up her nightdress.

She managed to get one arm free and tried to push him off her, but he was too strong and heavy, and although she pummelled him with her fist he didn't appear to feel it. But his hand was now pushing her thighs apart and he was forcing a finger inside her.

'You like that, don't you?' he said.

'Stop it,' she said frantically. 'I'll scream and wake

the girls up. They wouldn't like to see their father doing this to me.'

But even that didn't stop him. He put his left hand across her mouth to shut her up and with his right he unzipped his trousers. She tried so hard to fight him then, but his weight held her captive and all at once he was pushing himself into her. His hand across her nose and mouth was suffocating her.

It felt like he was tearing her insides apart as he thrust himself into her. His stale breath was hot on her face, he smelt of sweat and he grunted like a pig on each stroke into her. Nothing in her life so far had been as bad as this. He was shattering all her romantic dreams of true love and bliss in the arms of the man she would marry. She was crying silently, feeling even more wretched and abandoned than she used to feel when William Masters attacked her.

His grunting grew louder and suddenly he was still, flopping down like an overweight walrus, dripping with sweat.

Words formed in her mind – 'How could you do that? What will Mabel think of you?' – but she was too shocked to say anything. Somehow she managed to roll him off her and got out of the bed to rush to the bathroom to wash off the stink of him. She glanced round as she left the room, and saw he'd already fallen asleep. It crossed her mind to find a weapon, a knife to stick in him or something heavy to bash his head with. But she knew she would end up in prison: no one would believe a girl from Chatham's Dale Street wasn't a tart. She could almost hear people saying she must have coerced Roger Whitestone into bed with her when he was drunk, possibly intending to blackmail him. He was a respectable man who worked at the Stock Exchange, he had a beautiful home, a lovely wife and two adorable daughters: he wouldn't even look at a girl like her.

She locked the bathroom door and ran a bath, crying so hard she couldn't think straight. She had blood on her thighs, and she could smell something bestial. Who could she go to for help?

The answer to that question was so disturbing she wished she hadn't asked it. There was no one. Mabel was never going to believe what had happened. Neither would the police. Pamela's parents wouldn't want another person to feed. There was no one else.

As she sat in the bath, crying, she heard Roger come out of her room. He tried the bathroom door, then staggered away to his own room. She wondered if he was so drunk he didn't know what he'd done. But that didn't excuse him and she knew with utter certainty he would never admit to it.

She was on her own.

She noted the clock in the hall said it was just on four when, washed, dressed and her small case packed, she left the house. She was calmer now as she had found a way of getting her revenge on Roger. She'd pulled up the covers on her bed to hide the bloodstained sheet, but left a note under the covers for Mabel: she knew a woman would automatically want to strip her bed.

Dear Mabel,

Your husband came home tonight and raped me in this bed. You will see from the bloodstains I am speaking the truth. I had no choice but to leave as I knew Roger would lie his way out of it, and you'd have to throw me out. I took your housekeeping money from the tin on the dresser in lieu of a month's wages. Don't call me a thief. Roger is the thief. He stole my virginity, my dreams of university, my love of your daughters, and my dignity. He was an animal, and he's lucky I didn't get a knife and kill him. Believe me, I was tempted.

As low and humiliated as I feel now, and however uncertain my future, I feel sorry for you, Mabel. You can't trust your husband, and I know you won't forget what I've told you happened here tonight, whatever fairy story he weaves for you. Just bear in mind if you do waver and stay with him that he might look to your girls next. Men like him have no scruples. He proved that tonight.

Finally, I'm sure Roger will suggest tracking me down just to hide his own guilt. But be aware that if you should

do that, speaking to my old social worker or the police,
I will find ways to punish you for it. I'm sure your girls
wouldn't like to hear their father was a rapist.

She signed the letter and left it among the stained sheets. But writing it had brought her back some dignity. Roger couldn't take that away.

IO

Janet

Janet was shocked, she was incredibly sore and far too angry to make a plan before she left the Whitestones' house. Getting away, even though it was early and still dark, was all that was important to her. Reason said she should wait until at least seven, but she was afraid Roger would wake and try to talk to her, or that Mabel would come back early. Yet confrontation with either of her employers was nothing compared to the thought of the girls waking up and running to her room as they usually did. That would make her break down. She'd come to love them so much, and they would cling to her and try to stop her leaving, whatever reason she gave.

She couldn't go to Pamela's so early in the morning, and she doubted there would even be a café open. It was also chilly and her suitcase was heavy. She thought again of going to the police, but concluded that they would never take the word of a girl who'd been in care over a seemingly respectable man like Roger Whitestone. Besides, she couldn't bring herself to tell a policeman the embarrassing details of what he had done to her.

By five it was light and she found a seat in a little park to wait until a café was likely to open. The sky was heavy – she hoped it wouldn't rain. That was all she needed to push her over the edge.

At half past seven she walked up Haverstock Hill towards Hampstead. Instinct told her she'd be better going the other way towards Camden Town where cafés were cheaper and maybe she'd see a room to let on a postcard in a shop window. But she didn't like Camden Town: it was too rough and made her think of Dale Street. She bought a local paper in a newsagent's and, a few minutes later, found a café that was just opening.

Sitting by the window with a round of toast and a cup of tea, she kept nodding off and waking with a jerk. The café was filling with workmen. A couple of them glanced at her curiously, but fortunately didn't speak. She thought she ought to make up a story in case she was questioned, but she was so tired her mind had gone blank. She pretended to be engrossed in her newspaper, even though the print was swimming in front of her eyes.

'Are you intending to keep that seat warm all day, dear?'

A woman's voice brought Janet round. It was one of the café staff. She was middle-aged, wearing a vivid blue headscarf tied like a turban, her overall was a similar colour and she had a kindly face. Janet realized she must have dropped off, and the café was now packed.

'I'm sorry,' she said. 'I arrived in London late last night and I haven't slept. I'll leave now.'

'Where are you going?' The woman's voice was quiet and gentle.

Janet's eyes filled with tears. 'I don't know exactly. I need to find a room, and a job, but it's too early yet.'

'I'll get you another tea and a bacon sandwich,' the woman said, with a smile. She reached out and wiped away Janet's tears with a thumb. 'You can stay for a bit longer then.'

The woman refused Janet's money when she came back with the sandwich and tea. She suggested the YWCA hostel as somewhere she'd get a room. 'I think it's around the bottom of Oxford Street. But when I've got a minute I'll look in the phone book for you.'

Warmed by the woman's kindness Janet felt a little more hopeful, and the bacon sandwich was very good. It was almost nine when she left the café with the YWCA telephone number in her pocket and made her way up the hill to Hampstead village and the tube. She'd also circled a couple of bedsitters in the paper, and intended to telephone them and the YWCA when she got to the station.

She didn't really know why she crossed Fitzjohns Avenue away from the tube station, but the Everyman cinema was there, and whenever she had walked up to Hampstead with the little girls she had always checked to see what was playing. A girl around the same age as Janet was fitting posters of the latest film into the glass-fronted showcases. Janet put her case down as it was heavy and the girl looked round at her.

She had what Janet could only describe as a joyful face, not so much pretty but striking and 'country girl', with long blonde hair in a thick plait. She wore a rather old-fashioned heathery tweed dress with a wide white collar, and Janet guessed she was just a couple of years older than her.

'Are you looking for someone?' she asked Janet.

'No, just seeing what's on. Must be good to work here.'

'I like it. My parents say it isn't much of a job, but it's the closest I'll ever get to being a film star.' She laughed as she said this, and her large brown eyes sparkled.

'I daydream of becoming an actress,' Janet admitted. 'But right now I'd settle for any old job.' Almost as soon as the words left her lips she regretted them as she sounded plaintive and perhaps pathetic.

But the girl glanced down at her suitcase. 'Come in and have a cup of tea with me,' she said. 'You look tired and washed out. I'm Petula, but everyone calls me Pet. What's yours?'

Janet had passed a florist called 'Fleur' just a few minutes before, and the name had stuck in her head. 'Fleur,' she said, pausing for further inspiration. 'Fleur Faraday.'

'Gosh! That sounds like an actress's name,' Pet said, with a smile. 'Much better than mine. I'm Petula Goodwilly. Isn't that the worst you've ever heard? But come on in – we've got ages before the cleaner arrives.'

The smell of stale cigarette smoke in the Everyman took Janet back to the cinema in Chatham. As a child it had been a palace of dreams to her, somewhere there was no cruelty, no hunger, just vivid colour and wonderful stories. But the smell told her that dreams, however magical, disappeared as soon as the film ended. Tears welled in her eyes, spilled over and she couldn't stop them.

'What is it, Fleur?' Pet asked, taking her suitcase from her and placing it on the ground so she could embrace her. 'Have you run away from home? Or is it a boy?'

She wanted to tell her: she wanted this kind girl to understand what had happened and decide for her what she should do. But even though she was sore and her heart ached at how she had been violated by a man she trusted, she couldn't tell the story. All she could do was cry and allow Pet to hold her.

Pet led her into a tiny room off the foyer. It held a freezer, and the trays the usherettes filled with ices and drinks. There were two shabby armchairs. Pet nudged Janet into one and lit the gas under a kettle.

'Are there any jobs here?' Janet asked, trying to dry her eyes on an already wet handkerchief.

Pet wheeled round from the kettle. 'You ran out of a job? That's it! The people you worked for and lived with did something to you. Am I right?'

Janet couldn't answer. Her tears started again but she nodded. That was as close as she'd get to admitting the truth.

Pet asked her nothing further, just made the tea, putting extra sugar into Janet's, and handed her the biscuit tin. 'There's some chocolate ones,' she said. 'Mr Murphy, he's the manager, brought them in yesterday as it was his birthday. We wished we'd got him a cake because he's very kind to all of us.'

'How many people work here?' Janet asked.

'About twelve, but most of the usherettes are part-time.'

'Do you think your Mr Murphy would take me on?' she asked, as she nibbled a biscuit.

'He might if I ask him,' Pet said, looking hard at the younger girl, 'but I won't do that unless you tell me what you're running from. Is it home? Or a job that turned sour? You don't have to tell me details, just enough so I can get the picture.'

'A live-in job that turned sour.' Janet's voice shook and her eyes welled up again.

'And where's home and your parents?'

'I don't have any. I was in care before this job. I was going to night school too, hoping to go to university, but that hope is dashed now too.'

'It doesn't have to be.' Pet came to kneel in front of the younger girl, and dabbed at her face with a hanky. 'I can't promise anything but I do know a lady who takes in boarders. They're theatrical people who stay with her, and she's always looking for help in the house too. If she's willing to take you in you could still go to night school. She won't pay much, but she will feed you. I lived there for a time and it was fun, so many interesting people.'

'It sounds nice.' Janet sniffed back her tears. 'Do I have to phone her?'

'I'll do that,' Pet said. 'I'll go and ring her now. Then I must get back to work, but you can stay here and, with a bit of luck, I'll be able to whiz you down to meet Frankie once the cleaners get here. It's not far.'

As soon as Pet had gone out to the phone box at the station, Janet's eyelids were drooping with tiredness. 'You have to remember you're Fleur Faraday now,' she whispered to herself, and said the name over and over again. But she must have fallen asleep in the armchair as she was startled awake by voices just outside the office.

It was Pet and the two cleaners. 'I've got to pop out. Just tell Mr Murphy it was something important, but I'll be back within thirty minutes.'

Fleur heard sounds of equipment being taken out of a cupboard or a room nearby, doors opening and closing, and then Pet came back into the office.

'Frankie would like to see you,' she said, with a wide smile. 'She was a bit afraid you were a posh girl who wouldn't know how to clean or cook breakfast, a lot of her boarders are like that, but I put her straight. We'll go there now.'

A couple of hours later, Fleur was putting her clothes away in a tiny room at the top of a house in Haverstock Hill. She was surprised to find it was a rabbit warren of a place above a greengrocery shop that belonged to Frankie's brother. Behind the shop there was a huge kitchen, and it appeared everything happened in it. Frankie had only just finished cooking breakfast, and three young women were sitting around in housecoats, their hair in rollers. Frankie clapped her hands, said she had visitors and they scuttled off.

Pet introduced Fleur, then had to rush back to the cinema, and suddenly it was just Fleur, with Frankie looking at her curiously.

It was difficult to gauge Frankie's age. Her hair was grey, pinned up with iron curlers, her face was lined, and she wore an overall printed with mauve flowers, the kind Fleur associated with cleaners, factory hands and other working women. But her voice didn't go with her appearance. It wasn't plummy in the way Mabel's had been, but she spoke without a London accent.

'Well, Fleur, I know you didn't tell Pet why you ran away from your job, but I expect you to tell me because I won't let anyone stay in my home unless I know them well.'

Fleur hung her head.

'Pet said you were a mother's help,' Frankie went on, 'so either the children's mother was a tyrant or her husband couldn't keep his hands to himself. I'm guessing it was the latter. And as you ran out of the house during the night, I think he raped you. Am I right?'

Fleur hadn't expected such direct questioning, and to have Roger's crime flung at her like that was shocking. She burst into tears, and suddenly the full horror of what he had done to her came back as vividly as if it had just happened.

'They had gone out to visit a sick relative and Mabel said she'd be staying the night but Roger would be back,' Fleur burst out, through her tears. 'I was asleep and he just came into my room and did that. I couldn't stop him.'

'You didn't call the police, I take it.'

'I knew they wouldn't believe me. He's a wealthy businessman, and I'm just a girl brought up in care. I have no one to stand up for me.'

'Well, you have now,' Frankie said, and held out her arms to embrace Fleur. 'I can't tell you how many girls have told me that some man they trusted did this to them. But what you've got to keep firmly in your head is that it wasn't your fault. I know you probably feel dirty and that somehow you let him think that was what you wanted, but all the rape victims I've met feel like that. He's a beast who used his position to abuse you. It isn't your fault.'

Frankie had told her she was to lie down for a while as she looked worn out, and as she got under the eiderdown she felt safe at last. But it was funny that her dream was to be an actress, and now she was staying in a house for actors working at local theatres. Maybe there was a God up there.

11

Alice

Alice couldn't get out of her head the thought of her mother running a brothel. She could easily imagine her outmanoeuvring people, climbing over them to get what she wanted. She could even believe she would sleep with a man for some sort of gain. But not running a business where women were loaned like hire cars. Everything else Pet had told her had rung true, but not that.

Sally had never liked sleaze. She would turn off a TV programme if she thought the humour too near the mark. She would purse her lips at smutty jokes, and despised so-called sexy red and black lingerie. She didn't like people talking about sex or other bodily functions, yet if she was compelled to discuss such things, she was direct, never hiding behind euphemisms.

Alice couldn't talk to anyone she worked with about it, and other friends would press her to tell them why she was suddenly interested in such a subject. Eventually she rang Stuart and arranged to drop in to see him on her way back from work late in the afternoon.

It was still sunny and warm, and instead of inviting her in, Stuart suggested they walked on the Downs. 'Too nice to be in,' he said. 'Not quite warm enough yet for wearing shorts, but good walking weather.'

That suited Alice, and she soon got him up to speed with what she'd discovered so far.

'You can bet that sick fucker whose kids she looked after raped her,' he said. 'Why else would a young girl leave the house in the middle of the night?'

'If so, she appeared to recover quickly,' Alice said. 'I mean, going to stay in a guesthouse for actors and going on the stage herself.'

'I don't think any girl of her age would ever get over being raped,' he said. 'It's more likely she would remain wary of men, possibly even hate them. Did you ever get the idea your mum hated men?'

'Not hated, but she was very critical and dismissive of them. Dad used to tease her and say she was a bra-burning feminist. I can't see her running a brothel.'

Stuart looked thoughtful. 'In the course of my career I've met scores of women in the sex industry, from those on the streets to high-class call-girls. A huge proportion of them were sexually abused as young girls, some as children. I think some of them see it as a way of getting back at men, demeaning them by taking their money. Maybe your mum was one of those. But many more women who turn to prostitution have such low self-worth they believe they don't deserve anything better. Worse, they allow their pimps to control them and mostly give them a huge share of the money they've earned.'

'Do you think you could find out if it's true that Mum ran a brothel? I'd like to know where it was, whether she was prosecuted, and if Angus comes into this at all.'

'I can try,' Stuart said. 'If she was arrested there would be a record of it. It's possible that this story was made up, not perhaps by the lady you went to see but by someone with a grudge who wanted to discredit your mum.'

'Well, if there's no record it doesn't matter, does it?'

'No, but you've already got ugly images in your head, and delving a bit further is likely to make those images uglier still. This isn't a character in a book, it's your mum, Alice. I think you should drop it now.'

'I can't,' she retorted stubbornly. 'I want to know everything, warts and all. What she was and what she did. And perhaps why.'

'A friend of mine was told his great-grandfather was shot for cowardice in the First World War,' Stuart said. 'My friend left no stone unturned to get at the truth. He wanted to prove the man wasn't a coward, and perhaps was suffering from shell-shock as so many soldiers were back then. However, he found his great-grandfather had left his post and stolen an army truck full of provisions. He was discovered several days later holed up in an abandoned hotel near the coast. He'd sold all the provisions and concealed the truck. So, it turned out he was a thief as well as a deserter.'

Alice could see Stuart's reasoning. His friend was probably very sorry now that he'd dug into his ancestor's history. But she had to know about her mother. 'I can't find the words to explain why I need to know, but I have to carry on. Please help me, Stuart.'

He forced a smile. 'I will, Alice, but on your head be it. In the meantime, why don't you go and see Angus? You might find he has all the answers. I suspect he looked you up because he had more to tell you than just that he was your biological father. Listen to him with an open mind.'

A brief chat with Stuart turned into hours. After their walk he took her to a little bistro in Whiteladies Road where they had cannelloni washed down with a couple of glasses of very good red wine. As always, he was excellent company, a lively conversationalist and very astute. As they parted around nine thirty, he reminded Alice to ring Angus. 'He was a key figure in your mum's life, and from what you've told me about him, a reasonable man. So no more excuses, ring him. Tonight!'

Alice sat looking at Angus's telephone number for

some time, trying to weigh up whether it was too late to ring and if it might upset his wife. But in the end, she dialled the number and crossed her fingers hoping he'd answer.

He did, and as soon as she said her name, she heard a sharp intake of breath.

'Are you okay to speak?' she asked. 'I don't wish to put you in an awkward position.'

'I'm in my office working late, so there's no problem at all.'

'I'm sorry if I was sharp with you that day in Totnes,' she began. 'You gave me a massive shock.'

'I see that now,' he said. 'I regret approaching you at such a time. It was very thoughtless of me.'

Alice felt touched by the warmth in his voice and his apology. 'I'm over that now,' she said, 'but I can't tell Emily about you. She's having a few problems with her husband and until that's sorted I can't burden her with anything else. The reason I'm ringing now is because I hoped we could meet up and have a proper conversation about Mum. I've been delving into her past and many things puzzle me. How would you feel about that?'

'I'd love to meet up. I come over to Bristol quite often. Would that suit you?'

'I live and work in Bristol but it might be better if you came to the Shaldon – that's one of the hotels I manage. It's near Chepstow, so easy for you to reach.

I can book out a room we use for business meetings. It's quiet and we can talk uninterrupted.'

After giving him the address of the Shaldon, and promising to text him the date and time of their meeting when she'd checked her work diary, they ended the call.

It felt like a big step forward, arranging to meet him. But if her mother hadn't opened up to a good friend like Pet, it was unlikely she'd told Angus much. But he could give Alice a different perspective, and hopefully some new leads.

It was three days later that they met, on Thursday, late in the afternoon. The Shaldon was a rambling, quaint hotel. Built in 1820 as a gentleman's residence, it had been added to by subsequent owners in a piecemeal manner. After the war, with its views of the River Severn, it had been a fashionable place to stay but it had gone into a decline in the nineties: a hotel just outside Chepstow that had nothing more to offer than a view of the Severn no longer attracted crowds. People wanted to stay in either picturesque parts of Wales or the Cotswolds, or in cities like Bristol or Bath. So now the Headingly Hotel Group were concentrating their efforts on making the Shaldon a first-class wedding venue: the river looked great in the photographs.

Alice had taken great care with her appearance to meet Angus again. She wore a red fitted dress, very high-heeled shoes, and had blow-dried her hair that morning. As she was driving there, she wondered why she cared about how she looked, but it was just a matter of pride. She might find out disturbing things about her mother, but she could still shine.

Angus arrived at the room called Berkeley about five minutes after Alice. She'd taken a seat at the big desk with her back to the window so she could study him closely. She had to admit he was looking good for a man of seventy: a sprinkling of grey at his temples made him look distinguished. She thought he worked out as there was no hint of a paunch under the smart grey suit and crisp blue and white striped shirt. She could see similarities between him and herself, things she hadn't noticed in Totnes.

They shook hands. Alice poured him coffee and then she began.

'Did Sally – or should I call her Fleur for you? – ever tell you why she ran out on the people she was mother's help to in Belsize Park? Or perhaps she mentioned Hampstead. She would've been seventeen then.'

He frowned. 'Sally is fine, Alice, though I'll probably forget and go back to calling her Fleur. But, no, I didn't know she'd ever been a mother's help. But she did mention Hampstead. She spoke about a woman called Frankie at the house where she stayed while playing at London theatres.'

'Did she ever tell you which theatres or shows she was in?'

'Not really. She was always vague about details. I came to suspect she bigged herself up as an actress.'

Alice raised her eyebrows, and he blushed. 'I don't want to speak ill of her, Alice, but she wasn't terribly truthful. Maybe it would be more diplomatic if I called it exaggeration.'

'It's okay, Angus.' Alice smiled. 'I know what she was like. Frankie took her in thanks to a friend called Petula, known as Pet. Did you know her?'

'I never met her, but Sally mentioned her a few times.'

'I went to meet her and she lives in a beautiful house near Arundel in Sussex. She's a lovely person. She met Mum on the day she'd left her mother's-help job. She suspected something bad had happened there, maybe rape by her employer's husband, but Mum never admitted it to her. That's possibly why she was so hard-nosed with men. What do you think?'

'I agree that she must have been badly hurt by someone. I also suspect she either had an abortion or miscarried at some point when she was young. Maybe it was that man, but I always had a feeling the hurt went further back to when she was a child.'

'What did she tell you about growing up?'

'Almost nothing. I remember once she was offered a role in a play in Chatham and turned it down. When

I asked why, she said something like "I never want to set foot in that town again." I found out after a while that she was born there, and her father was in the merchant navy. That's probably where I got the idea that her problems started there. I think she was taken into care – she once mentioned something about climbing trees in a garden. I jumped on it and asked where it was, but she said she couldn't remember. As you probably know, when she didn't want to talk about something, it was like a steel shutter had come down.'

Alice nodded. That was exactly what Sally was like. 'Angus, where did you meet her?'

'In a hotel bar in Kensington in the late seventies. I was staying there for a couple of days while visiting a trade fair in Olympia. The place was full of buyers and exhibitors. Fleur was sitting at the same table. I think I asked her if she was working on a stand – back then lots of exhibitors would employ good-looking women to chat up buyers. She was around thirty-five or -six then, but could easily have passed for late twenties. She said she was thinking of opening a china and giftware shop and was visiting the fair to do a bit of research. I offered to help – after all, I'd been in the trade for some time. We had a few drinks together, then went for a steak across the road. By midnight I was totally smitten with her.'

Alice guessed that he'd fallen into bed with her

mother that night, but she could hardly ask him. 'Did she open a shop?'

He laughed. 'To be honest I don't think she had any particular interest in china and giftware. Later she told me she ran a small promotions agency, supplying girls for trade fairs and the like.'

'You say that as if she was the madam of a brothel,' Alice said, with a smile, hoping to catch him off guard.

He blushed furiously. 'Oh, gosh, no. I meant she was networking – well, sort of. She was trying to find companies who would use her agency. Mind you, there were a lot of odd things about Fleur. She said she ran her agency under the name of Sally Symonds – she'd taken over the woman's company.'

Alice nodded. 'I think she told porkies about more than her name. Angus, I was told she ran a brothel. I don't know if it's true, but do you think it could be?'

'If you'd asked me that back then I would have been angry you could think such a thing,' he said. 'As I told you before, I was totally bewitched by her. I just saw her beauty, the fun in her. I thought she was perfection.'

'But that wore off?' Alice raised her eyebrows questioningly.

'No. I adored everything about her. The way she spoke, dressed, laughed, danced, everything. I couldn't think of anything but her. It was wonderful, but terrible too. I had a wife back in Wales who I loved dearly.

I couldn't leave her. But Fleur came up with the solution: I would see her during the week and go home to Gwen every weekend. I thought Fleur was so noble not making me choose, though I think if she'd insisted, I'd have chosen her.'

'You bought a house in Bristol and put it in Fleur's name. Why was that?'

'Well, if I'd bought it in my name Gwen would have found out. Besides, Fleur was tired of London, the high rents, the dog-eat-dog atmosphere. She felt she could run her promotions agency in Bristol just as successfully as in London and have a higher profit margin because of the lower rents. I could see the advantage to me as it would make life easier, with less mileage between her and Gwen.'

'So you bought the house, and then what? Did you really think you could keep both women happy for ever?'

'Gwen was content, and Fleur seemed to blossom, when she told me she was pregnant with you. I saw that as security.'

'Really? Security? Having a baby was surely the recipe for chaos in your situation.'

He looked right into Alice's eyes. 'I was thrilled, and Fleur became a gentler, kinder woman. She wasn't striving for anything and she was really happy, glowing from within. That was when it occurred to me she might have miscarried or aborted a baby when she was young. She was often pensive, like she was remembering something from the past. But I don't mean she was miserable. It was a very happy time. I hoped you'd be a girl – I called you Alice right through the pregnancy.'

At that Alice felt a little twinge in her heart. 'But what possessed you to marry Mum?' she asked. 'That's what I can't understand.'

'It was Fleur who wanted it. She said she felt vulnerable, afraid I'd leave her alone with the baby. I argued against it, said I'd never abandon her and, after all, it was me who'd be punished if I got caught. But she argued that she was the only person who would know the truth and she wasn't going to broadcast it.'

'So you agreed?'

He sighed, 'Somewhat reluctantly. I was naive back then. I'd always stuck to rules, never so much as fiddled my expenses. She was telling me this baby meant the world to her and how she'd thought it would never happen. She said she was going to change her name to Helen, and as Helen Tweedy she'd be the happiest woman in the world once we were married. I swallowed that, hook, line and sinker. I was terrified when we booked the wedding that we'd be found out, but it went like clockwork. No problems at all. We married on Valentine's Day, she was three months pregnant, and wore a white coat with a fur collar. She looked like a beauty queen.'

'Who were the witnesses?' Alice asked.

'Two friends of hers, Roberta and Gregory Mullins, no one else. She said that as I couldn't invite anyone, she wouldn't either. She'd only known Bobbie and Greg since she changed her name to Helen. I had a job to remember the new name, but when I slipped up in public she'd make out that "Petite Fleur" had been my pet name for her.'

'And then? How was it when I was born?'

'Lovely – calm, happy . . . blissful, in fact. There was good weather that August, and I managed to wangle time off work to help out. We spent long lazy afternoons sitting in the garden with you.'

'But you must've been stressed keeping the two halves of your life separate?'

'Using the wrong name was the worst thing but luckily I managed to gloss over that.' He gave a rueful grin. 'Then I started to call them both darling to make it safer. But aside from the complications, the stress of pretending to Gwen I was in various hotels during the week and half expecting a policeman's hand on my shoulder or an officer at the door looking to arrest me, I coped.'

'So was Emily intended, or an accident?'

'She was intended. Neither of us wanted you to be an only child. Towards the end of the pregnancy Fleur became a little distant. Nothing to worry about, but I thought perhaps she felt a bit trapped, alone at home and me away at weekends, with no possibility of it ever being resolved. But I don't mean she regretted having you two. She adored you both and she was a good mum. I sometimes wonder now if, in those pensive moments, she was considering turning me in, like she was afraid I would be found out eventually and if you were older it would affect you two badly. But I didn't think any of those things when we were together. It was only once I was in prison that I found myself dwelling on odd remarks, little things that hadn't meant anything at the time. That's the trouble with prison. You have too much time to think.'

'That's a generous explanation.' Alice smiled at him, touched that he didn't mention her mother selling the house and pocketing the money. She was liking him more and more, and although she couldn't condone bigamy, she understood why he'd thought it was the only way to keep both of the women he loved happy. 'But about the brothel thing, could it have been true?'

'Maybe there was some truth in it,' he said, with a sigh. 'I did meet a couple of chaps in the trade at an exhibition who said they missed the parties they used to go to a few years before. They did that nudge-nudge-wink-wink thing men do when there's more to it than people having a drink and a dance. Then one said Fleur must have made a packet out of the parties. I was startled – your mum was the only Fleur

I'd ever heard of. But I couldn't question them. They were from Monmouth, and it might have got home to Gwen.'

'But it was before you two were together, so maybe it wasn't her,' Alice said, feeling sorry for him. 'And throwing parties isn't quite the same as running a brothel, is it? But I ought to go now, Angus. I've got to pop into one of the Bristol hotels on the way home. Another big wedding this weekend.'

He smiled with real warmth. 'It's been so good to see you and talk,' he said. Alice had her hands on the desk and he put one of his over them. 'I've thought about you and Emily so much over the years. If I'd known where you were I might have camped outside your door just to look at you. However, I want to assure you that if you decide this is our last meeting, that you've nothing more to say to me, I will accept it.'

'Thank you, Angus.' She felt a bit sad that she couldn't include him in her life, unless she passed him off as a friend. 'That's almost certainly for the best, but I'm really glad you got in touch. You've opened up a can of worms for me, but if I have to have a secret father, then I'm glad it's you.'

'And if I have to have a secret daughter, I'm very glad she is so beautiful, kind and clever.'

12

Fleur

Fleur pricked up her ears as Frankie's five paying guests chatted around the kitchen table. This week they were all women, aged from twenty to forty, one a novice, the others seasoned repertory performers. Fleur was washing the breakfast dishes and wished they would clear off and let her clean the kitchen, but even so their conversations were always interesting.

She had been living at Frankie's for a month now. The guests changed each week or ten days, going off to another town for a new production. She'd heard them learning their lines, discussing other plays they'd been in, listened to the intrigues, about who was doing what with whom, and now she wanted to become an actress more than ever.

But first she had a problem that must be fixed. Frankie thought she might be pregnant. It wouldn't have occurred to Fleur that she could be. It was only when Frankie asked her when her last monthly was that she was reminded of a double date with Pamela and a couple of lads they'd met in the Lyceum. She'd had a bad stomach-ache, and after only one glass of Babycham she'd had to go home, much to Pamela's annoyance. That was two weeks before the rape.

She hadn't spoken to Pamela since she'd explained why she couldn't go to the Empire with her. Without admitting to the events of that night, she didn't know how she could explain her sudden change of name and address. She often wondered if Pamela was hurt, but she had too much to worry about now to care about anyone else's feelings.

She hadn't thought anyone could get pregnant the first time. But Frankie said that was an old wives' tale, and each day they waited to see if her monthly would come.

But it hadn't, and Frankie said by now she must be five or six weeks gone and, in a couple more weeks she would take her to a woman she knew who would sort the problem.

'You don't have any other choice,' Frankie said firmly when Fleur cried. 'Bringing up a child as an unmarried mother is almost impossible. No one will give you accommodation or work. I couldn't keep you here with a baby, it's not suitable, and I don't want to lose you because you're a good little worker. Just do this and then get on with your life. I've had other girls here in the same position, and all of them were relieved when it was over.'

Fleur hadn't asked what an abortion entailed. She'd

rather not know, and instead she prayed fervently for her monthly to come and solve the problem. But time was running out. Frankie had arranged for her to visit the woman in King's Cross in two weeks' time.

At six in the evening Fleur and Frankie caught a bus to King's Cross.

'Is this it?' Fleur looked down the steep, litter-strewn stairs to the basement flat in trepidation.

'Yes, and it's not as bad inside as out,' Frankie said. 'Iris is doing you a favour, remember, so don't make a fuss, and by tomorrow morning it will all be over.'

The flat was dark, stank of mould and Iris looked none too clean. She was perhaps fifty, small and slightly built, with the grey skin of a chain smoker. Her bleached hair was stained yellow with nicotine. She said nothing to reassure Fleur, just looked her up and down, said, 'In there,' and pointed to the bathroom.

It was very grubby with cracked linoleum on the floor and an ancient geyser over the bath. A wooden stool was placed in the tub, next to a bowl of pink soapy water, which smelt of carbolic, with a length of rubber tubing in it.

'Take your knickers off and hop onto the stool,' Iris said curtly. 'I have to dilate your cervix, then pump the soapy water in. That acts as an irritant, and the foetus will come away in a few hours.'

Fleur hadn't expected this procedure would involve Iris putting her fingers inside her. She wanted to die of shame – and it hurt.

'Now I'll open the neck of your cervix. It seals up when you get pregnant,' Iris said, as she poked around. 'Keep still and take deep breaths. You'll feel a sharp or tugging pain when it's done.'

The sharp pain came. 'Good,' Iris said. 'Now for the carbolic.'

She reached down into the pink suds and pulled out the end of the tube, which had a solid tip on it. With her other hand she squeezed a rubber bulb. A jet of water spurted out of the tube. She squirted it until it was empty, then lowered the end back into the suds and pumped again.

'I have to be careful there's no air in the tube,' she said.

Fleur was really scared. She knew Frankie was just outside the open bathroom door, she could see her shadow, but wished she'd come in and hold her hand.

Iris held the tube carefully between two fingers to guide it and pushed it inside Fleur. There was a moment or two of resistance, then a dull ache and the tube went deeper. 'That's it,' Iris said. 'I pump in the soap now. Hold still.'

It didn't hurt, but it felt alien and wrong. So much water was going in and none coming out. Finally, Iris withdrew the tube, passed an old towel to Fleur to dry herself and told her brusquely to get dressed.

On the bus going home Fleur asked Frankie in a whisper what would happen next.

'You'll get pains later, like period pains,' she whispered back. 'Hopefully everything will come away, but if it goes on too long, I'll have to call an ambulance. We'll tell them you're having a miscarriage, and although the doctor who examines you may suspect it was an illegal abortion, you mustn't admit it. Promise me that? Iris, you and I could all end up in prison if you tell the truth. We were just helping you.'

The first rays of light were coming into the sky when Fleur got the first pain, which woke her. From the window in her bedroom at the top of the house she watched the pink glow in the sky gradually spread out over the Hampstead roof tops. Another pain followed the first and she felt the soapy water coming out too.

Frankie's bedroom was directly below hers, and she'd been given a broom handle to bang on the floor if the pain got too bad. But Fleur was determined to handle it alone. She had pads, a thick towel to lie on and a chamber pot to use, plus water and painkillers.

An hour later she wasn't quite so determined not to call Frankie: the pain was terrible, white-hot pangs that engulfed her and made her think she couldn't survive them. She clenched the side of the mattress so she wouldn't scream, and her bed was soaked with blood. She knew that if she did scream one of the guests might come running, and they would call an ambulance.

Around nine – the guests were calling to each other as they went down for breakfast so she knew what time it was – the pain had become so great she wanted to die. Somehow she managed to get up to sit on the chamber pot and in agony she passed what looked like lumps of liver. She didn't know if the tiny baby was among it, but she sobbed: it was wicked to have destroyed a life.

She'd lived with loneliness most of her life. Even when she was surrounded by people, she felt alone. Although there were times at Summer Fields when she had been happy, and the Duncans were very kind to her, she had still known she was alone. That was proved when she'd had to leave Summer Fields. Moving to London and working for the White-stones had made her think all the bad stuff was over: she could go to university and have a proper career.

But then Roger had done *that* to her, as if she was nothing but a lump of flesh to be used. It had left her feeling even more alone in the world.

She felt it now, so dark and strong it engulfed her, and she vowed to herself that if she survived this ordeal, she would forge a life for herself without ever considering or caring about anyone else.

Frankie came up a bit later with a cup of tea for her. Fleur was back in bed, and she'd covered the chamber pot with a cloth.

'Has it come away?' Frankie asked. She put down the tea then felt Fleur's forehead to check if she had a temperature.

'I don't know,' Fleur said, through tears. 'But there was a lot of blood and stuff.' She pointed towards the chamber pot.

Frankie looked into the pot. 'I think it has. Is the pain still bad?'

'No, just an ache, really,' Fleur replied. She hauled herself up to a sitting position to drink her tea. 'My bed is a mess and I'm still bleeding.'

'That's to be expected,' Frankie said. 'I'll get some clean sheets and water for you to wash. I'm going to tell the guests you aren't very well. If any of them pop in to see you, don't let on, will you?'

'I hope they don't come,' Fleur said fearfully. She might not be in terrible pain any longer, but she didn't think she would ever forget how bad it had been, or how frightening. 'Thank you, Frankie, for helping me.'

Frankie's face softened and she reached out her hand to stroke Fleur's cheek. 'That's all right, dear. I couldn't let any woman face that alone. You've been very brave, and I expect you'll feel weepy for some time yet. Now, do you think you could eat something? A boiled egg and soldiers?'

For the following couple of days Fleur lay in bed dozing fitfully, and she found her thoughts turned to how people reacted to certain situations. Frankie had offered her food, as if that would wipe out what she'd experienced. She guessed that was a typical maternal response and not one she had encountered before. Iris had hurried her out of her basement flat, not even looking at her directly: perhaps she was ashamed of what she did for a living. It had cost twenty pounds, which Frankie had paid and Fleur would have to pay back from her wages.

Roger and Mabel had seemed so nice, like she was an older daughter, not an employee. Yet he had taken advantage of Mabel being away for the night. Had he been waiting for such an opportunity? What he'd done to her was evil and she doubted the ball of hate inside her would ever go away. 'You must never trust a man again,' she whispered to herself.

On the fourth day she had recovered enough to pick up her life again, cooking and cleaning for the paying guests. She found herself watching and listening to them even more intently. Every one of the young women came from a good home. They were confident, poised and mostly very arrogant. They had style, too, and Fleur knew that to step out of her life as the girl who picked up the paying guests' clothes from the floor, and be on a stage like them, she needed to learn from them.

Perhaps Frankie had an inkling of how she felt because one day just after breakfast when they were alone in the kitchen, she tweaked Fleur's ponytail affectionately. 'You, my girl, are much prettier than any of them. You pay attention and you learn fast. I think you could be anything you want to be.'

'I want to be an actress,' she said.

Frankie just laughed, whether it was because she didn't think Fleur was the right type, or for some other reason, she didn't know.

Pet had been dropping into Frankie's once a week. They'd sit in the kitchen and chat, mostly Pet and Frankie talking and Fleur listening, but one evening, about two weeks after the abortion, Fleur and Pet were alone in the kitchen. Fleur was on the point of blurting out what she'd been through because Pet asked if she felt better.

It seemed that Pet had come round while Fleur was staying in bed and Frankie had said she wasn't well. Yet Fleur had a feeling that Pet had guessed what was really the matter because she had brought her some chocolates tonight and a couple of gorgeous dresses that were too tight for her.

Fleur tried on the emerald green one, a colour she'd never worn before, which looked surprisingly good. The dress was cut in a way that gave her an hourglass figure.

'You look ravishing,' Pet said. 'But you must stop wearing your hair in that ponytail. It does nothing for you, so let it loose.'

'Really?' Fleur couldn't think of anything else to say.

'Yes. You look like a stuffy old librarian with it pulled back. Long hair is sexy, especially when it's thick and blonde like yours.'

'So why do you wear yours plaited?' Fleur thought this was a case of the pot calling the kettle black. 'After all, yours is thick and blonde too.'

'Because at the Everyman we're made to keep it tied back. Frankie would insist you tie yours back when you're cooking. Anyway, I've got a much bigger face than you, which suits a plait, but your pretty elfin face needs to be framed.'

It felt good to be complimented. It reminded Fleur of how she'd felt when the braces finally came off her teeth and one of the teachers at school had remarked that she was a very pretty girl. She had been on cloud nine all that day, thinking that the past, her mother and William Masters were wiped out for good.

But Fleur knew now that the past could never be wiped out. She thought she'd banished her mother by not writing back to her, but she guessed letters from her were still going to the Whitestones'. Maybe they even opened them and guessed at the kind of home she'd come from. Roger would like that: he'd probably tell himself she was only a guttersnipe and deserved what he'd done. But his actions would never leave her. She could change her name, move to a new address, wear her hair differently, but the hurt and humiliation were still inside her.

'You're a funny girl,' Pet said, breaking through her reverie. 'You've got the looks and the intelligence to be anything you want to be. I just wish you could believe it.'

That remark made her cry, and suddenly Pet was holding her tightly and telling her she hadn't meant to upset her, only to encourage her.

'If you're serious about being an actress, I'll try to help you get into it,' Pet went on, rocking her in her arms. 'I don't know what makes you so sad, but if ever you want to let me in on it, I'll listen and try to make everything better.'

13

Fleur

Fleur paused in trepidation outside the scuffed door of the church hall in Camden Town where she was to attend an audition for a part in a play and looked to Pet for reassurance.

'You'll be fine,' Pet said. 'Or at least you will be with that rubber band out of your hair.' She didn't wait for Fleur to remove it from her ponytail, just pulled it out, then ran her fingers through her friend's hair. 'That's better, or it will be if you comb it and put a bit more lipstick on.'

The audition was not only for a small part in a comedy but to join a repertory company. The play had bombed in London's West End, but that was because there were no big names in it. A tour of seaside towns had been booked but one of the cast had been badly hurt in a car crash. Fleur was auditioning to take over her role, that of Imogen, the innocent younger sister of the main character. It was a very small part, but Pet and Frankie had harangued the producer, whom they knew well enough to bully, to take a look at Fleur, who, they believed, was perfect for it. Imogen was very pretty but gormless and the laughs came from her lack of understanding of what was going on.

'I'm scared,' Fleur admitted, as she combed her hair. 'What if I forget the lines?'

'You won't – there aren't many. Besides, it's all about how you look, bewildered, dumb, awkward, but don't forget the sexy wiggle when you walk across the stage. That's Imogen in a nutshell.' Pet pushed open the door of the hall and nudged Fleur in.

Under supervision from Pet, Fleur had bought a tight red pencil skirt, a clinging red and white sweater and was wearing them with a pair of high heels. As she walked across to a bench to sit down, it was clear that she didn't need to practise a bottom wiggle: it just somehow happened.

Four other girls were waiting, and Pet was glad to see none of them were as attractive as Fleur. As long as she delivered her lines just as she and Frankie had coached her, she should get the part.

Pet wasn't sure why she was going to such lengths to get this new friend acting work: Fleur was the cagiest person she'd ever met, revealing absolutely nothing about where she'd come from, her parents, or other friends. Frankie said she never got any letters and, in her opinion, the girl was a runaway.

But Pet couldn't help liking Fleur, even if she couldn't explain why. At times she thought of the girl as a stray cat, the kind that is so appealing you feel obliged to feed and offer it shelter. However, she knew from experience that stray cats take what they want, showing just enough affection that you don't lose patience. Then, when it suits them, they scratch you or move on.

Three people were sitting at a table in front of the small stage, the producer Mike Trelawney, and two other men Pet didn't know. Mike had told her that the two people who would be acting the audition scene with Fleur weren't members of the cast, just two drama students.

They watched a girl called Angela Bailey do her audition. She was very wooden, rather plain and didn't speak clearly.

Fleur's name was called next, and Pet had just enough time to whisper, 'Break a leg,' and push her towards the stage.

It couldn't have gone better. Fleur didn't forget her few lines, managed to keep up the bewildered, dumb-blonde wiggle across the stage and her voice was clear and crisp. Mike clapped – maybe not just because the drama students had been on the ball too. Pet thought he was going to take Fleur on.

Pet knew a great deal about theatre and acting, but had no aspirations to be onstage. She was far more interested in props and lighting. She thought she'd like to work for a theatrical agent, arranging auditions, finding new talent and suchlike.

After the audition she took Fleur to a nearby coffee bar, and they chatted about the acting world.

'I wonder if you'll get to meet Diane Lombard,' Pet said. 'She's the most terrifying agent who handles some of the biggest names in the acting world. I went to see her a few months back with a view to her taking me on. It was just as well I didn't want to act as she told me I walked like a carthorse.'

'That is so cruel,' Fleur exclaimed, astonished that her friend could laugh about it. 'I'd want to kill myself if someone said that to me. And it's not true anyway. You don't walk like a carthorse.'

Pet giggled. 'I do! I lumber along, and I'm not a honey-pot to men, not the way you are!'

Fleur suppressed a smile, which suggested she was well aware of the effect she had on men, and perhaps she intended to use it to her advantage.

Fleur was delighted to hear that she was to play Imogen, though not surprised as she had noted the way Mike Trelawney had looked at her. After just a week of rehearsals, she would be off to Margate for her debut on the stage. But even before she got to Margate, she had found the rest of the small cast didn't think much of her acting.

'She only got the part because Mike's got his eye on her,' she overheard someone say at a rehearsal.

Mike Trelawney had come to rehearsals most days, and he had been over-attentive, so maybe it was true. But Fleur wasn't fazed: she would learn from the cast, make friends with them and eventually get bigger parts. Marilyn Monroe had made her name playing dumb blondes, and people worshipped her. That might happen to her too.

Frankie was less than joyful about her going away. They were alone in the kitchen when Fleur told her, and she thought Frankie was cross because she would have to find another dogsbody to cook and clean. She couldn't resist saying so.

'It's true I'll have to find someone to take your place, and that won't be easy. But that isn't why I don't want you to go,' Frankie said, coming closer and putting her hands on Fleur's shoulders. 'I'm just not sure you're ready for travelling around with a bunch of strangers just yet. I was all for you going for an audition because it would prepare you for what you need to do as an actor. I also hoped it would make you more realistic if you got turned down. But now I'm worried you won't be able to cope with what's to come.'

'I'll be fine,' Fleur insisted. She didn't understand why someone like Frankie, who loved everything about theatre, acting and the people who lived in that world, would be so odd about her joining the ranks.

'Repertory is tough. I did it myself for a short while. A show each night and two matinees, and the digs aren't cosy like here. If you get a main meal included it will invariably be awful, so you and the rest of the cast will live on fish and chips. One bath a week. Some repertory companies stay in one town and put on a new play each week, and that means they have to rehearse while they're doing the current play. You're lucky in that your company does the same play, travelling to a new town each week for the summer season, but, Fleur, the digs are usually worse, and the only advantage is that there's no rehearsing. You'll get to see a lot of depressing new towns.'

'I need a challenge,' Fleur insisted. 'Maybe I'll hate it, and if I do, I'll come running back here, hoping you'll still need my help.'

'There will always be room for you here,' Frankie said, pulling her close for a hug. 'Just make sure that if you fall for some sweet-talking bloke he uses a johnny.'

When Fleur said goodbye to Frankie it was all she could do not to cry. They shared a secret and the older woman had given her love, comfort and security when no one else would. It was so typical of kind Frankie to say there would always be room for her. That, to Fleur, was a safety net.

*

A few weeks later Fleur resolved that she would never tell Frankie how often she felt like jumping on the next train back to London. She had never been so lonely. The rest of the cast merely acknowledged her presence with a nod, making no attempt at friendship. When it was a nice day and there was no matinee, they all palled up with someone either to go to the beach or to look around the town. Twice she heard them making arrangements and asked if she could join them. They pretended they hadn't heard. On both those occasions she'd gone off on her own and cried.

Pet had told her before she left that it was common practice for the cast to ignore the youngest person, and in time they would mellow when they felt she'd got what it took to be an actor. But it hurt terribly, and she didn't know what she could do to change things.

The first few times she went onstage, she felt sick with fright, and she thought the rest of the cast were hoping she'd forget her lines or fall over. But she didn't and, judging by the laughs she got and the frantic clapping for her at curtain calls, she was quite good. But the loneliness was corrosive, eating away at her and making her feel worthless.

Then, right at the end of the summer in Hastings, she met Barney Marsh. He was the stage manager at the theatre, and son of the owner, Michael Marsh.

He had green eyes, red hair and freckles, and wasn't much to look at, but when he smiled, he made her smile too, and for the first time since she'd been on the tour, she felt a bubble of happiness surge through her veins.

'Come to the beach with me this afternoon,' he suggested.

'I can't swim,' she said.

He came closer to her and brushed a strand of hair away from her eyes. 'You don't need to swim. You could just have a paddle. Or we can lie in the sun and talk. I want to know about you.'

'That'll be a short chat then,' she said, and smiled. 'I haven't done anything interesting.'

'Neither have I.' He grinned. 'I just run this theatre for my dad, and unless I disappoint him and run off to seek my fortune in London, I expect I'll be stuck in Hastings for ever.'

'So, maybe it'll be good to bore each other with our uneventful lives.' She giggled.

They arranged to meet at two by her digs. They'd had a run-through of the play that morning so he could be sure the lights and scenery were right, and all of the cast were slightly giddy with either excitement or trepidation as this was the last week of the tour. Fleur was happy to go back to Frankie's: although she had learned a great deal about acting during the tour, and knew she had improved, she was no longer so certain that this was the career for her. Often, she felt she had spent all these months in isolation, able to see and hear other people but they didn't see or hear her. Barney was the first person to show any interest in her.

'Do you know Hastings?' Barney asked, as they walked down towards the beach. It was a perfect afternoon, warm sun, no wind, and the sea as smooth as a sheet of glass. Fleur was wearing a pink and white striped sundress, her bare arms and legs lightly tanned.

'No, I've never been here before,' she said. 'But we've been to so many seaside towns these past months that they're all beginning to look alike. What's special about Hastings?'

'Well, apart from the battle, nothing much, but there's lovely places all around here. I love Rye and Romney Marsh in particular. My grandparents lived in Rye, and I spent a lot of time with them. My dad and mum were typical theatrical people, always off somewhere, waiting for the big break. Then Mum died when I was eighteen, and Dad bought the theatre.'

'So, if he was an actor before, why buy the theatre?'

Barney shook his head. 'I never really got that. Maybe he thought he could take on acting roles in the theatre and be at home with me. Or maybe he was just star-struck and couldn't be away from fellow actors. But he manages to make a fair living out of it, without doing a hand's turn. I'm the slave.'

'So do you hate it?' she asked. He walked fast and she was quickening her step to keep up.

'Sometimes,' he said, pausing for a moment and looking at her. 'I'd have liked to be able to choose my own destiny. I get fed up with all the petty squabbles, the egos of some of the actors. They make ridiculous demands, and they're never grateful. But, then, you'd know all that.'

'They don't speak to me,' she blurted out. 'I've never been so alone since I joined them.'

'They think you only got the part because you're beautiful?'

'No.' She hung her head. 'When they do mention how I came to be taken on they imply I ensnared the producer. I wouldn't know how to do that – I only spoke to him once and that was briefly.'

'Jealousy is a powerful emotion,' he said. 'And you are beautiful, Fleur. I think every man passing by us must be jealous of me.'

She blushed. 'I don't feel as if I'm beautiful.'

'I read a book once where the heroine said it was a curse to be beautiful. I couldn't see how that might be. But I suppose if everyone thinks you only get breaks because of how you look, it might become a curse.'

She thought then of all the times her mother and William Masters had said she was ugly, and she'd believed them. 'I'll be glad to go back to London and Frankie's house.' She went on to tell him about the theatrical people who stayed there and how she cleaned and cooked for Frankie. 'I feel safe and happy there and I get to see my friend Pet. She's another lovely person.'

'What about your family? Are they in London?'

That was the question she always dreaded, but she'd learned to lie.

'No family. Dad died in the war and Mum of a heart attack a few years back. There isn't anyone else and that's probably why I'm so fond of Frankie.'

'I'm sorry, Fleur, that's tough.'

'No, it isn't,' she said, with a laugh. 'At least I don't get any stick from anyone. Let's talk about something more cheerful.'

Once they were seated on towels on the pebble beach, they talked about what they would do if he wasn't running the theatre, and she wasn't acting.

'I'd go to medical school and train to be a doctor,' he said. 'Mind you, I'm not so sure my brain's sharp enough. What about you?'

'I had planned to go to university,' she said. 'I actually thought about studying psychology. But I got on a different path and forgot about it. Now I'd just like to get an acting role that would make me famous.'

He frowned. 'So, fame is important to you? What about happiness?'

'I'd be happy if I was famous,' she retorted, a little sharply.

'Would you? Not just cocking a snook at all those who were unkind to you?'

Her head jerked round to him. 'Whatever do you mean?'

He wiggled a finger at her. 'I might not have a degree in psychology, but I sense how much anger there is in you. Someone hurt you badly, and I'd say it was long before you started acting. Why don't you tell me about it and let it out?'

She jumped to her feet, her face flushed with either anger or embarrassment. 'I didn't come here to be cross-examined.'

Barney jumped up too and caught hold of her forearms. 'I wasn't cross-examining you. It was just a friendly observation. Okay, if you want to keep it to yourself that's fine, but I've always found that a true friend is someone who knows everything about you and likes you just the same.'

She didn't reply, or move away, just hung her head as if she was ashamed.

Barney reached out and, with one finger, lifted her chin. 'Let me be your friend, Fleur. I really like you.' On an impulse he leaned forward and kissed her lightly on the lips. She didn't break away.

'Shall we paddle now?' he suggested.

Barney Marsh couldn't boast of a great deal of

success with women. He blamed his red hair for that. But the moment he had seen Fleur on the stage for the first time he'd wanted her. An inner voice told him he would be punching above his weight: she wasn't just pretty, she was ravishingly beautiful with an ethereal quality. He casually asked around about her and heard comments like 'a recluse', 'uppity', 'thinks a lot of herself', 'strange'.

It was his opinion that all of those remarks were untrue and made by people who hadn't even tried to engage with her. Was that because of her beauty?

While the evening performance was taking place, Barney was in his room behind the box office, supposedly entering takings in a ledger. But he couldn't concentrate because he kept thinking about Fleur. They had held hands and paddled in the sea, and she'd laughed when a big wave came and soaked her dress. Her laugh was delightful, almost like the tinkling of a bell, but when she stubbed her toe on an unseen rock she swore like a trouper.

He thought then the best word to describe her was 'unpredictable'. Later they walked along the front and he bought her an ice cream. They talked of fairground rides they liked and the ones that scared them. Of food they loved or hated. She told him of some of the horrors she'd encountered in digs: on one occasion the previous guest had wet the bed and the landlady hadn't changed the sheets.

'I got in and the bed was soaking,' she said, with a grimace. 'I ran down the stairs to report it and she said I was making a fuss about nothing. I did make a fuss then so she moved me to another room. I inspected the new bed minutely – I expected bed-bugs at least.'

She was easy to talk to as long as he didn't ask anything personal, and on the way back to her digs he kissed her again. She responded with warmth and drew him close; the kiss was so good he wanted it never to stop, yet it was he who broke it off eventually, needing to hide his arousal.

The problem now was that she was returning to London next Sunday. He had just six days to make her like him enough to come down to Hastings to see him or invite him up to London to see her. Barney lived in a seafront apartment with his father, and while his father often spent a few days with a lady friend in Brighton, there was no knowing if he was planning to do so again anytime soon. Ideally, Barney would have liked the flat to himself from Saturday night onwards, so he could invite Fleur there.

'I've got to have you in my life, Fleur,' he said aloud.

14

Alice

Alice was stuck: she didn't know where to go in her investigations. It had been great to talk to Angus, to get to know him and stop seeing him as the villain of the piece. He'd said he thought she ought to talk to Ralph and admit what she knew. While that would round off her curiosity about her mother's past, she was too afraid of hurting Ralph and Emily.

Common sense told her to give up. Yet if she could just find out if it was true that her mother had run a brothel, she felt that would satisfy her.

Talking to Stuart again was the only answer, so she invited him round for dinner at her flat. She didn't get much time off work – usually she worked six days a week, but if there was a big wedding at the weekend, she had to go in on Sundays too, to check everything was all right. It meant she worked long days, sometimes till gone nine in the evening. Because of this she'd cheated with the food for their dinner and got a chef at work to make her a superb beef curry and a few accompaniments. All she had to cook was the rice.

Stuart arrived at eight bringing her some lilies and a bottle of expensive Merlot.

'So, I finally get to see your flat,' he said, with a wide grin. He stood just inside the door, looking around. Kitchen, sitting room and dining room were one large open space, with doors opening by the dining table to a Juliet balcony. He walked over to it and admired the view over the rooftops. As it was a lovely warm evening, Alice had the door wide open, the sun coming in, and the dining table was pretty, with a pink and white theme, including a small vase of pink rosebuds between the candles.

'It's gorgeous,' he said appreciatively. 'Pale pink and ivory together is always chic, but I expected nothing less of you. You couldn't have such a pale palette if you had small children.'

'When Emily brings her kids up here, she's on tenterhooks thinking they'll smear the sofas or drop drinks on the cream carpet. But they're always careful. However, I did it like this as almost a protest to my ex who insisted on strong colours. To be honest, I'm a bit tired of the girly vibe. I fancy some black with splashes of orange. But I haven't got the energy to change it.'

Stuart laughed. 'Why is it that women are always wanting to change the look of their home?'

'Maybe because they'd like to change their husband, but the décor is easier!'

181

Over a gin and tonic while she waited for the rice to cook, Alice told him the bare bones of what she'd discussed with Angus. 'I really like him,' she said. 'I don't like that he was so weak he went along with bigamy for Mum, but he'd have made a great dad. I feel a bit sad I can't have him in my life.'

'That's good, but clearly there's something more on your mind,' Stuart said. 'What is it?'

'The brothel thing. I really want to know for certain. Angus said he met Mum at a trade fair, and she lied and said she planned to open a china and gift shop. Later he found she ran an agency that supplied girls for promotion work. Was that a euphemism for call-girls? Was she actually there drumming up business?'

'After the last time I saw you, I tried to find out more. She was definitely charged with keeping a disorderly house, but the offence was "not proven". I found it odd there wasn't more detail on record. I was on the Vice Squad for a couple of years, and it was common for officers under certain circumstances to turn a blind eye to brothels because they approved of them. The girls were off the streets, they didn't usually become drug addicts and they were safe from vicious pimps. Besides, officers like me were realists. We knew prostitution was the oldest profession in the world and we could never wipe it out. To most of us it was stupid fining women for selling their bodies when they had to feed their kids. Especially as the punters got off scot-free.

'Now, from what you've told me about your mum, she wasn't a naive girl who'd been lured into bad company. She was an actor too. I think she was more of a party arranger, supplying girls to entertain the male guests. Those girls would have gone for it willingly. They probably enjoyed it and made good money.'

Alice winced. 'That fits with something Angus said. But it's so seedy.'

'A great deal of business has been created in Britain by captains of industry who enjoyed such parties,' Stuart said, with a shrug of his shoulders. 'Remember the Profumo scandal, with Christine Keeler and Mandy Rice-Davies? They used to be called on to make parties go with a swing. Swimming starkers in pools with captains of industry and cabinet ministers. Christine was just a year older than your mum, and not half as gorgeous. I can see nothing wrong with paying a few pretty girls to liven up a party. They weren't forced to go to bed with the men. It was their choice.'

Alice wasn't convinced it was as harmless as he'd made it sound. 'Maybe so, but I've got a feeling that around that time something bad happened to Mum, something that made her want to leave London, change her name and marry Angus for security. Was she being blackmailed? I know a court case would've been scary, but it wasn't proven, which meant she got off, so why marry Angus just for security?'

Stuart sighed. 'Why can't you believe she just fell in love with Angus? Why assume there was a darker reason?'

'I just sense it,' Alice said stubbornly. 'But the rice is ready now, so let's sit down and eat.'

'You're a funny girl,' Stuart said, a bit later. They'd got to the cheese and biscuits, and had drunk almost two bottles of wine. 'Your mum burned the candle at both ends it seems, whooped it up, tried a bit of everything, and I can't help feeling maybe you should follow her example. You work God knows how many hours a week, you hardly ever go anywhere, except to see an old codger like me, and there's no man in your life. Has it occurred to you yet that the real reason your mum settled on Angus might have been because she'd had enough of parties, acting and insincere men? Maybe she wanted children. She was cutting it fine there, wasn't she? Another couple of years and it might have been too late.'

Alice laughed. 'Only a man would come up with that. Or are you trying to say my clock is also ticking and maybe I'd better find a man to start breeding with?'

'You know I didn't mean that about you. But I could be right about your mum.'

*

A couple of evenings later Alice had an unexpected phone call from Petula in Sussex.

'I hope I'm not calling at a bad time, dear,' she said, 'only I remembered something and thought it might be useful to you – or have you got bored with trawling through the past?'

Alice smiled. She liked Pet, and as she was merely doing some ironing it was good to have a phone call that wasn't work-related. 'It's a very good time and, no, I haven't given up trawling, though a friend has told me I should. Besides, it's lovely to hear your voice.'

Pet laughed. 'That's not something my husband would ever say! Now, I remembered a phone call I had from your mum. I think it was about 1965 or '66, but dates are not my forte. I hadn't heard from her for ages, a year or more, I think – she never was a phone person and only ever five words on a Christmas card. But she had told me before when she did her first tour with repertory that she'd met a man she really liked. He was called Barney Marsh and he was the stage manager at the theatre in Hastings. I never met him, but from what Fleur said about him he sounded lovely. Anyway, she'd been with him all this time, and she was ringing me for sympathy because he'd gone off with another woman.'

'Oh dear,' Alice said. She hated calls like that from girlfriends as whatever she said it was always wrong. If she said he was a two-timing bastard, the response would be that he was perfect. If she said he was a good man, she'd be told he was a liar and a cheat. She couldn't win. 'Nothing worse than those calls.'

'I agree,' Pet said, 'so I was only half listening. Also I thought she probably deserved it. She wasn't the kindest of people, quite cutting. Anyway, she was distraught, all high drama. She said she couldn't live without him. I did my best to calm her down, with plenty-more-fish-in-the-sea type advice, and suddenly she said, "I'll make him pay." I didn't know whether she meant financially, or if she intended to harm him in some other way. I didn't ask because I thought it best not to know.'

Alice was afraid she was going to hear that her mother had stabbed him. 'Did you ever find out if she carried out her threat?'

'No, and it was several more years before I heard anything more from her. But, Alice, just a couple of days ago I was flicking through the local paper and there was a picture of him.'

'Barney?' Alice said. 'Doing what?'

'Yes, it was him. Barney Marsh is having an exhibition of his art here at a gallery in Arundel. I never knew he painted, but it's definitely the same man. There was a bit about him running his father's theatre in Hastings, then selling it to concentrate on his art. I've looked him up and he's a widower now, lives in Brighton. I thought he might be able to fill a few gaps in Fleur's life for you.'

'Gosh.' Alice was momentarily stunned.

'We could go to his exhibition together and you could stay the night with me. What do you say?' Pet suggested.

Alice pulled herself together. 'That would be good. It's probably inappropriate to talk about my mother at his exhibition but we could play it by ear. If he's nice, I could contact him at a later date. Besides, it would be lovely to see you again anyway.'

'So when?' Pet asked.

Alice opened her diary. 'I've got this coming Thursday and Friday off,' she said. 'Is that too soon? The big boss wants me to work the entire weekend, so this is to keep me sweet.'

'That would be perfect, and good for you to have a change of scene. You'll be coming by train, I assume, so just confirm the time you'll arrive in Arundel, and I'll be there to meet you. We can have lunch before we go to the gallery.'

Alice was excited as the train approached Arundel, not just because she'd meet her mother's old flame, but she'd be spending some time with Pet too. Stuart had rung her the day after they'd had dinner together and warned her again that she was becoming a bit obsessive about her mother's past. Perhaps she was, but it was no one else's business.

'Alice darling!' Pet came swooping down the station platform, looking like an exotic bird in a flamboyant multicoloured dress. 'How good to see you again.'

'And to see you too.' Alice was enveloped in a warm embrace and the heady scent of Shalimar perfume.

'I've booked us a window table at Woods, a little bistro where the food is divine, and we can people-watch. The gallery won't be open until two, so we've got plenty of time.'

As they ate, Alice could see why her mother and Pet had been friends. They had a similar exuberance, a sense of the ridiculous, and both flitted from topic to topic like butterflies on flowers. Pet was much warmer, more motherly than Sally, and without the touch of steel, but just as entertaining. She thought they must have been quite a force as young women.

They were looking at the dessert menu when a man spoke behind them. 'Petula Parks, I was just thinking about you!'

Both women turned to see a smartly dressed man of around forty beaming with delight.

'Flynn, how absolutely lovely to see you,' Pet exclaimed. 'What on earth are you doing here in Arundel?' She explained to Alice that Flynn had taught one of her sons to play the piano and they'd remained friends. 'Come and sit with us,' she suggested. 'Unless, of course, you're with someone.'

'I'm alone and I'd love to join you,' he said. 'I can't stay long as I've got to catch the train back to London. I'll just order a sandwich and a coffee if that's okay with you both.'

When Flynn had sat down, Pet explained, 'Alice is the daughter of an old friend of mine and lives in Bristol. What brings you here?'

Alice had a job not to stare at the man. She thought he seemed artistic. Whether that was because she already knew he played the piano, or his slightly too-long dark hair, long slender fingers, or his eyes like chocolate buttons, and sharp cheekbones, she didn't know, but it was a look she liked.

'I came to buy a guitar,' he said, 'but, sadly, they'd sold it just an hour before I arrived. It was that which made me think about you, Pet, your son and the piano lessons I gave him. How's he doing?'

'Very well,' she said, with a smile. 'He hasn't kept up with the practice, I'm sorry to say, just keeps saying he's going to get back to it. But no doubt you're used to hearing that excuse. What are you doing now? I remember back then you were playing guitar in restaurants and bars.'

'I still do a couple of gigs each week on guitar, and some session work,' he said, 'but my main work is teaching piano at the Guildhall School of Music at the Barbican.'

Alice was impressed. He had to be very good to be teaching there.

'So how about you, Alice from Bristol? What do you do?' he asked, his dark eyes boring into hers, like lasers.

A tremor ran through Alice. It was a very long time since any man had made that happen. 'I manage a group of hotels,' she said. 'I came down to find out a bit more about my mother, who died a few weeks back. Pet told me an old flame of hers is exhibiting his work here, so we're going to see it.'

'Not Barney Marsh?' he asked. 'I looked in the window of an art shop close to the guitar place. I love his stuff.'

'Yes, that's him,' Alice said. 'But until Pet told me about him today, I'd never heard of him.'

'I only learned about him a few months back. One of my colleagues is an art buff and she mentioned Barney. It's not the sort of name you associate with art, more like a circus act, but I'm told he's very well thought of.'

Flynn ordered his coffee and the sandwich, Pet and Alice had a dessert, and the three of them chatted about Arundel and nearby villages.

'I grew up in Amberley,' Flynn said. 'I loved it there. We moved to London when I was twelve, much to my disgust. Dad was offered a very good job, and my mother's heart was set on me becoming a world-famous concert pianist, so I needed excellent teachers and a music college. My gran was still living here, so I used to stay with her from time to time. That was how I came to teach Pet's son.'

Eventually he looked at his watch. 'I must catch the next train,' he said. 'It's been so lovely to see you again, Pet, and to meet you, Alice.'

'If you come down here again, ring me and you can stay with us,' Pet said.

'I may very well take you up on that,' he said, looking at Alice. 'And if I get to Bristol, could I take you out to dinner?'

'Yes,' Alice said, and, afraid she'd sounded too eager, added, 'That would be nice. I'll give you my card – it's got my work and home numbers – as I flit around a lot.'

They paid their bills, and outside the bistro they said goodbye to Flynn. He kissed Pet's cheek, but took Alice's hand. He didn't shake it, just squeezed it slightly and held it for longer than necessary, looking right into her eyes. Alice thought it was more sensual than a kiss and blushed.

'I'll be in touch,' he said, over his shoulder as he walked towards the station, and Alice knew he meant with her.

'He's become a real heart-throb,' Pet said, as they

moved towards the gallery. 'But I don't suppose you noticed. I think you have to be as old as me to appreciate talent.' She laughed and Alice knew she was aware of the effect Flynn had had on her.

The gallery was in a long, narrow building, and as soon as Alice walked through the door the vibrancy of the paintings hit her. It was like walking into a fairground at night. They were in the main large canvases, at first glance abstract, until you stood and looked more carefully. There was a series of six, each with a famous building almost hidden in swirls of colour. The Eiffel Tower, swathed in a gossamer-like green veil. St Paul's Cathedral behind a netting of purple. The Taj Mahal covered with semi-transparent red and yellow.

'How clever,' Alice gasped, thinking how much she'd like such a piece of art to liven up the sugared-almond colours in her flat.

'Astounding,' Pet exclaimed. 'Not at all what I'd expected of an old flame of your mum's. That's him over there.' She pointed to a tubby, bald man wearing an emerald green jacket. 'Shall we go and speak to him?'

Alice didn't answer: she was distracted by a portrait of a young woman, sitting on a swing in a garden. It looked as if it had been painted by a different artist from the other pictures as it was in the traditional style of portraits, using soft colours. The model had blonde, wavy shoulder-length hair and wore a pale pink dress.

'It's my mother.' Alice had never seen a photograph of her mother when she was young but she recognized the wide mouth, so like her own, the slight flare of the nostrils, like Emily's, and the amused expression, which she'd seen a million times.

'So it is!' Pet exclaimed. 'Oh, my goodness, this is going to be interesting!'

15

Fleur

'You've set your cap at Barney now, then?' Miranda, who played her older sister Barbara in the play, sniped at Fleur as they were taking off their stage make-up in the dressing room.

'Whatever do you mean?' Fleur's face was covered with cold cream.

'Don't come the innocent with me,' Miranda snapped. 'He's in the wings watching your every move, and you know it.'

Fleur had noticed Barney appeared to be spending a lot of time in the wings, but it hadn't occurred to her that he was watching her. 'It's more likely he's watching you,' she retorted. 'I expect Mr Trelawney's heard you were drunk the other night and asked him to check you aren't every night.'

Miranda had been drunk for one performance, slurring her words and stumbling around the stage. But Fleur didn't really think anyone in the cast would tell tales.

'You little bitch, I bet you told him,' Miranda hissed at her, her thin face alight with rage.

'Even if I knew his phone number, which I don't, I wouldn't waste money telling tales on you. I expect the reporter who was here that evening had already written it in his review.'

As far as Fleur knew there had been no reporter in the audience, but she was enjoying scaring Miranda and paying her back for all the slights and unpleasantness she'd dished out.

Miranda plonked herself down on her chair across the room, but Fleur could see her face reflected in the mirror. She looked as if she was about to start crying. Fleur felt no remorse: if someone was mean to her, she'd be twice as mean back. That had become her code since she discovered that everyone in the cast was against her.

Was Miranda right, though? Was Barney just watching her, not the rest of the cast? She hoped so because she liked him a lot. In fact, she had butterflies in her tummy just thinking about him. But could he be bothered to come to London to see her? She didn't think Frankie would let him stay on the sofa at her house. She'd be afraid of Fleur getting up to what she called hanky-panky. But Fleur was much too scared to do anything like that. Why would any girl do that when it hurt so much, and you ran the risk of pregnancy?

Yet Miranda and Ruth, who played Fleur's aunt, both had men friends and she was pretty certain they had sex with them as she'd overheard them cackling about underpants. Maybe it didn't hurt after the first time.

On Friday afternoon, the second to last day of the tour, Barney caught Fleur's arm as she was leaving by the stage door. 'Hold up,' he said, in a stage whisper. 'Can I meet you in a few minutes for a chat? We could go to the Copper Kettle tea shop. Do you know it?'

She did: it was in a back-street away from the sea-front. She supposed he was worried about being seen with her by one of the cast. She nodded.

'I'll see you there in twenty minutes,' he said.

'I won't be hidden away,' she muttered, and knew she ought to walk away and go to the shops as she'd intended. But she really wanted to see Barney and per-haps this wasn't the time for sticking to principles.

Barney arrived, hot and flustered, about ten min-utes after she'd got there. 'Miranda was on the warpath,' he said, as he sat down opposite Fleur. 'My father came in and she said I was behaving unprofes-sionally with what she called "the young upstart".'

'Meaning me?'

'Afraid so. That's why I didn't want Father to see us together – I expected him to take Miranda's part. But he didn't. Someone had told him about her being drunk onstage, and he considered that far more important. As I was leaving, he was telling her off. Unfortunately for you, Fleur, she'll probably think you told him. She's quite poisonous.'

'She can't do much now. We've only got two more evening shows and the matinee tomorrow to get through.'

Barney groaned. 'I'm fairly certain she'll think of something to show you up. Just be careful. Once before there was a young, pretty girl in the cast she turned against and she threw her by not sticking to the script. The girl was totally confused. I'm afraid she might do that again.'

'Forewarned is forearmed,' Fleur said, with a grin. 'I'm sure I can turn the tables on her if necessary.'

'The other thing I wanted to ask you is if you'd like to stay at mine on Saturday and Sunday. My father's going off to see his lady friend.'

'I won't share your bed, Barney,' she said primly. 'If that's what you had in mind I'll go back to London.'

He blushed till his face was almost as red as his hair. 'That wasn't my plan. We have a guest bedroom, and you can use it. I just wanted a chance to get to know you better, and to take you to some of the pretty villages and little towns around here that I love.'

As the Friday-evening performance began, Fleur took deep breaths to calm herself about what Miranda might do. She hoped it might only be that she was intending to try to confuse her by changing some of the dialogue. She felt she could deal with that. But she had to watch out for tripping too: a fall onstage would be awful.

A little later, while waiting in the wings for her cue from John, playing a house guest, she saw that Miranda, as Barbara, was in place on a sofa, doing needlepoint. John was looking out of the French windows.

'Where is Imogen?' John said. 'I asked her ages ago to come with me to the post office in the village.'

'I'm here, John, ready to go,' Fleur said, crossing the stage towards him. 'Didn't Barbara tell you I needed to change my shoes for the walk?'

'You said you were going to have a bath,' Miranda said.

Fleur was immediately alerted. Miranda should have said, 'It was me who said you ought to change your sandals for shoes as the lane is muddy, but then your head is always in the clouds.'

Fleur walked to centre stage behind where Barbara/Miranda sat, pulled a comic face and put one finger to her head in a gesture to imply her sister was daft.

The audience laughed. Barbara/Miranda turned on the sofa to look at what Fleur was doing and caught her pointing to her head.

'It's sad,' Fleur/Imogen said to the audience. 'My poor sister can't remember anything lately. It must be John coming to stay.'

Barbara/Miranda's face was twisted with anger. It took John to step forward and put things right.

'Let's get off to the post office before it rains again.'

Fleur looked back as she and John reached the wings. Miranda was clearly fuddled and had forgotten what she was supposed to say next. She stood up, looked out at the audience, then ran off the stage on the opposite side to Fleur.

Barney or his assistant stage manager had the presence of mind to bring the curtain down.

'What on earth was the matter with her?' John asked.

Fleur made the fake wide-eyed-innocent face she'd perfected during the run of the play. 'I'm sure I don't know. What was that about me having a bath?'

'At least you saved the day and made everyone laugh,' he said. 'Now we've all got to adjust our lines to make sense of what she said.'

Later, after the last curtain call, as everyone was rushing back to the dressing rooms, Miranda grabbed Fleur's arm. 'I suppose you think you're very clever,' she spat at her.

'Cleverer than you, that's for sure,' Fleur retorted. 'It backfired on you, didn't it?'

After the last performance on the following day, the cast were all preparing to leave Hastings and saying their goodbyes. Some were going in the coach to return to London with the costumes, others being picked up by family or friends in a car. Two were making for the last train.

'Are you coming in the coach?' John called to Fleur.

'No, I'm staying here for the weekend,' she said, with a smile. 'It's been good working with you. Hope to see you again one day.'

All of the cast, apart from Miranda, had been warmer to her today: it was clear they knew what Miranda had tried to do and admired Fleur for thwarting her.

It was only a very small victory for Fleur, but it made her feel good.

'I was afraid she'd try something again tonight,' Barney said, once they'd waved everyone off. 'Thank goodness she didn't.'

'So, it's just us now,' Fleur put her arm through his. 'The summer's over and I hope we're about to start something new.'

Fleur was impressed by Barney's father's apartment. It was on the second floor of a rather grand Victorian terraced house overlooking the promenade. Barney had said it had been a family house until 1958 when the owners had converted the upper floors into a big flat, as the ground floor was enough for them, and sold the upstairs to Barney's father.

There were three bedrooms, two bathrooms, a big kitchen, a sitting room that overlooked the sea, plus a couple more rooms in the attic. Fleur looked up at the huge bay windows with thick dark green floor-length velvet curtains and an ornate gold-braided pelmet and wondered how much they had cost. There was a chandelier too, silver candlesticks, Persian rugs and paintings that looked as if they belonged in a museum. Even the fireplace was splendid: it had one of those fenders with leather seats on it.

'This was Mr and Mrs Percival's drawing room before they converted downstairs into a flat,' Barney said. 'My father bought all the furniture from them as it looks so right here. The Percivals had no further use for it. It isn't my taste, I'd rather have something more contemporary, but it isn't my apartment.'

The rest of the apartment was equally grand, making Fleur feel small and out of place. But Barney took her into the kitchen, made her bacon sandwiches and tea and filled a hot-water bottle to put in her bed. 'My mother was a great believer in warming beds,' he said, with a smile. 'I've kept up the tradition.'

They chatted for a little while after the sandwiches, and when Fleur began yawning, he took her to her room. 'The bathroom is next door,' he said. 'Sleep well, and tomorrow I'll get the car out of our garage and take you on a tour of Sussex.'

He kissed her then, standing on the landing, and she felt shivers of delight run down her spine until she almost asked him to sleep with her.

'Night-night,' he said finally. 'See you in the morning.'

She thought she wouldn't sleep because he'd made her feel she was on fire. But the big soft bed, like Heaven after what she'd been used to in digs, the warmth of the hot-water bottle and the prospect of two days alone with Barney sent her to sleep in no time.

Three months later, at Christmas, Fleur stayed at the apartment again. She woke in the morning to hear someone raking out the grate in the sitting room to light a fresh fire, guessed it was Barney's father Michael, and thought back to the lovely memories she and Barney shared.

That first weekend she had spent with him had been so wonderful and she fell hopelessly in love. He drove her around showing her Rye, Winchelsea, Lydd and the marshes, chased her along the beach at Camber Sands, and they ate egg and chips for lunch in a transport café, then had a posh French dinner in Rye. But all that first day they kept kissing and touching, and by the time they got back to the apartment later in the evening, they were tearing off each other's clothes almost before they got through the door.

Somehow, she knew Barney wouldn't hurt her, and his love-making, once they were in the big soft bed, was so slow, gentle and sensual that all memory of her terrible ordeal in Belsize Park faded from her mind. She didn't know that the glorious, wonderful feeling that made her feel fireworks were going off inside her when he touched her was an orgasm – he had to tell her that. She didn't have to ask him to use what Frankie had called a johnny: he just produced one before he entered her, and it didn't hurt at all.

The following day they barely got out of bed, talking, making love, and more making love. When they went out to find a restaurant to eat, they stayed out only long enough to devour steak and chips, then went home for more love. Barney said he'd known the moment he set eyes on her that she was meant for him, and at his first kiss she'd known they had something special.

But as wonderful, erotic and all-encompassing as that first weekend was, she had to go back to London as his father was coming home, and Frankie was expecting her. They had to rush to tidy away all traces of her in the apartment, laughing at the number of used johnnies and discussing where best to dispose of them. She was sore with love-making, and on the train back to London she wondered how she could even stand a day without him, let alone a week or two.

But she had coped. She got a walk-on part in a West End play, which lasted four weeks before it folded. She helped Frankie paint one of the guests' rooms, she went out for odd nights with Pet, and never owned up to either of them that she was in love, or even told them about Barney.

Barney had to run the theatre. The only time he could get away was Sunday, and if his father stood in for him on Monday they could have a night in London, or she would catch the train to Hastings. Either way it was a cheap hotel for one night only. Once Fleur was so desperate to see him, she caught the train to Hastings, rushed to the theatre, and they had sex on the floor of the office behind the box office. Exciting as it was, it wasn't enough. Fleur was dreaming of living with him, cooking his meals, washing his clothes and sharing a bed every night. But when she told Barney this he laughed.

'You, my darling, aren't little-woman-at-home material. You'd be bored within weeks. You've got to make a name for yourself as an actress first.'

Finally it was Christmas. Barney had told his father about her, and he invited her to spend the holiday with them. There was a pantomime at the theatre, a matinee and an evening show on Boxing Day. But she could go with him, sell ice creams, watch the pantomime and be in the same building as him. That was enough for her.

But as she watched the show, laughing at the silliness, enjoying the dancing and singing, she knew she wanted to be up on that stage performing. She could play Cinderella, imagining herself in a beautiful ball gown and dancing with the prince. She was aware, of course, that the panto season lasted two months at most but, just as Barney had said, it was the stage she wanted and needed. It crossed her mind then that maybe she couldn't have that and Barney.

But getting work on the stage wasn't easy. At Frankie's she got to hear of new plays about to be produced, and where the auditions were being held. She went to them all, even if she didn't think a part was suitable for her: she believed that if she looked keen and in touch with what was going on it would be noted and approved of.

Again and again she read the parts for cheeky maids, younger sisters, the occasional nurse and even a nun, once.

'You'll never be a leading lady,' Giles Piggot, an arrogant producer, said dismissively. 'You have the looks, but you can't act.'

As she cleaned rooms and cooked meals at Frankie's, watching girls she was convinced couldn't act for toffee getting work, she smarted at his words. If no one ever gave her a chance to read for a lead role, how would they know she couldn't do it?

16

Alice

Alice was transfixed by the painting: it was a sharp jolt into the past to see the mother she remembered from when she was a small girl.

'Heavens above,' Pet exclaimed at her elbow. 'I didn't expect that. It's a fabulous painting and she looks exactly how she was when I first met her. But what a shock for you! I would have warned you had I known.'

Alice looked round to see Barney Marsh coming towards them. 'One of my earliest paintings,' he said. 'Not what I'm known for now, but I thought I'd bring it out of my studio where it's been languishing for years.'

Alice was no art expert but she sensed from the romantic softness of the work that Barney had been deeply in love with her mother.

'Mr Marsh, it's my mother. You would have known her as Fleur,' she said simply. 'I came to talk to you about her, but I didn't for one moment expect to see a portrait of her here.'

'Fleur was your mother?' The colour had left his face, and he suddenly looked his age, which had to be in the late seventies.

'I'm sorry to shock you,' she said. 'I'm Alice, and this is Petula, whom I'm sure Mum must have mentioned to you.'

'Pet, how do you do?' he said, holding out his hand to shake hers. 'Fleur often spoke of you. I always hoped to meet you one day, if only to learn a little more about Fleur. She was something of a mystery.'

'It's that mystery I wish to solve,' Alice said. 'My mother died recently. Can you spare us a moment to go somewhere more private?'

He looked from Alice to Pet. 'Of course. It's quiet here now and I have a couple of ladies taking care of things. Come into the office and I'll get you some coffee.'

Barney's colour returned as he took them into a small, rather cluttered office beyond the gallery. 'How did you find me?' he asked.

'I read in the local paper that you were exhibiting here. I just recognized your name from things Fleur had said,' Pet explained. 'I live locally, you see. I was in contact with Alice, so here we are.'

'Fleur rang me when you left her. She was in quite a state. Then I heard nothing more from her for several years.'

'It was the secrets she kept that made me give up

on her. Her past became a wall between us. Sometimes she'd tell me something, and I'd think we were finally getting somewhere, and I'd find out later it was a lie. She preferred to make something up rather than tell the truth about herself. But I knew in my heart she'd gone off being with me. She wanted far more than I could ever give her. But I went on my own. I only told her I was with another woman because I hoped she'd start telling me the truth and maybe value me. But instead, to get her revenge, she told a pack of lies about me to anyone who would listen.'

Alice said how sorry she was, then told him briefly about Angus being her true father and the bigamous marriage. 'I love Ralph Kent who brought Emily and me up. I never doubted he was my true father so it was a huge shock to find out he wasn't. I suppose one day I've got to talk to Ralph and tell my sister the truth, but I'm hoping by piecing together Mum's past, I might find a reason, a motive, an excuse. Anything so I can put the whole thing to bed.'

'I discovered after the first flush of falling in love with her steadied that she had more sides than a fifty-pence piece,' Barney said ruefully. 'She was passionate, yet could be ice cold. She was bright, funny, unpredictable, moody, untruthful, dangerous, spiteful, generous and at times very loving. She nearly drove me mad. She made me believe I couldn't be happy without her. But she was wrong about that. After we split I took up painting and through that I met Mary. We got married and were very happy. She died a few years back and I miss her terribly.'

'I'm sorry,' Alice said. She liked Barney: he was rather like Ralph, strong, stalwart and kind. 'Did you have any children?'

'Just one, a daughter, Amy. She's a doctor, working abroad. I hope she'll come back to Brighton and work at the local hospital. Now what else can I tell you?'

'Did you ever get a feeling of what Fleur's childhood was like?' Pet asked him.

'I think it must have been awful. She had a scar on her leg from when she must have broken it but she wouldn't tell me what had caused it. Who doesn't admit what caused a broken limb? You say, "A car crash, an accident skiing, I fell down a flight of stairs." Or "I had an operation." By evading the issue you're surely covering up something nasty. I think it was an injury inflicted by one of her parents.'

Alice nodded. She'd seen the scar too, and had asked about it. Her mother had laughed it off. Once she said she fell out of a tree she was climbing. Another time she said she'd swum into a rock under the sea. Alice hadn't bothered to ask again.

'I felt it was done by one of her parents too,' Pet said. 'She wouldn't open up about them, or anything else about her early life. Another pointer to a terrible childhood was how she watched the way I did things, simple things like holding a knife and fork, table manners and so on. She was always asking me what things were for, or how to say something. Like she was educating herself. This dropped off over the years when she felt she'd learned enough to pass as well brought-up.'

'How sad is that?' Alice exclaimed. 'To feel you can't admit where you come from or what your parents were like.'

'I think she may have been taken from them into care,' Pet said. 'That would explain a lot. Back then orphans or those in care were chucked out into the world at fifteen or sixteen to fend for themselves, which might explain, too, why she went to work as a mother's help. A seemingly better life, perhaps, but at the mercy of cruel or perverted employers. It's a shame Frankie isn't still with us. She took Fleur in at her theatrical digs when she ran away from the mother's-help job. She grew very fond of Fleur, and I think knew more than she ever told me.'

'Is it because Frankie had theatrical digs that she got the idea of being an actress?' Alice asked.

Barney smiled. 'I think Fleur's dislike of reality was responsible for that. She told me she'd had the ambition for as long as she could remember. She could have been a good comic actress – her timing was great – and she lit up the stage as a dizzy blonde. But she thought she should be playing serious dramatic roles. She'd never have pulled those off.'

Alice looked at Barney. 'So she carried on acting all the time she was with you?'

'Yes – well, when there was work. It's a precarious life, as I'm sure you know. But I got us a flat in Hastings and, of course, I was keeping her so when she went off on a tour she had nothing to worry about.'

'Barney, when she told me you'd left her for another woman, she said she'd make you pay. You say you didn't leave her for someone else, but did she carry out that threat?'

'She said some pretty unforgivable things to people about me. She demanded a big lump sum to set herself up in a flat in London, plus there was an arson attack on the theatre. She, of course, had an alibi – she was in a play in the Home Counties at the time, but I think she paid someone to do it. Luckily he wasn't very good at his job. The window he broke and shoved petrol-soaked rags through was just the men's lavatory, with tiled walls and nothing much to burn. I think she had directed him to the window in the props and scenery room. Had he got that right the whole theatre might have gone up. It was a nasty, vindictive thing to do.'

Alice wanted to protest that her mother would never have done such a thing, but she knew in her heart that she could. She had never liked to be thwarted, and she was vindictive.

Perhaps this showed in her face as Barney came over to her and took her hand in his. 'I wish I could have told you better things,' he said. 'I truly loved her, though, and I don't regret the time we had together. I look at the painting of her, which I did from memory over a year after we'd split up, and I just recall the best of her and how she made me feel. Would you like that painting, Alice?'

'I'd love it, but I can't take it from you.'

'You're absolutely the right person to have it,' he said firmly. 'And I sincerely hope you can accept what she was, good and bad. One thing you should remember is that she did a good job of mothering you. I'd call that redemption.'

Pet had invited a couple of friends of a similar age to Alice over for supper that evening.

'Shame Flynn wasn't staying in Arundel,' she said, with a mischievous grin, as she laid the table. 'He'd have been an ideal guest. But I bet he's on the phone to you very soon.'

Alice watched as Pet took a huge homemade lasagne out of the fridge, then pulled out salad stuff. 'You can do that.' She handed Alice a large bowl.

'I don't know that I've got anything to offer Flynn or any man any more.' Alice sighed, as she tore up the lettuce leaves. 'I work long hours, I've become selfish and I'm not a lot of fun, these days.'

'That would change with a new romance,' Pet insisted. 'Now tell me what you thought of Barney.'

'He's a really nice man,' Alice said, as she began slicing cucumber. 'He reminded me of Ralph, my dad. And what a brilliant artist. I can't wait to get the picture of Mum home.'

'How are you going to explain it to Emily and Ralph?' Pet asked. 'Are you thinking of telling them everything? Or an edited version?'

'I honestly don't know, Pet. With everything I've learned about Mum so far, editing seems to be a bad idea. It's adding more lies. And I haven't investigated the brothel business. It's just getting worse and worse.'

Pet rolled her eyes. 'The problem is we've got too many negatives. Fleur was essentially a fun person, a hothead, a big dreamer, selfish and egotistical. But she was fun. If we could find one person, other than me, who knew that side of her, maybe it would balance up the bad stuff.'

The subject of Fleur was postponed for the supper party. Pet's husband was out on business but the guests, Martha and Grant, were very entertaining. They ran a party-planning business and their stories about some of their projects were hilarious.

'We had one client putting on a party for his wife's fiftieth birthday,' Martha said. 'The wife was mad about elephants and he wanted life-size cut-outs of them all around the edge of the marquee. Then he asked if we could get a real elephant to bring in as the ultimate surprise. My jaw dropped. Did he think you could just google "Hire an elephant"?'

Grant took over. 'I told the client that was well nigh impossible, but I kept thinking about it, and it so happened there was a circus coming to Brighton around the same time as the party. To cut a long story short I managed to bribe the circus elephant man and he promised he'd do it. A deposit, then the balance on the night.'

'I kept saying no to this,' Martha chipped in. 'Who knows how an elephant will behave when faced with a marquee full of people?'

Grant grinned. 'Come the night, I got a call to come out to the field next to the one with the marquee. The man was unloading the elephant, name of Marigold. She seemed very calm, and he had even supplied a girl in bright blue livery and a cap to ride her. So, off we went, through the gate, and approached the marquee.'

'I was at the entrance ready to give the signal for the band to strike up "Nellie the Elephant".' Martha giggled. 'As Marigold got to the marquee, I gave the signal, the band started to play and in Marigold lumbered, the girl on her back smiling and waving. When the birthday girl saw the elephant she gave a whoop of delight. So far so good, I thought. People were clearing a path for Marigold, and the girl on her back guided her towards the top table where the birthday girl was.'

'I was as proud as punch,' Grant said. 'It couldn't have been better. But as Marigold reached the table, we all heard a fart, her bottom kind of opened and out came the biggest pile of shit you've ever seen. God, the smell! Everyone was covering their nose. Then Marigold reached out with her trunk, snatched up half the beautifully decorated cake, complete with candles, and turned away to get out, stuffing the cake into her chops.'

Alice roared with laughter. 'That is a wonderful, hilarious story,' she managed to get out, over her laughter. 'But what about the birthday girl?'

'She was thrilled,' Martha said. 'But she told her husband to get a big box, scrape all the mess into it, and forget using a real animal again for anything.'

'He looked a bit crestfallen,' Grant chipped in, 'but he cleared it up, and we all had a good laugh about it. His wife nipped outside and got her photo taken with Marigold too. So it ended well.'

When the guests had left, Pet poured them a small brandy each to round off the evening.

'That was fun,' Alice said. 'Maybe I shouldn't work so hard and get out more.'

'Abandon your mum's history?' Pet raised an eyebrow questioningly.

'I have to go on a bit more.'

'So what's next, then?'

'I really don't know.' Alice sighed. 'I feel I've got less than half of her story. But my ex-policeman friend Stuart might have come up with some new ideas when I get back. At some time I'm going to have to bite the bullet and tell Ralph and Emily at least some of what I've discovered, or I can never hang that lovely picture of Mum on my wall.'

'I hope you can find out something that shines a better light on her,' Pet said, her face clouding with concern. 'She wasn't a bad person, Alice. Both Frankie and I became very fond of her. You've got to remember Barney was possibly her first real love affair, and most of us mess things up the first time. I was cruel to my first love when I got bored.'

Alice had just got into bed that night when Stuart phoned her on her mobile.

'Sorry to ring you so late,' he said, 'but I knew you'd want to hear this. I've found a woman who was a character witness when your mum was in court for keeping a disorderly house. She spoke up for her, and I think it might shine a little more light on the events at that time if you see her.'

'You mean you've got her address?' Alice asked.

'Oh, yes, and a phone number too. She still lives in the same flat in Bayswater as she did then.'

'That's brilliant!' Alice gasped. 'But how come you found a phone number so long after?'

'Well, that was a stroke of luck. My mate who dug out this info remembered her name because it's an unusual one. He cross-referenced it and found three years ago she was called as a witness about a property scam. Her phone number was on record.'

'So what's her name?'

Stuart gave a little snigger. 'Seraphina Gauloise. Who'd forget that?'

'Well, yes.' Alice chortled. 'But how old is she? I don't think I want to chat to another ancient old girl.'

'Now, now, don't be ageist,' Stuart said. 'She was fifty-eight when she was called as a witness.'

Alice agreed that wasn't ancient. 'Of course she might not want to talk to me.'

'Maybe, but Bayswater is close to Paddington so phone her in the morning and you might be able to see her on your way home.'

Alice wrote down the name and telephone number, then filled Stuart in with the news of Barney Marsh and the painting of her mother.

'I think at some time you ought to go to Chatham and see the street your mum lived in as a girl,' he said. 'I've often been told by people that going back to where parents or grandparents lived opens up another perspective of their lives. Also, if, as has been suggested, she was taken into care as a child, that will be on record. I could come with you if you like. We could find a nice place to stay in Rochester, which I believe is a pretty town, maybe even explore a bit further afield too.'

'I don't know that I can take any more time off work for a while. Let's see what happens tomorrow,' Alice said. 'But it's a nice idea.'

The next morning Alice rang Seraphina. To her surprise the woman was in and agreed to see her.

An hour later, Alice was looking up at a house in Bayswater and wondering how close it was to the house where her mother had had a flat. Flats in that area had sky-high rents now. It was a different world from where she lived in Bristol and she felt a little nervous.

It was even more unnerving when she pressed the bell marked 'Gauloise' and the front door opened automatically, without anyone checking who she was. She walked tentatively up the stairs. The carpet was a deep red and very thick, the banisters glossy walnut, and the wallpaper was clearly expensive with grey and white stripes. She glanced up, hoping she hadn't to go to the fourth floor, but as she reached the first a lady in a pale pink linen dress came out onto the landing and smiled. 'Alice? Do come in.'

Seraphina had to be mid-sixties at least, but she could have passed for forty, with her unlined face, perfect figure and shoulder-length blonde hair held back with a velvet band. Alice wondered if that was what a face-lift looked like. If so, she wanted one.

She urged Alice to sit down in a grand drawing room, with huge chandeliers, Persian rugs, armchairs and sofas such as she'd only ever seen in National Trust properties. Tables and glass-fronted cabinets were valuable antiques.

'Your friend the retired policeman, such a nice man, explained you are Fleur Faraday's daughter. He knew I spoke up for her in court all those years ago, and you want to know why, I expect.'

'Well, yes.' Alice was really puzzled now. How did a woman who was clearly very wealthy have anything in common with someone in trouble with the police?

'I didn't always live like this,' Seraphina said. 'I was a lady's maid in Pembridge Gardens close to where Fleur lived. I am Portuguese and we are known for our needlework. My then mistress valued my skill. But she could be cruel, and her husband far, far worse. He came into my room one night and raped me.' Her voice shook as she said this, and her lips had tightened at the memory.

'I'm so sorry. How terrible for you,' Alice said. 'How can men be so brutish? Was it to do with this that you got to know my mother?'

'Yes. I had talked to her a few times when I saw her in the street. I couldn't speak much English then, but it was good to have someone smile at me and say hello as I was only young. She was so beautiful and wore such stylish clothes. I admired her. I didn't know another soul in London and on the night I was raped I ran to her for help because she had a kind face.'

'I see.' Alice was shocked that the connection between her mother and this poised, beautiful woman was so sordid.

'I don't think you do,' Seraphina said, shaking her head. 'You can't imagine me as a young, terrified girl far from home. You only see me as an elderly woman living in luxury. But your mother didn't hesitate. She gathered me into her arms and took me in. She let me cry until I could tell her what had happened. Then she tucked me into bed and said she would take care of me. She did just that. She kept me, fed me and nursed me for four weeks.'

It was so good to hear something positive about her mother that Alice felt tears welling up.

'But that is not all,' Seraphina said. 'She was so angry with my employers that she went round to Pembridge Gardens to tackle them. She was so brave, and she told them she was going to the police to report them if they didn't make reparation to me. Of course, I didn't really understand what Fleur told me then as my English was poor but I knew she had been fighting on my behalf.'

'And did they?'

'First you have to understand what she took on. My boss was a Russian shipping magnate, what they call an oligarch nowadays, his wife the daughter of a Member of Parliament. I wish I could have seen their reaction to a young lady like Fleur, in her mini skirt, charging into their mansion and making demands of them. But she must have frightened them badly for them to give in to her demands. She was a force to be reckoned with.'

'And what were her demands?'

'She said they had to give me a little mews cottage a few streets away. It was very basic, not modern at all – at that time it would have cost no more than a thousand pounds. But to me it was a home and safety. Fleur took me to the solicitor to check that the deed of gift was all done properly. She never for a moment forgot what I'd been through. I wondered if it had happened to her too.'

'That's been suggested by other people who knew her.'

Seraphina shook her head sadly. 'It is not an easy thing for a woman to admit to. We feel so ashamed. But she finally told me about it a couple of years later, when I could understand English better. She said it was at her first job as a mother's help. But she was worse off than me as she became pregnant through it and had a back-street abortion. She believed it had left her unable to have a child so I was glad to hear from your friend that she finally had you and your sister. I just wish I'd known where she was years ago as I would have contacted her to see if there was anything I could do to help her.'

Alice closed her eyes, feeling a bit sick to hear Pet's suspicion confirmed. 'Poor Mum. It does sort of explain why she went out of her way to take from men in the only way she could. But, Seraphina, how did you get from a mews cottage to here?'

She smiled. 'I worked hard at my needlework. I made clothes for wealthy women, and spent my earnings on making my little house beautiful. Its value rose dramatically. I always felt that Fleur had given me financial security. Then one day I met Jack. He came to collect a dress for his sister, a very good customer of mine. We became friends, and then . . .' She paused, blushing.

'Lovers?' Alice prompted.

Seraphina nodded. 'He is a banker. By then I spoke good English, and I had learned much from my clients. I was confident and poised. He asked me to marry him and before long I moved with him to this house. We have a little holiday house in the South of France too.'

'Will you explain how you came to speak up for Fleur?' Alice asked.

'Well, first I must tell you how it was for her long before she helped me. Her rent was high, she wasn't getting acting work, and she hated having to be a waitress. But it was only after she'd made life good for me that she told me about the parties she threw and how she made some money from them. I was scared for her, but she insisted she knew what she was doing. After that I saw her less. She came for a coffee sometimes. I made her a special jacket to thank her for helping me and took it round to her. That day she was very happy. But it was shortly after that I heard she had been arrested for running a brothel.'

'Were you shocked, horrified?'

'A little, but I understood. When things are bad you can't see the road ahead properly. And I remembered how she'd comforted and helped me when I most needed it. Jack got a good lawyer for her. I wasn't prepared to commit perjury, but I could say what was true, how kind she'd been to me. Of course I couldn't divulge exactly why, any more than I could say she was giving those parties because of what a man had done to her. But Jack, he is well known, and above reproach, and as such, my being his wife, I was a good character witness. The lawyer said in Fleur's defence that she was only guilty of throwing parties with a few fellow good-time girls, that no prostitution was involved. He asked for the prosecution to prove that money had changed hands, and of course they couldn't.'

'She was acquitted?'

'Well, they said it was "not proven". I'm not sure what that means legally. I think it means it stays on a police record. But they let her go. She came to see me just once before she left London for good. She thanked me for standing by her, and we hugged each other, shedding a few tears. We had much in common, and I hoped she would find a good man too. But I sensed I would never see her again. Jack said it was because I knew too much about her, and she was the kind of woman who liked to be a closed book. Was he right, Alice?'

Alice smiled. 'Indeed he was. She's probably looking down right now and wishing I hadn't opened the book. But I needed to know.'

'I suspect she was kind and generous to many other people, not just me,' Seraphina said. 'People always like to dish the dirt on folk, but don't so often remember the good things. But you will remember this. I'm so very glad she was able to have children and had you.'

17

Fleur

Fleur didn't know why she suddenly had the idea that marriage to Barney and having his children was a sinister trap. But it seemed like it to her.

Part of her problem with him, which she had no intention of admitting, was that her head had been turned by Percy Turnball, the producer of a West End play called *Perfect Strangers*. She had gone to the audition hoping for the leading-lady role: a glamorous blonde who entrapped men, then disappeared after robbing them. She was so sure she could handle the part – she had the looks and knew how to use men for her own ends.

In the three years she'd been with Barney he had been everything to her. Then, after the audition for *Perfect Strangers*, she felt suffocated by him, bored and wanting freedom. There was no way she could explain her feelings without hurting him still more, so she did what she always did when in doubt: she lied. She told him she couldn't live without being on the stage.

Barney, in his generous and reasonable way, said she could have both. But he also asked why she had to raise obstacles to them being happy together.

Disappointingly Percy Turnball picked Coral Atkins for the role in *Perfect Strangers*. She was a well-known actress who had been in *Emergency Ward 10* on television. He could only offer Fleur the part of her maid. After the audition Percy asked Fleur out to lunch and apologized. He said he'd had to pick Coral as she was a household name and, as such, she would ensure the play ran for months. He went on to tell Fleur that she was a far better actress than Coral, as charismatic as Marilyn Monroe, and he was going to arrange for a screen test to get her parts in major films.

Fleur believed him and slept with him that night at his flat in Pimlico and every night once the play was running. But despite all Percy's big talk that the play would run for months, it had terrible reviews and folded after only four weeks.

Fleur was devastated, not just about the play folding but by Percy's sudden chilliness. He had claimed he loved her, even talking about becoming her manager and taking her to Hollywood. She had fully expected him to beg her to leave Barney and come to live with him. Yet all at once he wasn't even interested in what she was going to do next. She saw then his claims of love were as false as the one about getting her into films.

She had no choice but to go back to Barney. There was nowhere else. She didn't feel any guilt at what she'd been doing, only anger that Percy had duped her.

But nothing was the same with her and Barney.

He bent over backwards to please her. He bought her beautiful dresses, paid for her to get her hair done at the hairdresser's, but the nicer he was to her, the more he repelled her.

Then there were all the questions. For the first couple of years they were together he didn't ask about her past, presumably thinking it was unimportant. But suddenly he wanted to know the complete works. About her parents, school, how she came to be living in Frankie's home and about everyone she'd ever worked with.

So, she lied about everything, making up a fictitious middle-class family who had rejected her because she wanted to go on the stage. How could she tell him that she was taken into care because her mother brutally attacked her? Or that her stepfather wouldn't stay in the same room as her because she was the offspring of some man her mother had gone with while he was away at sea?

She could see that Barney didn't believe a word of what she told him. His eyes, usually so warm and sparkling, were cold and dull, which made her feel even worse. So, when he said he was leaving her because he couldn't stand her lies any more, she let him go. She even packed a couple of suitcases for him as he intended to stay with his father until he found another flat.

She couldn't find a reason for why she was so contrary. She wanted him out of her life. Why she became jealous and angry she didn't understand. It made no sense to be a dog in the manger. Nevertheless, she demanded money from him so she could move to London, threatened him she would tell people he'd betrayed her, and finally hinted at doing something far worse. Was it just because she felt guilty for sleeping with Percy?

She set off to London with three hundred pounds from Barney in her handbag, and she truly believed the world was her oyster. It was 1966, she was twenty-six and the world was changing dramatically. Great new shops called boutiques with fabulous clothes were popping up everywhere, skirts shrinking shorter and shorter, clubs for younger people, known as discothèques, were open until two or three in the morning, and people talked about 'free love' all the time. There was even a birth-control pill: no more johnnies or fear of an accident resulting in pregnancy. This was the time to be young, free and single. She was going to have a ball.

But first she had to make good her threat to Barney. The man she paid to set fire to his beloved theatre was useless: all he succeeded in doing was minor damage. But perhaps that was just as well as the police didn't try too hard to find him. If they had caught him, no doubt he would have pointed the finger at her.

With the money Barney gave her she took a lease on a smart flat in Bayswater and set out to find acting work. To her dismay she was turned down at every audition she attended. The plays they called farces, which had always featured pretty, rather dumb girls being chased by the men of the house, had disappeared in favour of more gritty subjects, which she wasn't suitable for. She felt as if she was being punished for leaving Barney, and she knew that if she didn't get work before long, she'd lose the flat.

She was forced to take a waitressing job to keep the wolf from the door. She hated picking up half-eaten plates of food, despised the men who pinched her bottom and loathed people who didn't leave her a tip. But she had to stick at it or lose the flat, and at least she got a free meal every day.

Then she saw a postcard in the newsagent's window: 'Would you like a career in modelling? Ring this number . . .' She felt a little flurry of excitement and wrote it on her hand, then hurried home to ring it.

Quentin Holmes said he would see her at his studio

at five thirty that same afternoon. He had a distinguished voice, and she saw him in her mind's eye as Donald Sinden, the actor. His address in Craven Mews was just a few streets away. He'd told her to bring an evening dress, a swimsuit and a tea dress. She wasn't quite sure what a tea dress was – it sounded very old-fashioned, the kind of frock women wore to church.

Quentin might have sounded like Donald Sinden, but he didn't look like him. He was short, balding, at least fifty, and he had bad teeth. 'Come into the studio, my dear,' he said, and opened another door to his left, which led into what was a converted garage. It was painted white and well-appointed with a large white umbrella, huge spotlights, several different-themed backdrops on rails for easy changing, and a quantity of seating, ranging from a chesterfield to an ordinary kitchen chair. His camera on a tripod was at the centre of the furniture.

'My usual procedure with potential models is to take a few pictures *au naturel* before the evening dress or swimsuit. I can, of course, see from a glance that the camera will love you. So, if you'd like to take a seat on the arm of that sofa . . .' He pointed to a large green one.

Fleur put down the bag holding her other clothes and did as he asked. Her mini dress was white, as were her new Courrèges boots and she thought the green of the sofa would set them off well.

'Very nice,' he said, from behind the camera. 'Lick your lips and leave them slightly apart, looking right at the camera.' She flicked back her hair, pouted, moved to different positions. He kept saying, 'That's good', and 'Perfect', which she liked.

She loved her off-the-shoulder sapphire blue evening dress. It fitted like a glove and made her feel like royalty. Quentin wolf-whistled and rolled out a new background for her of a bridge over a river.

Next came the tea dress: it had a pink background with sprigs of flowers, a sweetheart neckline and puffed sleeves. Barney had liked her in it, which was probably why she disliked it.

'Not quite your style that dress,' Quentin remarked. 'Let's try the swimsuit.'

As she couldn't swim, buying a new swimsuit had never seemed important, and the one she had was a bit old-fashioned with elastic ruching. But it was a pretty turquoise blue and Quentin looked pleased with her appearance. He took a great many more pictures of her in it than he had of her in other clothes, including one picture of her astride the metal kitchen chair. She hadn't thought to check herself before coming here and hoped fervently that no pubic hair showed.

'You, my dear, are made for glamour modelling,' Quentin said, as he finally stopped snapping away. 'A great body, long legs and a face that suggests you can be naughty. How do you feel about that?'

'Are you suggesting topless pictures or nude ones?' she asked nervously.

'Not necessarily,' he said airily. 'I can get the right look with a skirt hitched up, buttons left undone. The money is really good, even better for topless or nude. For fashion modelling you could be on an agency's books for weeks and not get offered one job. All they want now in magazines is skinny girls like Twiggy in the latest fashions, but I can get you work and money immediately.'

At his words Fleur knew he never did fashion photography. He was no David Bailey, just a seedy man involved in a somewhat grubby business.

But she couldn't afford to be critical, not with the rent due and an electricity bill to pay. 'How much are we talking about?' she asked, hoping she didn't sound too desperate.

'If I get you in *Tit-Bits* or similar magazines you'll get twenty-five for one picture. But I can sell just one good glamour shot over and over again to collectors. You can easily make a couple of hundred.'

'Is this nude work?' She felt faint at the prospect of having to take her clothes off for this man, but she needed money, and quickly.

'That's what my customers want,' he said nonchalantly, as if he was flogging car parts. 'You'll soon get used to it, love. And you don't have to worry about me. I've got a lovely wife at home. To me, taking

pictures of girls is no different from snapping animals or flowers. It's up to you,' he said, lifting his
camera off the tripod, as if he was packing things
away. 'I can print up and charge you a hundred quid
for the pictures I've taken today, so you can put them
in a portfolio and tout them round the agencies. You
could get signed up straight away, you're a very pretty
girl, but the chances are you'll walk miles, wear yourself out doing the rounds and getting nowhere. But
if you need money fast, I'm your man.'

He suggested she thought about it overnight and
rang him in the morning. Fleur left, wanting to retort
he wouldn't see her for dust, but deep down she
knew she would be coming back to him.

Two days later she was at his studio at ten. He'd
told her just to bring a dressing-gown. He'd supply
any props that were needed. She hadn't expected that
the first pictures would be of her wearing a black
suspender belt, fishnet stockings, a striped waistcoat
that didn't cover her breasts, and a top hat. He made
her pose in ways that made her blush. More astride
the kitchen chair, bent over the sofa, bottom in the
air, lying on the sofa legs apart, showing everything.

Next, she wore skimpy diaphanous baby-doll pyja-
mas and he photographed her pretending to vacuum
the studio. After a couple of pictures, he got her to
take the little shorts off.

'A lot of men like to see semi-naked women doing

household chores,' he said, with a rumbling laugh. 'They're probably married to women who look better covered up.'

An hour later he told her she could get dressed as she'd done enough for one day. He handed her twenty-five pounds. 'That's on account. I'll get the pictures printed and take them to the man who buys them. Come back on Friday for another session and I'll pay you what I owe.'

Fleur didn't want to think about the men who would be leering over her, or that she'd left Barney to end up doing this. Twenty-five pounds was more than she'd earn in a week as a waitress, and Quentin hadn't laid a finger on her.

The following evening, Pet called on her – she came most Wednesday evenings, usually bringing something for supper. That night it was fish and chips.

'So, what auditions have you been to?' was almost the first thing she asked, as she put plates to warm in the oven.

'None this week,' Fleur said, getting out some knives and forks. 'But I got a few pictures taken for a portfolio. I thought I'd try some modelling.'

'Oh, really, Fleur! I know you're pretty, but you're hardly the model type!' Pet exclaimed, as if her friend had just signed up to be a missionary. 'You need to look like a greyhound, these days, to get anywhere.

Why don't you get a lodger? In this area, with their own room in your nice flat, you could get twenty pounds a week.'

'I don't want a lodger.'

'Then go to a proper employment agency and get a real job. You're worth far more than being a waitress.'

Fleur hated it when Pet did the aged-aunt thing with her. She wished she could say she was sick of being rejected at auditions, and afraid she'd never make it. And she couldn't go to an employment agency because she hadn't got a National Insurance card as she wasn't Janet Masters any more. But she couldn't admit that now, not after all this time.

So she did what she always did and lied. 'The photographer who took my pictures works with various women's magazines. He's confident he can get me work with them.'

Pet looked her up and down as if she was tempted to tell Fleur she knew she was lying, but all she said was 'Let's eat.'

That night was the first ever that Fleur was glad when Pet went home. She couldn't stand the probing, the suggestion she was barking up the wrong tree, and a definite hint that, if she wasn't careful, she'd be in deep shit. But why did she have to be so irritating and such a know-all?

*

The following day Fleur went over to Hampstead to see Frankie. When she'd first come back to London, she'd told her over the telephone that she'd left Barney because he had another woman. But Frankie wasn't sympathetic. In fact she'd sounded like she didn't believe her.

Fleur liked Frankie too much to cut off their friendship over a lie, and her visit that day was to make amends. Frankie was very pleased to see her. They sat in the kitchen and chatted, Frankie telling her, among other things, how difficult one of her latest guests was. 'One more criticism and she'll be out,' she said. 'Now, are you going to admit you lied to me about Barney?'

Fleur hadn't expected that. She'd thought Frankie would have forgotten about it by now. 'Well, it was easier to tell you he had someone else,' Fleur reluctantly admitted. 'The truth was that I just felt trapped because I wasn't getting acting work and he made me feel suffocated too. That's hard for anyone to understand.'

Frankie shook her head ruefully. 'You should have stayed with him, Fleur. You loved him, I know you did, and maybe the truth is that you aren't cut out to be an actress. Sometimes we have to be brutally honest with ourselves. I wanted to be a ballerina as a young girl, but I wasn't prepared to practise until my feet bled.'

On her way home that day Fleur wished she'd had the guts to tell Frankie the whole story. If she had, maybe her old friend would have suggested she gave up her expensive flat and came back to work for her. The thought of that was appealing: there'd be no more striving for anything, and she'd feel safe and protected. She wondered how Frankie would react if she knew Fleur was intending to pose naked just to pay her rent.

Whether it was right or wrong, Fleur didn't care. Quentin paid her well. Mostly she earned between fifty and sixty pounds a week. Only a few hours' work, with no questions asked. It would do until an acting job came along. But as time went by Quentin began to expect more from her than just nudity. The day he took a dildo from a box and said he wanted to photograph her using it was a very large step too far. She flounced off to get her clothes, angry that he'd thought she'd go along with it.

After that, she had to go back to being a waitress, but she was still desperate to be on a stage. She'd been in London for eighteen months now and finally plucked up courage to make an appointment to see Diane Lombard, a well-known theatrical agent, at her office in Shepherd's Bush.

She'd been told at auditions that this terrifying woman ate newborn babies, chopped off penises and scalped anyone she'd didn't like. While she knew those were dramatic exaggerations, she'd also heard that Diane had the ear of the best directors and playwrights in the business. Fleur rang her office to make an appointment but the secretary said, 'She doesn't make appointments with unknowns. Come to the office between three thirty and five, and if she isn't busy, she'll get you to do a reading.'

Such a dismissive response was daunting, as was being told she'd have to do a reading but not what it would be so she could practise. But Fleur was determined, and the next day she went to Shepherd's Bush.

Diane Lombard had bright red dyed hair and sharp features, and Fleur was scared of her even before she barked the oddest questions at her. One was 'On a scale of one to ten, what number would you give your acting ability?'

'About seven,' Fleur said. 'But I'm still learning.'

'Are you familiar with *Twelfth Night*?' was the next.

Fleur could only look at the woman in dismay: she had no idea what it was.

'Shakespeare, you fool,' the woman snapped, and flung a sheet of paper at her. 'Read it, and let me find out if you're a real number seven.'

Fleur had studied Shakespeare's *Romeo and Juliet* at school, but she knew nothing of his other works, and as she glanced down at the passage typed on the piece of paper, her legs turned to jelly. 'If music be the food of love, play on,' she read, in a loud, clear voice. She doubted Diane handled any Shakespearean actors, so she probably only wanted to see if Fleur would fall apart with nerves. She gave it her best shot, and as she got to the last couple of words, 'highly fantastical', she glanced at Diane, who was smiling.

'Not bad,' she said. 'I'll send you for an audition in a new musical stage show called *Hair*.'

Fleur could barely speak she was so surprised.

'Can you sing and dance? Are you prepared to be naked on the stage?' Diane asked.

Fleur gulped, but having performed for Quentin almost completely naked, she felt she could do it if she had to. 'I'm not a trained dancer or singer, but I'm told I'm good at it,' she said. 'As for nudity, I can do that.'

'I'll be the judge of whether or not you're any good.' Looking Fleur up and down, noting her smart suit and hair neat in a chignon, she winced. 'You'd better look at what these flower children are wearing and copy it for the audition,' she said. 'I doubt you'll do any better than back row of the chorus but getting into a show that'll be talked about a great deal, even in a very small part, is a good career move.'

Wildly excited, Fleur was on the way out of Diane's office when she bumped into an athletic-looking blond man on his way in. 'Whoa,' he said, catching her by the shoulders. 'Has Diane scared you so much you've got to run out?'

'No,' she said, gazing into dark blue eyes and a tanned face. She also detected an Australian accent, which suited his faded denim shirt and the slightly too-long hair. 'I was just excited as she's told me about an audition that sounds good for me.'

'That'll be *Hair*,' he said. 'Yup, I can picture you in that. Do you know what it's about?'

When she said she didn't, he suggested they went for a coffee so he could explain. He said his name was Bruce but omitted to mention he was Diane's husband. In the café he told her that *Hair* was about a bunch of hippies in New York who were protesting against the war in Vietnam. 'To them life is about freedom, smoking dope and love. But the music is terrific. You come out with it ringing in your head.'

'And they do it nude?' she asked, a little fearful. She might have exposed herself to Quentin, but a whole theatre full of people?

'Only a tiny part. I saw it in New York and loved it. Go up to Kensington Market and you'll see what you need to look like. You're a natural. I bet naked with your hair down you look great.'

The only response appropriate was a blush and he put one finger under her chin, lifted it and leaned in to kiss her on the lips. 'On second thoughts let's have lunch. Then I'll take you to Kensington and buy you something.'

He didn't say that was going to lead to bed, but she knew it was and wanted it.

They had a lot of wine at lunch, a simple yet perfect spaghetti Bolognese, and then he hailed a taxi to take them to Kensington Market. Fleur had heard of this market, which sold vintage dresses from the 1920s, and other such things, but never visited it. The smell of cannabis was strong, Jimi Hendrix's music deafening as they walked into a space crowded with hundreds of stalls full of brightly coloured clothes. Along with the gorgeous vintage clothes there were vivid kaftans, shawls, cheesecloth shirts, and jeans – the legs had been slashed, then printed fabric stitched in to make them into flares.

Bruce took her to a stall at the far end. 'This is my favourite,' he said, waving a hand at dresses reminiscent of what dairymaids had once worn. 'If I had my way all pretty girls would dress like this, glimpses of firm bouncy breasts, tiny waists and a swirl to the skirt. I imagine tossing a girl onto some straw in a barn and having my wicked way with her.'

Fleur had seen dresses along the same lines in Laura Ashley, but her fabrics were soft prints and far more demure. On this stall the colours were vibrant and the material flimsier giving more than a hint of what was beneath.

'That blue one would be perfect for you,' Bruce said. 'Try it on.'

He was as unstoppable as a tank. She knew she would put the dress on and allow herself to be seduced wearing it. She also sensed that sex with Bruce would be mind-blowing.

She tried it on at the back of the stall as there was no changing room. It made her feel wanton, and as she walked towards him, he reached out and removed the pins from her hair, running his fingers through it to loosen it.

'Perfect,' he said, as she gave him a twirl. 'I'll have that one, please,' he said to the stall owner, who had a small baby in a sling across her chest. 'Keep it on,' he said to Fleur.

They went back to her flat and he fell upon her the moment they were through the door. 'You can't wear a bra with that dress,' he said, as he undressed her. 'And preferably no knickers either.'

She had been right: sex with him was indeed mind-blowing.

After her day with Bruce she joined a dance class, so she didn't show herself up at the audition for *Hair*, and studied magazines and reports from America so she knew what Flower Power was all about. Three months later, in May 1968, when she got her reminder of the auditions, she had become a hippie, an embroidered band round her head, beads everywhere, and clothes from Kensington Market. Bruce had introduced her to cannabis – she'd even learned where to buy it and how to roll her own spliffs.

The whole of London seemed to have caught on to Flower Power. There was a 'love-in' at Crystal Palace – no booze, just people high on cannabis, LSD and the idea of universal love. Fleur was a little too cynical to embrace what she suspected was just a clever move on someone's part to keep youth comatose and pliant, but she didn't share that subversive thought. After all, it was fun, and Bruce was the biggest part of it.

She didn't see him often – he swooped in when she least expected him. He made her doubt everything she'd once believed in, and gave her new, radical ideas. Somewhere along the line he told her he was married to Diane, and she knew that if the agent found out, she'd never set foot on a stage again. But Bruce was worth the risk. He was ten years older than her, but an amazing lover, a fun companion, and beneath all the gloss he was kind.

She was accepted at the audition in June, and rehearsals began immediately as the show was to open in September. She was just chorus, but that didn't matter: she could sing in tune, she could dance well enough to pass muster, and she was to be in a West End show and on her way up. The director had even referred to her as 'the pretty blonde with the long legs'. That was like getting ten gold stars.

Fleur had just a week of glory when *Hair* opened. So many curtain calls, standing ovations, and she'd made friends, real ones, she hoped. She had been with the rest of the cast going down into the audience as they'd sung 'Let the Sunshine In'. She had sat on unsuspecting laps, kissed faces, and encouraged the audience to follow the cast up onto the stage. It was wild, heady stuff, and the whole of London was talking about the nudity. In reality that part was very brief. They were behind a huge sheet that was pulled off momentarily, but people spoke about it as if the whole show was done without clothes. It had been totally liberating. An experience she would never forget.

But a week later Diane Lombard found out about the affair, and Fleur got her marching orders from *Hair*.

Fleur was floored. She'd finally got to where she wanted to be when her career was ended by a jealous woman. She'd known Bruce would never leave Diane – not once had he suggested a future with Fleur. He was a player. He would always be chasing women and catching them. So why should Diane single her out for punishment?

One of the cast, an American called Storm, hugged her when she got the order to leave the theatre. 'You know what that bitch is really afraid of, honey? That he fell for you. You've got the full set, the looks, brains, the figure, and he really liked you. Remind yourself of that, honey, and put two fingers up to her.'

A couple of days later Bruce came round to see her. He looked crushed. 'Fleur, I'm so very sorry. I told Diane you didn't know I was her husband, but she's like a tigress when she's jealous – she'd have torn you to pieces if she ever saw you again. She hates it that I'm upset about you, and I am, Fleur, but I can't afford to walk away from her. She has a stranglehold on my finances.'

Fleur didn't ask what that meant, what his finances were, why he couldn't start again with her. She just knew that this was her destiny: brief periods of happiness, then misery. It was never going to change.

He made love to her one more time that day. It was long, slow, and so tender it made her cry. She vowed then she would find a man who would put himself in front of a cannon for her, who would never consider his finances or anything else. She had to be the prize for all time.

After her brief period of fame in *Hair*, and being with Bruce, she was back to waitressing, a short spell of posing topless in a café for artists in Bayswater, and a spot of promotion work for a cigarette company. She quite liked the cigarettes: she was in all-male company at race meetings, plying men with the cigarettes the sponsor manufactured. She hoped she might find someone as nice as Bruce but the ones she met all seemed to be weak-chinned public-school boys who had about as much sex appeal as a toilet roll.

She slept with men who promised her everything, but the only thing she got, apart from a few trinkets and pretty dresses, was a sense of desolation and failure. Then one day, many months since the glory of *Hair*, she ran into Percy Turnball again. She had been impressed by his good looks when they'd first met. He could have passed for an Italian, with his dark hair, olive skin, sultry eyes and high cheekbones, and apart from a few lines around his eyes he still looked good.

A small voice inside her reminded her he was bad news. But as he came out of Whiteleys, the department store in Bayswater, and his face lit up to see her, she chose to believe he was remembering she was as good an actress as she was in bed. When he asked her out to dinner, she was certain he had a part in a play for her. She dressed herself up to the nines in a stunning cobalt blue mini dress and used up the last of her precious Joy perfume.

'You look wonderful,' he said, when he came to collect her. 'I've booked a table at the Ritz, and you can tell me all about leaving Barney Marsh. I was pleased to hear about that on the grapevine – you're worth much more than a man who runs a rather squalid provincial theatre.'

There was no point in pretending she had acting work, he would soon find out that was a lie, so she told him she thought Barney had spread bad things about her: no one wanted to give her a part.

'So, you must be feeling the pinch financially?' he asked in a kindly way, as if he intended to help her out.

'I'm almost skint,' she admitted. 'I need work and I regret taking on that big flat, but I can't get out of the lease.' She had shown him round her home when he'd come to collect her. His only comment was that it would be good for parties.

'Parties!' she exclaimed. 'I've got a job to feed myself just now, so a party is out of the question.'

Dinner at the Ritz was wonderful: superb food, attentive waiters, and it was good to be in a place full of elegant, wealthy people. But she couldn't help thinking that the cost of the meal and the wine would have kept her comfortably for two or three weeks.

Percy was lovely when he took her home, cuddling her on the sofa but not pushing to go to bed with her, so she relaxed. He was a lot nicer than she remembered.

'When I said parties earlier,' he said, after a bit, as he poured her more wine, 'I didn't mean with your friends, or that you pay for food and drink. There's a lot of money to be made by giving corporate parties. Businessmen from out of town, having a good time with some pretty girls. I could arrange it all for you, at least until you felt confident enough to organize it yourself. I know a lot of great girls, who get paid a flat rate for coming. The men pay enough to cover all the expenses and much more. You'd get a percentage of the profit, which can be considerable.'

'But what would I have to do?' she asked warily.

'Just be the hostess,' he said. 'We get a local catering company to supply party food, drink and glasses. They'd deliver it here. You'd just make it all look attractive and welcoming, which this flat already does. Glam yourself up and put on some music. The guests make the magic happen.'

'How much would I make?'

'I had another woman running a similar thing. She made fifty pounds a party, and her flat wasn't as big as this or as well appointed. She ran one every Thursday night. That's a good night to have them as most men go home on Friday afternoon to their wives and family.'

Fleur felt a flurry of excitement. It sounded like money for almost nothing. It was January and very cold. Heating the flat was so expensive, but the parties would solve that problem. She was also likely to meet a wealthy man who might be a potential husband, or she could be his mistress.

'But are the women who'd be at the parties call-girls?' she asked.

Paddington, which was close by, was well known for prostitutes, or street-walkers, as some people called them. In Bayswater there were call-girls, and their clients made appointments to see them, either in the girl's apartment, or she would go to their hotel room. It had crossed her mind recently that perhaps she could do that. But she had no idea how to go about it.

'No, of course not,' Percy said sharply. 'They'd sleep with a man if they really liked him, or he made an offer they couldn't refuse, but basically they're free-thinkers who like parties and fun. Much like yourself.'

It sounded to Fleur the answer to everything. One night a week would bring in more than she could earn waitressing in almost a month. Her flat was on the ground floor so it wasn't like people would be stomping up the stairs or thundering around above the other tenants' heads.

Percy arranged her first party nine days after their night out at the Ritz. He came during the afternoon to check that the drink and food had arrived and helped her set up a table as a bar in her kitchen. He checked the bedrooms for cleanliness and clean sheets, telling her quite casually that sometimes guests would be going into them for sex. Fleur didn't like the idea of that, but it was too late to back out.

'Send the bedlinen and towels to the laundry,' he said airily. 'It's all included in your expenses. You just need to write me a little note. You can lock your own bedroom, so they don't go in there.'

Six girls arrived at nine o'clock, all very pretty eighteen- and nineteen-year-olds in tightly fitting short dresses with low necklines. They were warm and friendly, admiring her flat and thanking her for hosting the party. By the time they'd all had their first drink of the night Fleur had lost her nerves and was really enjoying the company – she'd been alone a great deal recently.

Then Percy arrived, and soon after, the other men were coming in. Percy introduced everyone, saying they'd all got to behave as Fleur was a novice hostess.

Every one of the eight men looked like the kind of businessmen Fleur had met when she was promoting cigarettes: smart dark suits, highly polished shoes, weariness in their eyes. None was younger than thirty, and she wondered how their wives would react if they knew what their men got up to when they were away on business. All of them were well mannered, and in fact quite charming, so she relaxed and drank more than she normally would.

She danced with a couple of men, plied them with drink and food, and found she was enjoying herself. She saw couples going to the bedroom, but they weren't bothering her, and the time passed very quickly. As midnight drew closer, they began to leave. Fleur washed up the glasses, stacked the plates to wash in the morning, and went to bed satisfied that her immediate money worries were over.

She said after that first night she would do it for three months and then stop. But two years later she was still holding the parties and it had been a long time since she needed Percy to hold her hand. He was still involved: he took a fee from the men he sent to her, ringing to tell her their names, and how many, but she found the girls. That was easy: she had a whole book full of names now. Some had arrived via Percy and they introduced her to their friends. Fleur still did some promotion work and met other girls there. She learned which ones pleased the men most and used them frequently.

The cost of laundry, ordering food and drink was all billed to Percy. She didn't care if a man took two girls into the bedroom with him, or if one girl had sex with three or four men in the course of the evening. She'd soothed a couple who had been slapped or punched by the man they were with, but she made sure that the man responsible never came a second time. She'd had girls get so drunk they passed out, and the police had turned up a couple of times with a complaint about loud music, but mostly the parties passed without incident. She'd learned after the first to take the men's money in advance on the girl's behalf, and at the end of the evening she gave the girls exactly half of what she had been given. The girls were happy, the men too, and Fleur considered herself astute to make money at a party, in her own home.

On her thirtieth birthday she studied her face in the mirror, and saw it was harder than it had been when she was twenty and tiny lines showed around her eyes, but she was still stunning and had a better figure than most of her girls. But the lines were something of a wake-up call, and a reminder she should start putting money away for a rainy day.

In February 1972 she met a man called Rupert at one of her parties. She knew by the way he was looking at her that he wanted her, not one of the younger girls. He was attractive in as much as he had a full head of hair, nice teeth and a pleasant way about him, but was hardly a dream boat. But she thought, from the quality of his suit, the gold cufflinks and smart shoes, he was wealthy.

Later he asked her to dance with him, and as he held her close, he whispered in her ear, 'I'll give you a hundred pounds to have sex with me.'

Fleur was shocked. He didn't seem the type to buy a woman. He'd been to a couple of parties before tonight's, and she recalled he'd chatted to girls, including her, but never paired off with anyone. She had always promised herself she would never go to bed with any of the men, no matter how much they sweet-talked her. But a hundred pounds was a great deal of money, and when she hesitated before answering, he laughed. 'Every woman has her price,' he said. 'A hundred pounds it is.'

She took him into her bedroom and held out her hand for the money before he began to undress. As she put it into a drawer she closed her eyes, knowing she was about to step over the line she'd drawn for herself.

It was surprisingly good sex. Rupert knew what he was doing, but when she woke the next morning, he had gone, and only then did she feel ashamed of herself.

18

Alice

The telephone was ringing and Alice was out of breath from carrying the heavy painting up the stairs. She put it down and rushed to answer the call.

'Hello, Alice. It's Flynn – I hope this is a good time.'

She sat down at her desk. 'It's perfect. I've just got back from Sussex, and I'm only out of breath as I was carrying a heavy painting.'

'You bought one, then?'

'You're never going to believe this, but in the gallery there was a portrait of my mother.'

'Good God!' Flynn said. 'How weird. You mean it was painted by Barney Marsh?'

'Yes! The reason I wanted to meet him was because Mum had a fling with him years ago. Anyway, to cut a long story short, I spoke to Barney and he said Mum left him back in the sixties. He took up painting then. He was clearly smitten by her and painted the portrait from memory. He got married soon after, very happily it seems, and wanted to give me the painting. It was enthralling.'

'I'd love to know more,' Flynn said. 'It just so happens I'm coming to Bristol next Thursday. Can I take you out to lunch? I've got to see a colleague in the morning about a recital in St George's Church later in the year, but I'll be done by twelve thirty. Can you escape from your job?'

Alice's heart beat a little faster. She knew that even if she couldn't get time off officially she'd make up some plausible excuse. It crossed her mind it was one trait she'd inherited from her mother. 'That should be fine. Any idea where you want to eat?'

'I've always liked that restaurant called the Glass Boat. Would you like to go there?'

'I'd love to,' she said. 'It's always been a favourite of mine.'

'I'll make a reservation then. One thirty okay for you? I'll see you there. If by chance they're full that day, I'll ring you.'

She got a feeling he didn't want to end the call, but was aware they didn't know enough about each other to prolong it. 'I can't wait to see you again,' she said truthfully, thinking she might as well own up.

'Me too, but it's not long to wait.'

Alice remained sitting and gazing into space long after she'd put the phone down. She couldn't remember feeling like this with anyone before. Mooning over someone usually arrived after kissing, not just from the touch of his hand.

She took down a rather ordinary print from the wall by her dining table and hung the picture of her mother in its place. It looked superb, and even if it had been of some unknown woman she would still have loved it.

'How strange that two old friends of yours have brought a very promising man into my life,' she said aloud. 'What are the chances of that happening?'

She didn't want to hide the picture, and wondered if she could just tell Emily and Ralph a shortened version of Sally's past. Perhaps she could say Angus was an old flame: he knew Pet, so she had gone to see her. Pet had taken her to the gallery where she'd met Barney Marsh and found the painting.

The trouble with that was that Emily had a nose for intrigue. Alice knew she'd keep asking questions, and although Alice could manage a few white lies, she wasn't in the same league as their mother.

A little later Stuart came round, all fired up to arrange a hotel in Rochester for them, rabbiting on about where they would go, where they would stay. As soon as he saw the painting, though, he was stunned into silence. 'Wow,' he said eventually. 'She was gorgeous, and that is such a brilliant painting. I can see you in her, your mouth, the shape of your eyes, even if her colouring is different.'

'I see that, and Emily too – her hair is much lighter

than mine, and she used to bleach it before she had her children.'

'So how are you feeling about all this,' Stuart said, once they'd sat down with a glass of wine.

'Puzzled, excited, a bit guilty that I'm poking into Mum's past, yet meeting Pet, Barney and even Angus has been good.'

'You appear to have a hint of sparkle in your eyes,' he said sagely. 'And I don't think it's to do with your mum.'

Alice giggled at his powers of perception. 'I've met someone through Pet,' she said. 'A musician called Flynn. I'm having lunch with him on Thursday.'

He put one of his hands over hers and squeezed. 'I'm glad. You're much too lovely to do nothing but work. I hope it works out.'

Alice grinned. 'I feel eighteen again. I wish you could find someone too.'

Stuart laughed. 'I don't! I'm perfectly happy with friends, an occasional round of golf, and a stack of good books. I never had time for anything when I was working and I really don't want a woman coming into my life and reorganizing me. But are you still up for a trip to Rochester? If so, when?'

'Next week?' she suggested. 'I can get Tuesday and Wednesday off. We've got a huge wedding at the hotel at the end of the week so I know I'll have to work all hours before and after the wedding. The boss will owe me a break.'

'Great. How about leaving on Monday evening when the roads will be quieter so it won't take more than three hours? That way we'll be there for Tuesday morning to explore. I've found a nice little boutique hotel. Say the word and I'll book two rooms.'

'That sounds great. Stuart, you're a treasure. But I really think after this maybe I ought to knock it on the head. Do I need to know more?'

'I think it will come to a natural end, possibly when you tell your dad and sister about it. Looking at that lovely picture, I suspect your mum would like you to give them edited highlights only.'

Alice nodded. 'Umm, carry on the family tradition, then?'

Stuart finished his drink and stood up. 'Time to go, before it's pitch dark on the Downs. You won't be telling lies, Alice. You'll just leave out the bad things. It's not the same.'

As Alice walked along King Street to the Glass Boat she was fizzing inside. She loved this part of Bristol, where it was possible to see and touch the rich history of the city: the cobbles underneath her feet, the Old Vic Theatre, the Naval Volunteer pub and further along the seventeenth-century Llandoger Trow where Robert Louis Stevenson had written *Treasure Island*. Daniel Defoe was also a drinker there. She caught a glimpse of herself in a window and was glad she'd chosen to wear the turquoise linen dress and jacket she'd bought in a Clifton boutique sale at the end of last summer. She knew she looked her best: she spent most of her life in black, which didn't raise the spirits.

Turning off King Street onto Welsh Back she smiled at the riverside with its tall buildings that had once been warehouses and shipping offices. It looked so pretty with old Bristol Bridge as a backdrop.

The Glass Boat was perfect in the leafy setting, with sparkling windows, polished decks and a glimpse of immaculately laid tables inside. There were four swans cruising close by: she knew the restaurant owner always fed them.

She couldn't count how many meals she'd had here, but this was the first time there was a possibility of romance, and the fizzing inside her grew stronger.

Flynn leaped to his feet when he saw her. He was wearing a cream linen jacket, navy blue trousers and a blue and white striped open-necked shirt. He looked as if he'd even had a haircut for the occasion. 'You look wonderful,' he said softly, as his lips brushed her cheek. 'I thought today would never come.'

'You say the nicest things,' she murmured, and took

one of his hands. 'You also look wonderful, and I feel the same.'

As Flynn ordered wine, she wondered how she'd been able to drop her customary frostiness so easily – she'd stuck to it with men ever since her marriage had failed – and why she wasn't afraid of showing her feelings.

Conversation flowed effortlessly between them, as if they were old friends. She told him about her mother and her mysterious past, which she was trying to unravel. But she was keener to hear about him and his music.

Like her he'd married young and found it was a mistake. He said it was lucky they didn't have children, or he doubted he would have been able to leave his wife so easily. 'I wanted kids back then but it just didn't happen. Now I'm not so sure I would've been cut out for it. Teaching kids piano for years sort of put me off.'

'I adore my sister's children,' Alice mused, 'but I'm always glad to give them back. I don't feel deprived having none of my own. People, usually mothers, claim my life must be very empty. But you said you're at the Barbican. Surely not playing all the time?'

He smiled, and she loved the way his lips curled upwards at the corners. 'No, that would be exhausting. I'm involved with organizing recitals, giving lectures to students about music, and I do an outreach programme where I visit London schools to talk about careers in music. Not just playing an instrument well enough to perform, but background work in studios with sound systems and suchlike. My main objective, though, is to give as many children as possible a love and understanding of music. Like all the arts, it colours and gives meaning to even the most ordinary life.'

She learned he had a Down's Syndrome brother called Fergus. 'He's thirty now and shares a flat with two other men. Fergus is quite a high achiever. He loves cooking and gardening. The three of them are supported, but they manage very well with shopping and cleaning. Fergus loves music too. I used to play for him all the time when he was small and I still lived at home. He could be in the most ratty, confrontational mood, but when I sat down to play, he'd calm right down and just listen. I keep him supplied with CDs and take him to concerts when I can.'

'That's lovely,' Alice said. 'I don't know much about Down's Syndrome, but I'd like to know more.'

'It's good that we can accept anyone who has it as just a person, unlike the way they were treated in the past,' he said. 'But on a lighter note, how is the food?'

They had ordered their lunch and when it arrived at the table, they were so engrossed in conversation they were hardly aware of what they were eating. Alice had ordered bouillabaisse, one of her favourite dishes, and Flynn had a fishy risotto.

'It's fabulous,' Alice said. 'One of the best I've ever eaten. And yours?'

'Yummy,' he said. 'I'm always trying to make risotto myself and failing.'

'I'm not good at it either,' she said, with a smile. 'I get bored stirring it and it burns on the bottom. I'm better cooking comfort food, roasts, cottage pie, spag bol. I wouldn't win any prizes for my cooking.'

'I like it, but I make a horrible mess. So, I tend to go for ping-ping meals, microwaved stuff. Fergus tells me I'm lazy, but when I cook for him, he's happy to clear up.'

'What about your parents? Are they still in London?'

'Dad died of a heart attack a few years back. Mum is in her late sixties, still sprightly, thank goodness, and she lives in Chiswick. She downsized from the family house there after Dad died, and she's now got a ground-floor two-bedroom flat close to Turnham Green tube station, with a little garden. Fergus is in Acton so he can see her easily. She keeps up with all her old friends so I don't have to worry about her.'

By the time they ordered desserts, they had got through two bottles of wine and were holding hands across the table and looking into each other's eyes. She wanted to ask him what time his train left, but she was loath to break the spell. For her at least, it was as if they were completely alone, in a kind of bubble that prevented the outside world intruding.

'I don't want today to end,' he said quietly. 'Am I being unrealistic to think you feel the same?'

'No, you aren't,' she said. 'I feel exactly the same. I don't even want you to catch your train.'

'Then I won't,' he said, and reached up to caress her cheek. 'I could go in the morning?'

She knew he was asking if he could stay with her. 'Yes. Please do that, and shall we go now while we're still capable of getting a taxi?'

It was nearly five in the afternoon as they went up to the high street to find a taxi. They hadn't realized they'd been on the Glass Boat for so long. It felt odd to be seeing people leaving work, breathing a sigh of relief that they had escaped the office and the sun was still shining. Flynn held her hand and it felt so natural.

He kissed her in the taxi and Alice felt as if it was her first ever kiss. In reality the first had been about bumping noses, and the boy had held her so tightly she'd thought he would crack her ribs. Flynn's kiss was sensual, hinting at what was to come. By the time they arrived at the flat, Alice felt she was on fire.

He kissed her all the way up the stairs. Even when she was unlocking her door he was kissing the back of her neck. Once they were in her flat they were pulling each other's clothes off.

Alice hadn't been with a man since she'd moved into the flat, and she'd always thought it would remain that way, a virgin bed, bath and everything else. In fact whenever she'd contemplated whether or not she wanted to change that, she'd been scared. She felt she couldn't expose herself again, not just her body but having to talk about where she came from, why her marriage had broken up, how she felt about things. To start from scratch with a stranger.

But as they fell onto her bed it felt right: his body fitted into hers as if it had been designed for her. She loved the way he smelt, the delicate touch of his fingers on her skin, his hair, eyes. Everything was perfect. He was a superb lover too, and it seemed to her that he was touching her body with the same sensitivity as he would play the piano.

No words were necessary: it was a meeting of bodies and minds.

They must have fallen asleep because when they woke it was dark outside. Alice pulled on a négligée and went into the kitchen to make tea. As she waited for the kettle to boil she stood at the open doors by her Juliet balcony and looked out over Bristol. So many twinkling lights, like handfuls of diamonds thrown onto black velvet. She couldn't hear any traffic, just a steel band somewhere in the distance.

Flynn came up behind her and slid his arms around

her middle, bending his head to her shoulders and kissing her neck. 'It looks beautiful,' he said softly. 'Is it my imagination that everything's been perfect today because we're meant for each other?'

'I hope so,' she said.

'I feel I'm falling in love with you,' he whispered. 'Is that completely crazy?'

'Maybe, but I feel it too,' she said. 'In a few days we might see we've been a bit hasty, but I hope not.'

19

Alice

The small hotel Alice and Stuart were staying in wasn't far from Dale Street, but the owner had advised them to walk there as parking was difficult.

The hotel, with its pretty garden, spacious elegantly decorated rooms, and en-suite bathrooms, was far removed from the street where Alice's mother had been a child. 'It's as grim as I feared,' Alice said, as she and Stuart turned a corner onto it and she saw a long narrow road of scruffy terraced houses. 'And it doesn't take much imagination to know how it was in the forties.'

'Be fair, there are roads like this in Bristol and every other city,' Stuart said.

'I know,' Alice agreed. 'Imagine how it must've looked just after the war, though! Gaps in the terrace where houses had been bombed. No gardens, front doors opening onto the pavement. There might have been a shop or two, but the houses would all have had soot-blackened brick, a couple of families at least to each one, no bathrooms or even electric light, the lavatory out back somewhere.'

'You're making me see it.' Stuart chuckled. 'There's not been much improvement in seventy odd years. It's still just cheap housing, mostly rented out. Students, immigrants, those on benefits, and old people hanging on in the hope of being rehoused.'

'I can't help but make the comparison with our family home in Totnes,' Alice said, in little more than a whisper. She was very aware that whatever she thought about the street, it was home to the people who lived in it. 'I understand now why Mum never spoke of it.'

'There's a Catholic school at the bottom of the road. I expect that's where your mum went,' Stuart said. 'And I've made an appointment at the council offices to see the equivalent of what they used to call the children's officer. This woman, a Cynthia Turner, will show us the old records. If they exist, of course. When I rang them they were helpful and sounded positive. But let's go on into town.'

Alice said nothing as they walked down the long street. She was imagining her mother as a six-year-old sitting on the doorstep, perhaps even then dreaming of something better.

'That's the house she was born in,' Stuart said, pointing out number thirty. 'I found it in a census.

Father a seaman, mother a housewife, and lodgers Stanley Whethers and his wife Nancy. Stanley worked in the dockyard. I guess most of these houses were inhabited by dock workers or seamen then. In fact, they were probably built for them.'

Alice looked across at number thirty and shuddered. She had a strong sense that that was where her mother's troubles had begun.

Cynthia Turner was a voluptuous redhead of about forty. She greeted Stuart and Alice with warmth and enthusiasm. 'I've found your mother's file, Alice, but it isn't easy reading, I'm afraid.'

'I didn't think it would be,' Alice said. She was touched that the social worker was sensitive.

'I just need to remind you before I reveal all that we mustn't view the past with present-day standards. Giving a child a good hiding was considered perfectly all right at that time, and kids from poor families were often hungry and malnourished. Miss Cooling, the children's officer involved with your mother, was one of the more enlightened ones, a qualified nurse and midwife. She moved heaven and earth to get young Janet to safety.'

'As bad as that?' Alice said.

'I'm afraid so. Now, I'm going to let you read her reports because they tell a powerful story.'

She put the file on the desk in front of Alice. 'I'll

'come back when you've had time to go through it,' she said.

Stuart sat next to Alice and together they read the handwritten report. It wasn't easy to decipher the woman's spidery writing, but how the social worker felt about abused children was soon apparent.

I called at 30 Dale Street in response to being told by the school nurse that Janet Masters was seriously underweight. I found Freda Masters, the mother, drunk although it was just late afternoon. The house was filthy, no food in the kitchen, evidence that the mother is an alcoholic, and rat droppings on the floor. Janet was not just very underweight but seriously malnourished. I instructed the mother on what constituted a balanced diet and said I would be returning shortly to check on the child in the hope there would be an improvement.

The next report was dated two days later:

I was informed today by the ward sister in Chatham Hospital that Janet Masters was brought in as an emergency just a few hours after I had called at 30 Dale Street. While the child did not admit her injuries were inflicted by her mother, a neighbour, Mrs Lovett, confirmed that they were. Freda Masters had beaten Janet ferociously with a poker. Her right leg was broken in two places, her arm too, and she had innumerable weals all over her body and her head. It is my belief that but for the intervention of Mrs Lovett, who stopped the beating and called the ambulance, Janet would have been killed.

The child is very poorly. Even if she recovers physically from this brutal attack I think the mental trauma is likely to stay with her.

A couple of days later Miss Cooling reported again:

I was at the court this morning at Freda Masters's hearing. I was called as a witness and I reported in detail Janet's injuries inflicted by her mother. I am dismayed that the police and indeed the judge did not take this crime seriously enough. In my opinion Masters should have been sent to prison. But she was let off with a fine. I feel it is a travesty of justice.

The next report was dated two weeks later:

Janet is still in considerable pain and has had an operation to re-set her leg as it had become infected. Freda Masters has made no attempt to visit her daughter, or even write her a letter. I am calling at the hospital almost every day to check on Janet's recovery.

The next update came a few weeks later:

Janet Masters's recovery has been long, slow and painful. One of the most remarkable things is that that child is so loyal to her mother. She didn't blame her for the attack, saying her mother had a hard life. I am determined Janet will never be allowed to go home to such a mother, and by all accounts her stepfather, William Masters, was equally cruel to the child. I hope to arrange for Janet to go to Summer Fields, a very highly thought of children's home on Rochester Way.

The next reports were of how Janet was settling into Summer Fields. Miss Cooling had written that the child was gaining weight but it would be some time before it was normal for her height. She said Janet was happy at the home, making friends with the other children and liked by the staff. She especially enjoyed the garden.

Another telling report was dated around six weeks after Janet had been placed in Summer Fields, some three months after she was taken to hospital.

I went to see Freda Masters today, but I was shocked that she showed no remorse, or indeed any interest in how her daughter was. She didn't even ask me where she was now.

There were a few more reports on Janet's health. Miss Cooling also mentioned that Janet had been seeing an orthodontist to have her teeth straightened, which, in Miss Cooling's opinion, would give her more confidence.

After a long gap, which suggested that all was well with Janet, there was a very brief report saying that Janet had passed her eleven-plus and would be going to Maidstone Grammar School for Girls.

The final report was when Janet was fifteen:

Every now and then in a children's officer's career there is a child who makes the hazards and disappointments of the job worthwhile. Janet Masters is one such child. She has charm, beauty and is highly intelligent. She has done so well at school that her teachers would like her to go on to university. This would mean staying at school until she is eighteen to do further exams. But such are the rules for children in care that this won't be possible: at sixteen they are considered adults, able to live alone and earn their own living. There is no provision for children to go on with further or higher education.

I wish to put down on record here my view on this. Janet is being let down again by the social services. If she could go on to university, which she deserves, she could enter one of the professions, but as it is she will have to get a job in a shop or office, and live on her own without any family support.

I do not believe she has recovered from the trauma she suffered at the hands of both her parents. I know she carries the scars internally. Having to fend for herself, she is likely to fall in with bad company. The scars she bears could make her behave irrationally, tell lies, make her cruel to her own children, or to have no respect for the law. I ask that her case be reviewed, a good foster home found for Janet so she can stay on at school till she is eighteen and able to go to university. If it is made clear to her that an exception was made for her I am sure she will work hard, and it will also heal her to know she is important to us.

'Wow,' Stuart said. 'Clearly no one above Miss Cooling took a blind bit of notice of what she recommended. Now we're beginning to see why your mum kept the past a secret.'

'I don't suppose she was even told how Miss Cooling fought for her,' Alice said sadly.

Cynthia Turner came into the room again. 'What did you think?' she asked. 'Was it what you expected?'

Alice shook her head. 'After seeing Dale Street I expected poverty, but for her mother to beat her like that –' She stopped, too stunned to say more.

'Miss Cooling was forced to resign after that last

report,' Cynthia said. 'She was ahead of her time, and her superiors didn't approve of her views. She went on to study psychology and called for all children to have protection and rights. She had died a couple of years before I came here, but people admired her work and her name was always cropping up. We social workers get some very bad press, these days, some deserved, some not, but back when Janet was a little girl, enlightened ones, like Miss Cooling, were as rare as hen's teeth.'

'Thank you for showing this to me,' Alice said, her eyes filling with tears. 'Miss Cooling was right about Janet's scars. I'm beginning to understand why she was so secretive.'

'I prepared a copy of it for you, just in case you wanted to show it to family,' Cynthia said. She held out a blue cardboard file. 'Would you like it?'

'Yes, please.' She thought Ralph and Emily should see it. Maybe it would ease them into what came later. Or, after they knew her mother's more recent history, as mitigation.

Alice didn't speak for some time after they had left the council offices.

'Poor kid,' Stuart said softly, clearly as shocked as she was. 'But she brought you and Emily up with love and kindness, so whatever went on in the interim years, that in itself is proof she wasn't mad or bad.'

They spent the rest of the day exploring the historic naval dockyard in Chatham, and went on to nearby Rochester to find out more about Charles Dickens and to look at the Norman castle.

'Let's go to Hever Castle tomorrow,' Stuart suggested, 'the birthplace of another misunderstood woman, Anne Boleyn. I'm told the gardens are astoundingly beautiful, and we'll be close to the M25 to get home.'

Alice said goodbye to Stuart outside her flat. It was just after seven thirty and they'd had an interesting time at Hever Castle, plus a wonderful late lunch in a nearby village. But she was anxious to be alone now, to think things over. She was sure Stuart would be glad to sink into an armchair with a drink after such a long drive.

A little later Alice was lying on her bed considering the events in Chatham and adding that to what Seraphina had had to say about her mother. Would it all make up for Emily and herself being allowed to believe Ralph was their true father?

Alice felt she knew more than enough now to forgive and forget. But she couldn't speak for her stubborn sister.

To Alice, the missing part of the story was what had made her mother marry Angus when she knew he already had a wife. However she looked at that, it didn't make sense. Until she'd unravelled that mystery she couldn't give up.

The following day at work, on an impulse Alice dialled Mira Lombard. The previous evening it had occurred to her that Mira had answered only direct questions: she hadn't volunteered any further information. But in her line of work it was more than likely she'd heard about the court case for keeping a disorderly house, and about Fleur's bigamous marriage.

Alice just hoped she enjoyed a bit of gossip.

'Alice!' Mira said her name with some enthusiasm when she picked up her extension. 'How good to hear from you again. Pet spoke very highly of you.'

Alice put her cards on the table, saying she had found out a great deal about her mother, but now she wanted to shine a little light on why Fleur had chosen to marry a man knowing he was already married. 'I'm assuming she felt she had to lie low after the court case about her house parties and moved away from Bayswater. But have you any idea of what she was doing? Angus told me he met her at a trade fair, but that was a few years later.'

'I heard she was running an agency for promotion work,' Mira said. 'There were a few sniggers about it, people assuming she was still providing girls for parties, but I think she'd got her fingers burned so she wouldn't do that again. Another story I heard was that there was a man on her tail because she'd either owed him money or he was blackmailing her.'

'Really? Blackmailing her about what?'

'Well, dear, it could've been anything – a dalliance with the judge who heard her case, proof she was running a brothel, anything. But that was just a rumour. However, she did hightail it out of London rather quickly. Later, and she'd been gone a few years, presumably having you, a whisper went round about the bigamy, and word was that the same man who had been blackmailing her had grassed her up.'

'I wonder who that could have been. Does Pet know?'

'No, dear. Pet didn't have any idea where she was during that time. When she spoke to me the other day and said you'd visited her, she said she never knew she'd married Tweedy or that she'd had you and your sister until the bigamy case. You've got to remember Pet was a new mother during that time so she wouldn't have been in touch with people in London. But she did say she put out feelers for you then, but couldn't find out even what town or city you were in.'

'So no one knew?' Alice said.

She heard Mira suck in her breath. 'There is one woman. She came to me hoping for acting work – she said Fleur had recommended me. She was good. I got her some TV adverts and she did voiceovers. Name of Jackie Moore. She married some actor, a rather successful one too, stopped working and had twins. She's divorced now and lives in Reading. I can't give you her number, that would be unethical, but I could ask if she was willing to speak to you, and give her yours.'

'That would be very helpful,' Alice said, punching the air in excitement. 'Do stress I only want to piece together Mum's former life and that I'm not a weirdo or a stalker.'

'I'll do that,' Mira said. 'Jackie liked your mother. In many ways they were similar – ambitious, beautiful and with a colourful past. Next time you're in London, ring me and we'll go out to lunch.'

20

Fleur

Fleur woke to the sound of crying. At first, she thought it was coming from inside her flat, but as she woke properly, she realized it was outside.

She got up, went to the window, which was open, and saw a girl looking up at the house. Even though it was dark, her face was illuminated by a nearby streetlamp. She knew immediately the girl was maid to wealthy people who lived nearby. She had spoken to her in the street several times, and knew her to be Portuguese, a sweet, gentle girl of seventeen or eighteen.

Fleur sensed the girl, whose name she'd never learned, was looking for her, and probably couldn't work out which bell to press as it was so dark. Only an emergency would have made her come out at night to find someone she barely knew.

Hastily Fleur flung on a housecoat and rushed out of her flat to the front door of the house. The girl's crying was a sharp and unwanted reminder of the night she had run away from Roger Whitestone. As she appeared on the top step, the girl rushed towards her. 'Please help,' she cried, in broken English. 'I am hurt by him.'

At those words a chill ran down Fleur's spine. She wrapped her arms round the girl and half carried, half dragged her inside. She was wearing a raincoat over a nightdress, and when Fleur switched on a light, she saw a bloodstain on the nightdress.

'What is your name?' she said slowly, making the girl sit down.

'Seraphina Gauloise. I sorry I wake you. I –' She began to cry again.

'Seraphina, it's okay. You're safe with me. But you must tell me, if you can, what happened.'

'He – my boss makes . . .' The way she put her hand on her lap made clear enough what he'd forced her to do.

'I will phone the police,' Fleur said.

'No, no!' Seraphina caught hold of her hand, dark eyes begging. 'If police come, big trouble. He will say bad things.'

This was all so familiar to Fleur. Seraphina was right: she would be put through hours of questioning, her employer would deny it and almost certainly claim she had instigated sex with him. Or he would tell the police she'd been out for the evening, had had sex with a boyfriend, then got back to find the front door locked and made up this story because she knew she'd be in trouble. Never mind that she was wearing nightclothes under her raincoat: the police were far more likely to take the word of a rich man than a distressed Portuguese maid.

Fleur didn't know anything about the people Seraphina worked for, but the house in Pembridge Gardens was huge and very grand. She'd noted crystal chandeliers when she walked past after dark and had seen the chauffeur pulling up in a Rolls-Royce. Knowing how she had felt when it had happened to her, she couldn't bring herself to let the poor girl be humiliated or violated further by the police.

'You can stay here,' she said slowly, so Seraphina would understand. 'In the morning we'll decide what to do. I will make you tea now and run a bath. You are safe.'

When she handed the girl a cup of tea, she noted that her hands were shaking so much she could barely hold it. Fleur stroked her hair, murmuring words of comfort that she knew would have little effect, then ran the bath for her and dug out a clean nightdress.

Fleur felt white-hot anger at men who could do this to women. Seraphina was little more than a child, just as she'd been when it had happened to her, and Fleur was well aware that the rape had coloured and spoiled her life.

Maybe she couldn't take Seraphina to the police, but she could take on that disgusting man. She'd shame him in front of his wife, and make him pay, one way or another. He might, of course, call it blackmail, but he was the bastard who had taken an innocent and delicate young girl by force.

After Seraphina had had her bath, Fleur tucked her into the bed in the spare room. 'Go to sleep. Don't worry, I'll make sure no one hurts you.'

Fleur couldn't sleep, she was too wound up, and she remembered how she'd taken on Brenda at Summer Fields. It had felt so good to expose and punish her for what she'd been doing to other children. Perhaps it had made her stop stealing and being nasty to those smaller than herself. She would do the same to the man who had hurt Seraphina.

At ten the next morning Fleur left the house. She had the bloodstained nightdress tucked into her handbag, and she'd told Seraphina she had to get a few things from the shop. She was fired up with anger. Seraphina had told her on one of their meetings in the street that she'd got the job for her sewing. She'd said Portuguese needlework was much prized, and that was why rich ladies took on girls like her.

The door of the house in Pembridge Gardens was opened by a thin-faced older woman, who was perhaps the housekeeper, judging by the starched apron over the dark blue high-necked dress. Behind her, Fleur could see a palatial hall with black and white checked tiles, huge green plants and a very grand staircase.

'I wish to see the lady of the house,' she said, in a loud voice. 'It's to do with her maid, Seraphina.'

'She does not wish to see anyone this morning,' the older woman said. 'Seraphina didn't come home and she's struggling with her clothes alone.'

'She'll struggle even more if she doesn't see me immediately,' Fleur said. 'She needs to know what happened to the poor girl.'

That seemed to do the trick. The housekeeper scuttled up the stairs, and Fleur took the liberty of going right into the hall and shutting the door behind her. The door to what had to be the drawing room was open. It was vast, decorated in mainly green and cream. Three sumptuous green velvet sofas, antique-style lamps and heavy brocade curtains gave Fleur the impression it had been designed by someone with endless funds but no imagination.

'What on earth is it?' A cross-sounding woman's voice rang out from the top of the stairs. She was wearing a full-length velvet coat in deep rose. Fleur assumed it was a dressing-gown as the woman didn't appear to have brushed her hair. She came on down the stairs and Fleur noticed her slippers matched the coat perfectly. 'Foster tells me you've come about Seraphina. What's the matter with her, and why isn't she here?'

Foster, the housekeeper, was standing behind her mistress wringing her hands nervously.

As well she might, Fleur thought.

'I think we should discuss this in your drawing room, unless you want your entire staff to know what your husband has done,' she said curtly, and walked into the room.

'Excuse me, miss,' the woman said behind her. 'You do not go into people's homes and make veiled threats or enter rooms without an invitation.'

'Your husband didn't wait for an invitation to rape Seraphina last night,' Fleur snapped at the woman, and enjoyed seeing her mouth drop open. 'She was distraught outside my house in the early hours of the morning, and I took her in. This is the nightdress she was wearing.' She took it out of her bag and thrust it at the woman, showing her the blood.

She dropped it, like a hot potato, but her face was drained of colour. 'How do I know you aren't lying?' she said. 'The pair of you could have made it up.'

'If you could even think that you must be extremely stupid,' Fleur said. 'Seraphina is distraught, and although I want to take her to the police to make an official complaint and see your husband arrested, she's afraid. You should make reparation.'

'Money, you mean?' the woman said haughtily.

'Your sort of people makes me sick,' Fleur hissed. 'Not money at all, though God knows you should pay through the nose for that man's sick behaviour to a member of his staff. Seraphina will need a place to live, because obviously she is not coming back here. And I intend to see you give it to her. She may, of course, be pregnant too, but we won't know that for a few weeks. In the meantime, I shall ask my doctor to examine her, and I suggest you talk to your husband and make sure he's prepared to treat Seraphina kindly and generously. If not, I'll go to the press. Is that clear?'

Fleur saw the woman was badly shaken, but she felt no sympathy. 'Just remember that Seraphina came to you in the belief she was bettering herself, using her considerable talents to look after your clothes. But you allowed your husband to treat her in a way that meant she had to run out into the street to find an almost complete stranger to help her. You should thank God it was me she ran to. Anyone else would have rung the police immediately. And by tea-time today everyone in London would know what a beast your husband is.'

Fleur swept to the door, stopping only to pick up a business card that was in a dish on a side table. It read 'Alexis Akatov, 21 Pembridge Gardens, Bayswater'. She turned to the woman. 'Goodbye, Mrs Akatov, I shall be in touch again shortly when I have talked this over with my solicitor. I suggest you do the same with your husband. And don't allow him to think he can brow-beat me. He won't be able to. I am too angry at the crime he has committed against a helpless young woman to back down.'

Foster was standing in the hall and had clearly heard every word. She looked shell-shocked. 'Will you pack up Seraphina's belongings, please,' Fleur asked her. 'I'll send someone round in an hour or two to collect them. Plus, any wages owing to her and her P45. Needless to say, she doesn't want to step over this threshold ever again.'

It was only once she was out on the pavement that Fleur realized how reckless her actions had been. She hadn't known he was Russian or even his name. His wife might have called the police. Or he could have come in and wiped the floor with her. But she hoped the terror she'd evoked in his wife would make her attack her husband and insist he did as Fleur had said.

Fleur got home to find Seraphina crying again – she said she was very sore. Fleur rang her doctor and was told to come immediately to the surgery in Sussex Gardens. 'We have to see a doctor, sweetie,' Fleur insisted. 'If I'm to make the bastard pay for what he did, you'll need medical proof. You need a doctor on your side.'

At seven that evening Seraphina was much calmer. Fleur's doctor had been very kind and confirmed there was evidence of forced sexual activity and he promised he would act as a witness if required. Fleur had sent James, a twenty-year-old boy who often did odd jobs for her, to collect Seraphina's clothes and other belongings. With them, there was a month's wages and a note from Mrs Akatov: '*The least I can do under the circumstances is offer a month's pay, and I can only apologize to Seraphina.*'

'Guilt money,' Fleur said, tucking the note into a drawer for safe keeping. 'Good job she didn't consult the old man before she wrote that.' She sniggered to herself. It was an admission of sorts. But Seraphina's English wasn't quite good enough to understand what she had said, which she thought was probably just as well.

Seraphina stayed with Fleur for a month, but by the third week of her stay Fleur had upped her visits to the Akatovs to twice a week. She had discovered they owned a small mews house a couple of streets away from Pembridge Gardens, and their chauffeur lived in it. She had gone round there one day and stopped to talk to the man as he was cleaning the Rolls-Royce. She said she was looking for a mews house and asked if he knew of any for sale. He obviously had no idea who she was and not only told her about two houses he thought might be coming up for sale but flirted with her.

She asked him if she could use his bathroom and he agreed. It gave her just enough time to check it would be the perfect house for Seraphina to set up a dressmaking business. It needed redecorating, and the kitchen was ancient, but apart from that it was in reasonable condition. The chauffeur volunteered it was probably worth about a thousand pounds: others in the mews had gone for that amount if they needed work on them.

She still hadn't met Alexis Akatov, but she knew now he was a shipping magnate. On her last visit to the house Mrs Akatov had tried a different tactic, saying Fleur could call her Isabella, perhaps imagining that if she could befriend her all this would go away. Her father was a Member of Parliament, which she had mentioned as if that might frighten Fleur off, but to Fleur that was just another weapon in her armoury. She had insisted Alexis Akatov be there on Friday when she would call again, as this must be resolved now. If not, she might have to take more direct action.

On Friday she presented herself as promised, heart thumping. Akatov was there, and made an imposing figure. He was tall, about six foot two, and wide without being fat. He had a full head of reddish-brown hair, with just a touch of grey at the temples, and a beard with red tones. He wore a colourful embroidered waistcoat under his pale grey suit, and Fleur got the impression he saw himself as something of a dandy.

He launched into a tirade at her, claiming that the maid should be dealing directly with him, not using a go-between.

Fleur said that was ridiculous as he had terrified and hurt Seraphina very badly. 'Don't you have a conscience? Surely a man in your position can get a woman easily enough without resorting to rape – and what a thing to do with your wife so close by. It was appalling behaviour. But, as I said in the beginning to Isabella, you must make reparation to Seraphina. She cannot stay with me for much longer and she needs to earn a living. I suggest you give her, free and clear, the mews cottage your chauffeur lives in so she can start a dressmaking business from there. Plus a thousand pounds to make necessary improvements on the house.'

He gave a great guffaw of laughter. 'Why should I do that? What possible power do you, an out-of-work actress, have to make me?'

She knew then he'd been making enquiries about her. But she was fired up now and didn't care. 'We have the testimony of the doctor who examined Seraphina later that morning. He found traces of sperm and severe bruising, which proves you had used considerable force to rape her. Also, he found a few of your red pubic hairs caught on her own, and there is the blood on her nightdress, which your wife has seen. But if this isn't enough to convince you that I have power, I also have a great many connections with journalists, and every one of them would bite my hand off to get this story. Especially as Isabella's father is a Member of Parliament.'

Fleur glanced at Isabella, saw her stricken face and felt just a little sorry for her. She'd made up the bit about the red pubic hair, and as Seraphina had bathed after the rape the doctor had found it hard to get a sample of sperm. But she worked on the principle that if she lied with conviction, Akatov would believe her.

'The cottage and cash will not stop Seraphina's nightmares. She will probably never trust a man again or get the evil you did to her out of her head. But a secure place to live and the chance to rebuild her life will help. So do this, Mr Akatov, and we will draw a line under this sordid, disgusting business. If you choose to refuse, you have my word that you and your wife will live to regret it.'

She paused, looking from one face to the other, wondering how on earth she managed to get all that out without faltering. He was trying to appear blasé, but she noticed he had a little tic by his eye, a sure sign he wasn't so confident. Isabella looked as if she might collapse. Fleur actually felt sympathy for her – after all, she had to live with this beast.

She swept out then, satisfied she'd had the last word.

In the street, though, she could hardly walk because her legs were shaking so much and her heart was thumping, like a steam hammer. It crossed her mind that if she'd delivered that speech in a film she might have won an Oscar.

*

They won. Seraphina's solicitor, Mr Agnew, rang to say that Akatov's legal people wished to set up a deed of gift of the cottage and sent a cheque for Seraphina too.

'Does Mr Agnew know what he did to me?' Seraphina asked.

'Not exactly. I thought it better not to say until we were forced to. But Alexis Akatov doesn't know that. Collect the cheque, cash it and perhaps spend a bit of it going home to see your mother,' Fleur suggested. 'By the time you get back the cottage will be yours.'

Fleur wasn't altruistic by nature, and she felt she'd done all she could for her friend now. Besides, she needed to organize another party and she couldn't do that with Seraphina in the flat.

21

Fleur

Nearly two years after Seraphina came to her for help, Fleur was trying on a beautiful velvet jacket she had just made for her as a belated thank-you present. It was dark red scattered with exquisite gold embroidery.

Fleur loved it. It was, she thought, the best jacket she'd ever seen. Seraphina had even embroidered on the lining 'Fleur, how can I ever thank you enough?'

So much had happened since the awful night she had shared with Seraphina. When the girl had come back from Portugal to move into her little house, they discovered the Akatovs had left their home and put it up for sale. Fleur made a few enquiries and found their chauffeur and the housekeeper had gone with them. It was thought they had moved to the country.

Seraphina set to work and made her place very attractive. She bought a brass plaque to put on her door that said 'Seraphina Gauloise, Court Dressmaker'. It wasn't long before the wealthy ladies of Bayswater and Kensington were beating a path to her door, and within six months she told Fleur she had more work than she could handle. That was why she'd taken so long to make Fleur's jacket.

Fleur had continued to go to auditions, but she suspected Diane Lombard was still putting out her poison and preventing her getting parts. But she had had quite a lot of interesting promotion work at exhibitions in London, demonstrating everything from non-stick saucepans, jewellery cleaner and lawn mowers to vacuum cleaners. There were also the outside events, at horse-racing, motor-racing, flower shows and the like. It was fun mixing with other girls and she found she had a lot in common with them.

There were a couple of romances too, with Bill, who worked in advertising, and Ambrose, who was an accountant, but both turned out to be bores, however much they wined and dined her. The parties at her flat were a great deal more entertaining, and she made money from them.

Percy Turnball was still in the background finding the male guests. He and Fleur had become quite close friends and Fleur had managed to forgive him for the callous way he had treated her after the closing of *Perfect Strangers*.

On the whole she was very happy with her life now. While she hadn't quite accepted that she would never act again, and wished she could fall in love with a man who would love her and look after her, there was always the hope of something. She had not seen Pet for a long time: she'd married her farmer and was now Petula Parks. She suspected Pet was angry that she hadn't gone to her wedding, but that weekend Bill had invited her to a house party in Scotland, which had seemed a more fun event.

As it turned out, it wasn't fun. It rained the whole time, the house was like a fridge, and everyone there could talk of nothing but horses and hunting. She also realized Bill wasn't for her.

As for Frankie, she had sold her place in Hampstead and moved out to Kent. Fleur went to see her and, to her surprise, found she was living in sheltered accommodation, which family members had talked her into. Perhaps they were right: she seemed vacant, as if the old Frankie had vanished, but they could have installed some of her favourite pieces of furniture, pictures and ornaments in her room, which would have helped her to feel more at home.

Fleur felt ashamed that she had neglected her friend for so long – maybe if she'd kept in closer touch she could have had some say in what Frankie took to that place. But, to her further shame, she didn't go again after that one visit as it was so depressing. She knew she owed Frankie and Pet a huge amount, and ought to have been more appreciative of them both.

Now she twirled in front of the mirror, admiring her new jacket. She couldn't wait for the right occasion to wear it. The years had been kind to her: she was still slender, her face still smooth but for a few tiny lines round her eyes, and she had no grey hairs at all. It took a bit more effort with make-up to pass for a twenty-five-year-old now, though. Tonight she was throwing one of her parties and she'd be wearing a new midi-length shocking pink dress. She never wore minis now: they were very passé.

The party kicked off at eight. The seven male guests were part of the crew at the motor-show at Earls Court and they were all over forty, with receding hairlines and pot bellies. There were five girls, all of whom Fleur knew well. She had no doubt they'd make the men feel like gods.

With Tamla Motown sounds on the record player, a good buffet and plenty to drink, in no time almost everyone was dancing and enjoying themselves. Fleur always stood back from the revelry and never drank much as she needed to have her wits about her.

Percy was always careful to tell the men he sent that it was a party they had to pay to attend, and stressed that the girls were party girls, not call-girls. Occasionally a man would get drunk and be abusive towards one of the girls, usually about why they were expected to pay to go to a party. Fleur defused any tension by pointing out that if they had gone up west to a nightclub they'd have had to pay a steep entrance fee, and buy their own drink and food. That was usually enough, but now and then she would be compelled to ask a guest to leave.

Fortunately, tonight everyone seemed happy, the buffet was good, the girls were making the men dance with them and there was a lot of laughter. Fleur noticed Robina leading a big guy from Hull into the bedroom, and Sandra was snogging on the sofa with Will, who often came to these parties when he was in town.

Suddenly there was hammering at the street door, which Fleur ignored. But one of the other tenants in the house must have let the person into the hall as all at once the banging was on her front door. Suddenly she heard, 'Police! Open up!' At that her blood ran cold with fright.

She had prepared for a raid back when she had first started, but as it had never happened she'd more or less forgotten it might.

'Keep calm. It's a private party,' she warned the guests quietly. 'But I must open the door or they'll kick it in.'

Six policemen charged in as she opened the door, and it was only then that Fleur remembered she hadn't warned Robina in the bedroom.

Before she could attempt to charm the officers, they were opening the bedroom door and found Robina and her man in bed.

The senior officer told Fleur he was arresting her for 'keeping a disorderly house'. But she protested and said everyone there was a personal friend.

'So you can give me all their names, then?' he said, and smirked.

Percy always told her the men's names, and normally she wrote them down and even tried to commit them to memory. But she hadn't this time.

To be fair to the male guests they all tried to help, calling out their names, claiming they always came to see her when they were in London. But two of the officers took each of them into the hall to write down their names, addresses and reason for being in London.

A burly policewoman took down all the girls' details, and asked how much they were paid to come to the party. While all this was going on, Fleur was frog-marched into the kitchen and given the third degree.

'You're running a brothel here, simple as that,' insisted the senior officer, who had a badly pock-marked face. 'You take money to let them in, then get a share of what they pay the girls.'

He read her her rights, snapped on handcuffs, then led her outside to a police car.

In terror she begged the policeman to let her back in for a moment to ask one of her friends to lock up for her. But he said gruffly, 'One of the officers will do that, after they've questioned everyone.'

*

Four hours of questioning later, they locked her into a cell for the night. A duty solicitor was called, a skinny little man with a disconcerting squint, called James Kernow. She didn't think he believed a word of her explanation that she threw these parties for fun, and they were men she'd worked with at trade fairs and become friends with. 'We like to get together when they're in London. They chip in with the cost of drink and food, but that's all they pay for.'

The police were a little less tactful: they insisted she was running a brothel and tried to catch her out with the names of the men, where she'd met them and what company they worked for.

Luckily some of the men's names came back to her but she glossed over the other questions with flirtatious banter. 'All of us girls who work in promotions get chatting to men in bars after a trade fair closes for the evening. Do you really think men who have been promoting their goods and taking orders all day want to discuss their work in the evening over a drink?'

It was awful being locked into a cell. The pillow was like a rock and grubby too, and the one blanket was scratchy. Still wearing her slinky dress, she was cold, and the prospect of a court appearance in the morning without being able to have a bath or put on fresh make-up was terrifying. She hadn't even got a comb with her.

She was allowed to make one phone call, but she

didn't dare ring Percy for help as he might be dragged into this. Pet was out of the question. Even if she'd been in London Fleur wouldn't have wanted her to know she was in this kind of trouble.

What worried her most was that Alexis Akatov might have been behind this to get back at her. He could have found out about the parties and rung the police. She was also concerned at the police being in her flat without her there. What if they were poking around, looking for anything more they could throw at her?

She couldn't think of anything incriminating there, but what if someone had been snorting cocaine, or rolling spliffs and left evidence of it? Such things were so commonplace she wouldn't have noticed, but if it was found in her home, she would be charged with possession.

James Kernow hadn't said whether she'd be fined or sent to prison, and she didn't have much faith that he'd be able to convince a judge she was innocent. She'd been in some tight corners in her life, but this was very scary. Eventually she fell into an uneasy sleep huddled under the scratchy blanket.

22

Fleur, 1975

Dust particles danced in a shaft of weak sunshine as Fleur lay on her bed, reminding her of school. She'd often lost all track of what her teacher was saying because she liked to think those dust particles were fairies.

She pulled herself back to the here and now, and considered what being charged with keeping a disorderly house really meant. While the case was found 'not proven', that didn't exactly wipe the slate clean. Not only had it been in the papers, but she had also received a twenty-eight-day notice to quit her flat.

As for her acting career, she had no idea how it would affect that as she'd worked so little in the last few years. But she knew that mud sticks and that many people who knew her must be clapping their hands at her misfortune. No one was going to believe she hadn't been making a small fortune from her parties.

She'd had it coming, she knew that, so there was no point in saying 'if only', or 'it isn't fair'. She had at least a thousand pounds in a post office savings account from the proceeds, not to mention a wardrobe full of smart clothes and some very nice jewellery, which she could always sell if she had to, and she could look back on a few lovely holidays in Spain and expensive meals out.

In one respect it was good she'd been told to vacate the flat. It was too expensive and most of the neighbours knew she'd been arrested. It was time to turn over a new leaf, maybe move somewhere out of London, perhaps change her name too.

But where? And what new line of work could she do?

The years had sped by. She was well into her thirties now, and what she really wanted was stability. To be able to wake up each morning without anxiety. To be loved by someone and to love him back. To have a forever home with furniture she'd chosen herself. Maybe even have children before it was too late – if she was able to become pregnant, that was.

Aside from acting, promotion work was the only other employment she enjoyed. When she thought about it, the two had similarities. Promotion work was like acting in as much as you had to pretend you loved the goods you were selling to get people to buy them. But she couldn't go to one of the agencies as they would want a P45, which she'd never had, and she would have the very devil of a job explaining to someone at a labour exchange or tax office how she'd kept herself all these years. However, lots of companies employed promotion girls on a casual, self-employed basis, so she could go to some trade fairs and talk to people.

As always when Fleur made a plan, she executed it immediately. The following morning she set off for Olympia in a smart navy suit, high heels and her hair tied back at the nape of her neck with a navy ribbon. She looked sexy but businesslike, and men liked that.

The trade fair in progress was for stationery, and that didn't offer many opportunities for promotion work. But she had always been good at picking out the top dog in a company: she stopped at the stands where she saw such a candidate, expressed an interest in his products, told him she was thinking of starting a promotions agency, and asked him if his company would consider using one.

Most said they used in-house people, a few said they would be interested, so she took down their details. Two men said they would consider her on a casual basis and proceeded to tell her about fairs in other cities where they would be exhibiting.

Fleur went home at the end of the day feeling quite pleased with her day's work. Stationery didn't need promotion; buyers looked at the stuff on the stand, and if they liked it, they ordered it. She needed companies that supplied products that required a big element of salesmanship, like toys, giftware, kitchen utensils.

But her priority for now was to find a new place to live, somewhere no one knew her.

It was at the start of September that Fleur saw an advertisement for a gifts and fancy goods trade fair at Olympia. She had picked up a few casual promotion jobs during the summer, moved to a small studio flat in South Kensington and spent many hot sunny days sunbathing in Hyde Park. She hadn't seen or spoken to any old friends, not even Pet or Frankie. That was mainly out of embarrassment because they were sure to have heard about her arrest.

She had made one new friend, Cora, the girl in the flat above her. They went out to a pub or the cinema now and then. Cora was a dental nurse who had a boyfriend in the Royal Navy. She was the complete opposite to Fleur, a bit shy and serious, but their friendship felt rather nice and tranquil after all the scatterbrained, noisy, narcissistic girls she'd been involved with for so long.

She managed to get a pass into the gift fair by saying she was looking for stock for a shop she was opening in Bristol. As soon as she was inside she found herself becoming excited by the stands, which were full of interesting items from all corners of the world. Glass, lamps, pottery, wood, soft toys, hats and scarves, posters, key-rings and greetings cards, a regular Aladdin's cave of treasure.

Stopping here and there to talk to people on the stands, she asked if they used regular employees to work on their stand or promotion girls. To her disappointment she learned most used their own employees as they enjoyed trade fairs, especially with a three- or four-day stay in a hotel.

After a few hours she had collected only three business cards from companies who thought they might be interested in her girls. But she had also learned that most of the buyers, stand-holders and other people involved with the fair tended to gather in their hotel bars in the evening. She picked the Kensington Palace Hotel as she knew it was popular with salesmen and buyers with rather deeper pockets than the average man.

The best bar in the hotel was on the top floor with a view over Hyde Park. She sat down, ordered a gin and tonic, and studied the various leaflets she'd picked up that afternoon. The bar was about three-quarters full, mainly businessmen, but a few women who, judging by the way they were in discussion with their male companions, were employees. The conversations were muted, she didn't know why. Perhaps they were all talking quietly or there was something odd about the room's acoustics. When two men took the sofa opposite hers, the other side of a low coffee-table, she couldn't hear a word of what they were saying.

Just after the two men had sat down, a dark-haired man joined them. He glanced at Fleur, perhaps wondering if she was with the others, and sat on a padded stool between the two sofas. He took some papers out of his briefcase, and Fleur felt he was handing over sales figures for the day. The other men seemed pleased, and ordered drinks from a waitress. They continued to talk, not looking at her, and Fleur thought she'd picked the wrong seat. She considered getting up, visiting the powder room, then coming back and sitting elsewhere. But suddenly the first two men stood up and left.

'See you tomorrow, Angus,' she heard one say, and they were gone, leaving Angus alone.

'Have you been at the trade fair today too?' he asked Fleur, as if he was a bit shocked that he was suddenly alone.

'Yes, I have,' she replied. Maybe he'd thought the other two men would be spending the evening with him. 'What line are you in?'

'China and glass mainly,' he said. 'We import from Italy and Portugal. How about you? A buyer or a supplier?'

'Neither,' she said. 'But come and sit on this sofa. You look really uncomfortable on that stool, and there's something weird with the acoustics in here.'

'I thought that was just me,' he said, and got up to move next to her. 'I could hardly hear what the directors of my firm were saying. I hope they heard the figures I was giving them.'

'They looked pleased, so I shouldn't worry,' she said. 'Were they going off to eat, leaving you on your own?'

He smiled, and she saw how dark brown his eyes were. His face was very tanned, teeth very white. In fact he looked almost Spanish or Italian, but his accent held a hint of Welsh. 'I wouldn't go with them even if they asked,' he said. 'They're very dull company, only interested in figures.'

He introduced himself then as Angus Tweedy and she said she was Fleur Faraday, adding that she was thinking of opening a gift shop and was doing some research. Sitting next to one another they could hear perfectly, and his nervousness seemed to disappear as he talked about his job. He was a representative for his company, covering South Wales, Bristol, Somerset, Gloucestershire and the whole M4 corridor, as he called it, to London. At first she thought he was going to be a total bore, but he was surprisingly amusing, going on to tell her about some of his strangest customers.

When he asked where she was thinking of opening a shop, she said, 'Bristol,' without any real thought, merely because he'd mentioned it.

'Clifton would be a good area,' he said. 'Plenty of visitors in the summer, and the university. Mind you, they do say Bristol is the salesman's graveyard. If you can make it there you'll do well anywhere else.'

He bought them both another drink, and before long Fleur felt she'd known him for years. Later she would try to analyse what it was about him that was so attractive. He was nice-looking, he had good manners and a lovely deep voice, but it was more than that. She thought the main thing was that he didn't try to impress her, no making out he was the top salesman or a demon sportsman. He spoke of buying trips to Italy and Portugal and how much he loved those countries' style, and indeed wished he could live in one or the other. Fleur had been to Lisbon just once, and to Naples and Venice. She had fallen in love with Italy and wanted to see a great deal more of it.

After several more drinks Angus said they should eat and suggested they went to an Italian restaurant across the road from the hotel. 'You are very lovely, Fleur,' he said, halfway through the meal. 'But I need to tell you now that I'm married.'

She waited, half expecting him to come up with the line she'd heard so often: 'It's not a happy marriage. We both want out, but we're staying together for the children.'

But Angus said, 'My wife is a gem, we're happy together, and I know that the right thing to do would be to finish this meal, go back to my hotel room and forget about you. But somehow I know I'm going to find that hard.'

Such honesty was disarming and unusual. 'We aren't doing anything wrong,' she said. 'Just a meal with a new friend. So relax, enjoy the moment. It will be okay.'

Fleur was used to leading men on – she'd done it her entire adult life. To her it was a game: the more reluctant they were to be swept away by her charms, the more she wanted to play. But it wasn't like that with Angus. She realized he had never picked up a woman in a bar before. Perhaps his wife, at home in Wales, was the only woman he'd ever been with.

But that reluctance, the shyness, the utter decency of the man worked like an aphrodisiac on her. She looked at his full lips, thought how much she'd like to kiss them, and felt twinges of desire in her belly. She took his hand over the table, ran one finger down his palm and saw his eyes close momentarily, proving he felt the same pangs as her.

More wine, and Fleur knew he was past the point of going back to his hotel room alone. As they left the restaurant she drew him to her and kissed him, there on the pavement, regardless of people walking by. That kiss went on and on, then taking his hand she led him back to the hotel.

'I'll just see you to your room,' she said, knowing

full well she had no intention of leaving it till the next morning.

At his door, he attempted to do the right thing and say goodnight. But she kissed him again and felt him lean into her, unable to resist.

She had been to bed with more men than she could count, but that night was the very best. He wanted her so badly, yet he still had a boyish innocence and a desire to please that were utterly disarming.

'You've bewitched me,' he murmured, in the early hours of the morning, when both were sated and sleepy. Fleur did not chalk that up as a triumph because she felt bewitched too. Tears ran down her cheeks because he could never be hers.

She eased herself out of his arms at five in the morning, gathered up her clothes and dressed in the bathroom. She didn't want anyone to see her and cause him trouble, but she left her phone number on his pillow because she knew she had to see him again.

Falling in love had not been in her plan, and for the next two days she swung from hoping he would never phone her to thinking she'd shrivel up and die if he didn't. Again and again she told herself that affairs with married men were always a bad idea. They didn't leave their wives, so a mistress had to accept she would only get the crumbs from the table, never the full meal. Yes, there might be a weekend in Paris or Rome, but mostly it would be meetings in dreary hotels far from his home, no dinner parties with friends, no walks in woods, or paddling in the sea. A married man just wanted sex, nothing more. He got the rest at home.

He phoned her on the third day, and she knew from his voice he was in the same place as her, half hoping she'd say they must end this before someone got hurt. Of course she didn't, and that was how it began. Each time he ended his working day within fifty miles of her flat, he came to her. Each Friday night through to Sunday she knew he was home with Gwen.

Once when she cried and said a couple of nights in the week wasn't enough for her, he comforted her: 'Gwen gets the father, the man who puts the dustbin out and cuts the grass. You get the younger Angus, the lover, the man who idolizes you. It's you I think of all day, not Gwen. I think of touching your body and I'm aroused. You get the best part of me.'

23

Alice

A week after she'd spoken to Mira Lombard, Alice took a call from Jackie Moore. 'Jackie!' she exclaimed. 'How good of you to phone. I was afraid you might have thought it was a weird request.'

'Not at all, I liked your mum very much and I'm sorry for your loss, Alice. If I'd known earlier I would have written to you to say so. What can I help you with?'

'You appear to be the last girlfriend Mum kept in touch with. I wondered when you last spoke to her and if you could shed any light on why she married Angus.'

'Let me see,' she said thoughtfully. 'It was such a long time ago I can't remember the year. But I visited her in Bristol. You were just a toddler and your sister Emily was around six months old.'

'My goodness, that's very exact,' Alice said.

'That's because it's engraved on my memory,' Jackie said. 'Soon after, she was in deep trouble, people saying all sorts about her. As for why she married Angus, it was because she loved him, and wanted security for you two with a wedding ring on her finger.'

Alice gulped. That was not what she'd been expecting. 'But I've been told some very unpleasant things about her.'

'Fleur was many things. She told fibs, she was mostly out for number one, she was deceitful, secretive and at times completely barmy, but there was another side I loved about her. Her generosity of spirit. I suspect from what Mira told me about you, that's something you've inherited.'

It was flattering to hear that Mira approved of her. 'But why did she grass Angus up about the bigamy if she loved him?'

'I don't believe she did that. Many people claimed she did, but I believe she was blackmailed by someone who said they'd get Angus arrested if she didn't pay. Angus gave himself up because he was afraid they would come for Fleur.'

'Really? Did she tell you this?'

'I'll come to what Fleur told me later. But I'm absolutely sure Angus gave himself up willingly for Fleur. He was the blackmailer's trump card, even though I'm sure his grievance was something Fleur did to him. I'm assuming it was related to her parties. Maybe he had evidence that she was running a brothel.'

'The verdict was "not proven", though.'

'That doesn't convince everyone of innocence,'

Jackie said. 'There is often a disgruntled person who wanted a different outcome. Maybe Fleur threw someone out or it was someone who fell for her and she didn't reciprocate. Or even someone she got into a dodgy deal with. I wouldn't put that past her. Many people have long memories, and the longer they wait, the more bitter they become.'

'If it was that, why wait so long to act?' Alice asked.

'Maybe he found someone to back his theories. It could have taken a long time to find her – she had changed her name, remember. Possibly he hired a private detective. If so he must have thought he'd won the jackpot to find your mum had married bigamously and had two daughters. That would have made it easy to squeeze money out of her.'

'Do you have any proof of that?' Alice asked. 'Or is this just supposition?'

'I was with her just a couple of weeks before Angus was charged. But Fleur, or Helen as she'd called herself since she'd married Angus, was so happy when I saw her. No one can fake that kind of bliss. We sat in her little garden with you playing in a paddling pool and we took it in turns to cuddle Emily. She said she'd never known happiness like it and she loved every bone of Angus's body. Of course I didn't know then that Angus was married to someone else, but I'd been in their company and I promise you he was no sleaze ball. He truly loved your mum.'

'She didn't tell you then that Angus was married to someone else?'

'No. But you must know how secretive she was?'

Alice agreed she did. 'Did you speak to her after Angus was arrested?'

'I tried to, but the phone was cut off. Her name was in the paper but it only stated that Angus had married her bigamously. I don't think newspapers can start printing sleaze until a court case, though I'm sure they were already compiling it. Then I got a letter from her, the saddest one I've ever received, with no address, of course. She said she'd run for it. She admitted it was all her fault. She'd talked Angus into the marriage, and because of her, someone was trying to blackmail him so he'd given himself up to keep her safe. She said she was frightened, but Angus had insisted she must run away with her girls to escape the hue and cry. She thanked me for being such a good friend, and said she'd be in touch again once it was all over. But I guess she couldn't deal with it. I never heard anything again.'

'She met and married Ralph, who I thought was my true father, then she became Sally Kent. She was like a snake shedding her skin and setting out in a new one,' Alice said, a trifle bitterly.

'She would have had good reason for that,' Jackie said firmly. 'I wouldn't mind betting it was to protect you and Emily. I recall her once saying to me that she

314

wanted a man who would stand in front of a cannon ball to protect her. To me Angus was that man, though possibly Ralph was too. But I didn't see her with Ralph as I did with Angus. Besides, why would she run away so fast, or say someone was blackmailing them if it wasn't true?'

'I don't buy it,' Alice said. 'It's a kinder alternative to what I'd already been told, but a bit too far-fetched for me.'

Eventually Jackie rang off, and Alice continued to sit at the table staring out of the window thinking about what she'd just heard.

She was confused. She wanted to find something to redeem her mother, and if Jackie was right, the one person who might know the whole truth was Ralph. But how could she open what might be a can of worms for him?

She rang Stuart then, hoping he might put a different slant on it. He was pleased to hear from her and didn't appear to be watching something unmissable on TV so she told him what Jackie had said.

'Mmm,' he said, as she finished. 'It kind of conflicts with the facts on record. There was nothing about blackmail or that Angus had given himself up.'

'It was a long time ago. Did they keep accurate records of everything that was said and done?'

'Usually. It is possible he didn't report the blackmail because he was afraid that whoever made the threat might hurt you and Emily. But he could have told the police and they would have protected your mother and you two kids.'

'Perhaps he didn't believe that.'

'A career in the police force is a real eye-opener to what some people are capable of,' Stuart said sadly. 'I've seen terrific courage and compassion, pure evil and everything in between. It's made me a cynic, but you've got Ralph, who is a good man, and your sister. Some of the people I've met didn't have one decent person in their corner.'

'I'm sure,' she said thoughtfully. 'But the real question is where do I go from here, Stuart? I've dug a hole for myself that I feel I can't scramble out of. I hate poking into areas of Mum's life that she wouldn't have wanted me to know about.'

'Then stop,' he said. 'My best advice is you go and see Ralph. You don't have to reveal everything, just the parts that affect him. Tell him who Angus is. You don't need to get heavy about it, just say you know now that he's your biological dad. Ask him how he met Sally, or Fleur, and when they got married. From what you've told me about him he's level-headed, calm and truthful. Maybe he's kept quiet all these years because your mother said he must!'

'Okay, I'll think about it. Maybe when I've got a day off I could go down there and talk. I just don't want to upset him by revealing something he didn't already know.'

'And how about the romance?' Stuart asked. 'Please don't tell me it's over already.'

'No.' Alice giggled. 'It can't gallop along because his work is in London and mine is here, but he's coming down on Thursday night. He has to go home on Friday morning as there's a concert and I've got a big wedding on. But we've talked on the phone about booking some holiday from our respective work and going away together. Hopefully that will be next month.'

'Get this thing sorted with Ralph before then,' he said. 'You can't relax fully if you have something serious on your mind.'

24

Helen Tweedy, 1983

Helen stood at the French windows looking at the daffodils in the garden and her heart seemed to swell with happiness, as it did so often these days. She turned to look at her two daughters. Alice, now nearly three, was sitting on the floor, trying vainly to put a dress on a doll that, just moments before, she'd pulled off. Emily was in her little bouncy seat, smiling and gurgling at her older sister.

They were such beauties, Alice with her dark hair, so much like Angus, and Emily blonde like her. Both had a sweet nature too, and she felt blessed.

While she knew it was perhaps wrong to insist Angus married her, she so needed the stability of marriage. She'd changed her name to Helen, which went well with the surname Tweedy, and felt safe that the past was gone and forgotten. She had been reborn as a mother of two, and she loved that role.

The little house on Windmill Hill in south Bristol was only a two-up-two-down, but it was cosy, and the tiny garden was south-facing. Victoria Park was close by, and she often took the girls to Windmill City Farm to see the animals there. It was a little lonely at the weekends when Angus had to go to his other home in Wales, but she'd made a few girlfriends at the local mother-and-toddler group, so two days a week on her own with the girls wasn't enough to be upset by.

She knew she had changed a great deal since falling for Angus. She still kept her secrets – he wouldn't want to know all that horrible stuff from way back – but she was honest with him in every other way. She didn't ask for anything – after all, he had bought and furnished this house for her, and had given her more happiness and contentment than she deserved.

A ring at the doorbell startled her. Glancing first at the children, and seeing they were happy together, she went to open the door. Standing there was a heavy-set man in a Norfolk jacket and corduroy trousers. He was bald and around fifty.

'Mrs Helen Tweedy?' he asked.

'Yes, what is it?'

'I have a message for you from Mr Alexis Akatov,' he said, his voice sounding Russian or Polish. He pulled a letter out of his pocket. 'You must respond to this within a week. Failure to do so will be damaging to you and your family.'

'Excuse me!' she said indignantly. 'How dare you come to my home and make threats?'

'Read the letter and you will see,' he said, turning on his heel and walking away down the street. 'One week!' he called.

She went back indoors and, once she'd shut the front door, opened the envelope with shaking hands. At the top of the typed letter there was a London phone number.

Mrs Tweedy, or should I call you by your real name Fleur Faraday? Several years ago, you accused me of a crime and blackmailed me into providing a home for a former employee you said I had abused. I allowed you to do this at the time as my wife was sick and I didn't want her upset by anything. However, I am not a man to take such accusations lightly, and after my wife's death I decided to make you pay me back that which you took from me.

I already knew you were a common prostitute, and now I have learned you married bigamously. I want Five Thousand Pounds, or I will inform the police of Mr Tweedy's crime, contact the newspapers to tell them of your former occupation, and should you think of taking this to the police, you may be putting those two little girls you have in grave danger.

Alexis Akatov

She read it three times in the hope that she had somehow misunderstood it. But no, the man's intention was quite plain. She recalled how joyful she had been and how surprised all those years ago when Akatov had done as she demanded and given Seraphina the little house. She had forgotten that was his name – it hadn't been worth remembering. But she might have known that nothing came so easy.

What was she to do? She didn't have five thousand pounds. Buying this house had cleaned out Angus, and it cost a great deal to keep two homes going. But even if he had it, who would pay that, knowing a blackmailer would just come back for more?

Tears sprang into her eyes at the thought he might harm her babies. There had to be a way out of this, but she couldn't think of one. Go to the police and Angus would be arrested. Do nothing and the man would come back. Running away wouldn't work either. If he'd found her here, he could find her anywhere.

She remembered Frankie once laughingly saying, 'Be sure that no good deed goes unpunished.' She'd called Frankie a cynic, even though it had made her laugh. But it had been a good deed she'd done, for no personal gain, and now she was being punished, just as Angus would be for doing something good when he knew it was wrong.

It was the worst day she ever remembered. She

grew hot, then icy cold. She felt sick with fear and the children picked up on it and began to cry. Eventually she put them into the double buggy and went out, walking almost blindly through Bedminster and on to Ashton while trying to find a solution. But there was none. Her children were snivelling – they must be hungry: she remembered she hadn't given them any lunch and it was nearly five o'clock.

She walked faster going home, trying to avoid thinking about the letter by planning dinner for that night. It didn't work: it kept coming back stronger and darker, and her desperation grew.

As she walked along Coronation Road, she considered throwing herself into the Avon later that night. But that would only make things worse. Her children would be motherless, and Angus would still be exposed.

She asked herself why it had been so important to her to be legally married. Angus would have looked after her and the children anyway. Just the thought of him going to prison for something she'd talked him into was terrible. A gentle, mild-mannered man like him wouldn't survive the harshness of prison. And what about poor Gwen? What would it do to her? She had done nothing to deserve such trouble.

Yet, above all, there was the threat to her girls. She loved them so much, and how could she be sure that the Russian wouldn't make good his threat? She'd be looking over her shoulder for years wondering when he might do it. Some things never went away.

'What's the matter, darling?' Angus asked later. She'd made home-cooked ham, eggs and chips for dinner, a meal he loved, but she'd eaten hardly any of hers, and she'd barely spoken.

He got up from the table and came round to where she sat, pulling her to her feet and into his arms. 'Don't even think of telling me a lie. I know this is something bad. Have you spent too much money, or are you about to leave me for another man?'

'God, no,' she said, shocked he would even consider she'd do the latter. 'Don't try and get me to tell you, it's just too awful.'

'If I found out you'd put poison in that ham and I'd got only minutes before I started fitting, that would be awful,' he said, with a smile. 'The second worst thing would be that you'd sold this house and we have to leave tomorrow.'

That he could joke about reasons for her being quiet and troubled made it even worse.

'Don't, Angus. Please don't make jokes.'

'Then tell me. However bad it is we can face it together. It won't get any better by you locking it away inside you.'

She knew that much was true and she was at breaking point anyway. She went over to the shelves where she'd shoved the letter between two books, pulled it out and handed it to him.

His face turned white as he read it, and he looked at her with dark eyes full of fear.

'That's why I didn't want to tell you,' she cried out, bursting into the tears she'd held back since the man had called. 'I can't let you go to prison, but even if we could somehow get the money together, he's bound to come back for more.'

She had to explain then about Seraphina and how it had all come about. But even as she told the story she wondered if he believed her. Barney had once said to her, 'You can lock up a thief but not a liar.' And although she didn't remember lying to Angus, wasn't concealing her past the same as lying?

When she'd finished, Angus sat on the sofa without saying a word. She didn't try to make him speak. She knew that, like her, he was trying to think of a way out of this.

Eventually he got up, pulled on his jacket and went to the door. 'I'm going to the police,' he said. 'I'll never let that man harm a hair on my children's heads. It will be bad for them if they find out about the bigamy when they're older, so best to deal with it now while they're small.'

With that he opened the door and swept out, leaving her sobbing into her hands.

*

Angus never came back to live with her. He was held in custody overnight, and the following morning he had his first court appearance in Bristol. The duty solicitor made a bail application, but it was refused, so he was taken straight to Bristol prison.

He refused Helen permission to visit him there as he said he knew she'd have to bring the girls and he didn't want them to see him in a prison. He also pointed out that he didn't want any reporters photographing her as the pictures would appear in newspapers once he was convicted. Likewise he implored her not to come to court for the same reason.

At the second court appearance a month later, he was granted bail on the condition he stayed at his house in Wales with Gwen.

It was only then that he wrote to Helen, almost certainly because he knew any letters he wrote in prison would be read. He explained that the judge considered he was a flight risk staying with her and insisted that he resided with his legal wife.

Gwen has been a marvel [he wrote]. *Shocked and hurt as she is, she is willing to forgive me and stand by me. So, it is up to me now to do the right thing, to be a real husband to her, and set you free, darling. I do not wish to taint my daughters with this or ruin your life. Leave Bristol, put the house in the hands of an estate agent. Once they've sold it you will have the means to support our girls. In the meantime, there is some money I hid away for a rainy day in a box in my filing cabinet in the dining room. This is the rainy day now. Thank goodness you learned to drive. Call a taxi and take enough things for you and the girls for now. You can hire a car later. Send the keys of my company car back to them. A removal company will pack and deliver the rest to a storage company once the house is sold. Leave no forwarding address with anyone. Just go. It breaks my heart to know I will never see you again, but I am reminded that if I'd done what was right in the first place, none of this would have happened.*

The police tell me they are investigating Akatov. Should he or an employee ever find you, go immediately to the police, but it is their belief he won't now I've been charged. Don't listen to what people say about either of us, darling. We both know the truth. Hold your head up high and teach our girls to do that too.

My love and sadness at how this has ended, Angus

The day that letter arrived, she was neither Helen nor Fleur, but Janet Masters in her head. Once again, she'd been dealt a body blow just as painful as those her mother had inflicted on her. She was an outcast, someone destined never to hang on to happiness. She felt so alone, even as Alice and Emily, sensing her sadness, climbed onto her lap for cuddles.

She knew Angus wouldn't change his mind and, as much as it hurt, she knew she had brought this down on him, so he was right to say it was enough. Her job now was to keep her girls safe, well away from gossips and out of reach of scandals.

25

Sally

With a hired red Audi packed with children, clothes and toys, she made her way out of Bristol towards the West Country.

When she took her driving test before she met Angus, she'd used the name Sally Symonds, because at the time she was considering abandoning Fleur Faraday for good. She'd never told Angus that her licence and insurance were in a false name, and the address she'd given was where she had lived when she first came to Bristol. She had also opened a bank account in the same name and over the years had put small amounts of money into it, her rainy-day account. It had been a nuisance having to go to the old address every few weeks to check for mail, but it seemed fortuitous now. At least bully-boy Alexis Akatov would have difficulty in tracing her again. It was sadly ironic that Angus, too, had been putting money away for a rainy day.

Somewhat reluctantly Helen Tweedy was no more and she would be Sally Symonds.

Every other time she'd moved she'd felt excited, a new start, a clean slate. But not this time. First she'd had to get a taxi with all her stuff and the two little ones. She told the driver she'd been staying with friends and had had a tiff with her husband: he'd driven off leaving her high and dry at the side of the road with their clothes, the buggy and two small children. She had put on her sunglasses and made out she was crying as she asked him to get her to the nearest car-hire company. Then, when she was mobile, she'd go to her mother's in Exeter.

In the past such an enormous lie would have delighted the actress in her. But not this time. For one, the taxi driver who came was a kind man, and said her husband should be horsewhipped. When they got to the car-hire place, he refused her fare, wished her well and carried all her stuff inside, where he told the staff to be gentle with her. They made a fuss of Alice and Emily, putting baby and child seats into the car without charging her extra for them.

Once the children were dozing in the back and she was driving on the open road, the magnitude of it all hit her. She was forty-three now, not a teenager, and once again her life had blown up in her face. She'd got by under the radar all her life with no real documentation, living on her wits and making no provision for the future. Her looks were fading, and she had two small children dependent on her. How could it have come to this?

It was then she thought of Totnes. She'd been there just once in the early stages of pregnancy. Angus had had to stand in for his company's regular Devon and Cornwall salesman, who was in hospital. He had suggested she went with him as it was a pretty drive and she would like Totnes because it was a bit hippie-dippy, as she could be sometimes.

She did like it, the long, steep high street full of intriguing independent shops, the river at the bottom with ferries going to places like Dartmouth. There were funny little alleys, and even stranger-looking people. She liked its alternative vibe, a shop where you could buy soft handmade leather shoes and boots in rainbow colours, art shops, studios with the wackiest ceramics she'd ever seen, and clothes she couldn't imagine anyone wearing except to a pop concert.

So that was where she would find somewhere to live. She'd abandon her smart, city clothes and high heels. She'd reinvent herself as a studious, vegetarian, bohemian sort of woman, and start again.

Six weeks later Sally Symonds closed the door on the fitter who had just put down a new carpet in her living room. He'd been very kind, helping her put back the furniture, and as he left he wished her happiness in her new home.

She had spent the first week in Totnes in a bed-and-breakfast, which wasn't so good with a lively three-year-old and a baby who was just starting to crawl, while trying to feed fussy children in cafés was expensive and exhausting. The owner of the bed-and-breakfast, though, had a friend with a studio flat she was willing to let to Sally on a week-by-week basis until she found somewhere permanent.

Then she found the ground-floor flat in Alexandra Terrace and signed a six-month lease. It was small, just one bedroom, a bathroom, a studio-style kitchen-dining-living room, and she had use of the back garden. She'd been told a young couple lived upstairs.

The terrace was similar to where they'd lived in Windmill Hill, Victorian and a bit down-at-heel, but she embraced it eagerly: it was ideal until the house in Bristol was sold and she could buy somewhere permanent. All her belongings and furniture had arrived three days ago, and this had been a nightmare: although the Bristol house had been small, she and Angus had acquired quite a lot since they'd bought it. The boxes were piled up to the ceiling in the main room, and the packer had adopted a random method, so kitchen equipment might be in with baby clothes. Trying to sort stuff, with Alice pushing her way through toppling piles of bedlinen and Emily pulling herself up on boxes, was a waking nightmare. When she'd finally got the cot, Alice's bed and her own erected and made up, she was tempted to push them into the room and shut the door on them.

But that evening after they were in bed and sleeping, she managed to sort out the kitchen area, pile up the furniture she wouldn't have room for and pack Angus's belongings. In the morning she would contact the storage company and ask them to collect it.

It was two in the morning when she finally crawled into bed, completely exhausted. She silently prayed that Emily wouldn't wake at five as she often did. That prayer at least was answered: the children slept till after eight.

Since then she had managed to stow away, arrange and sort almost everything. She'd even hung curtains at the windows, and had a telephone installed. Now the carpet was laid it looked like a home, and if she could just find someone to plumb in the washing-machine she'd feel she'd won a jackpot.

It was the washing-machine that brought her and Ralph together. That same day, in the afternoon they went out for a walk because it was a lovely day. Emily was in the buggy but Alice insisted she was a big girl and could walk. They were making for St Peter's Quay, to look at the boats and Alice insisted on walking along every garden wall she saw. Sally remembered Bridgetown vaguely from when Angus had brought her there for the day. She loved the

Georgian houses, neat front gardens, the timeless and serene atmosphere of the area.

She didn't see the man on his knees in his garden until Alice climbed onto his wall. He bounded up, said hello to her, and she held out her arms to him, expecting him to lift her down into his garden.

'I'm sorry,' Sally said. 'She's a pushy little minx. Alice! That's the gentleman's garden, not a park.'

The man laughed and lifted her down anyway. 'If you want a closer look at my weed-filled patch, you're very welcome.'

'It doesn't look weed-filled to me,' Sally said, looking admiringly at the profusion of flowers. 'I've just moved into a flat and the garden there has absolutely nothing but weeds. I shall have to get to grips with it.'

The man began telling Alice the names of his flowers and she took his hand as if she'd known him for ever. Sally thought how nice-looking he was, suntanned, dark brown eyes, thick brown hair with just a touch of grey at the temples. He looked so right in his khaki shorts, T-shirt and plimsolls. She thought he must be about forty, but his body was slender, like a younger man's, and his skin was smooth. He turned back to her and held out his hand to shake hers. 'Ralph Kent,' he said. 'I know the little one is Alice, but what about you and the pretty baby?'

'I'm Sally Symonds, and Emily would thank you for the compliment if she wasn't asleep.'

They continued to chat over the garden wall, and she half expected his wife to come charging out to see who he was talking to. 'I need to find someone to plumb in the washing-machine,' she said. 'You wouldn't know anyone, would you?'

'I could come and do that for you,' he said immediately. 'It's a simple job but a plumber will charge you far too much.'

She said she couldn't expect him to do that, but he insisted it was no trouble. 'I've taken a couple of weeks' holiday from work,' he said, 'but, apart from weeding today, I've got nothing else organized. I'd love to do it for you and see this lovely girl again.' He smiled down at Alice who was still holding his hand, and Sally's heart melted a little. 'Shall we pick some flowers for you to take home?' he said to Alice.

As Sally pushed the buggy with both children in it, the bunch of flowers resting on the folded hood, she felt a warm glow from meeting Ralph. He was so kind and easy to talk to. She had no doubt he had a wife: a treasure like him wouldn't be on his own.

Since leaving Bristol she'd never felt so alone, even with her children close at hand. She'd barely spoken to anyone, except about accommodation. To make a new friend, especially one with plumbing skills, was truly marvellous. He'd written her address on a scrap of paper and said he'd come after tea, as he was sure with two little ones she needed the washing-machine working promptly.

Another six weeks passed. It was September now and Sally dreaded winter arriving, with its dark evenings, but she tried hard not to think of such things. Angus's trial was coming up next month and she hoped that if his defence was good he might be let off with a fine, or a short prison sentence. Being unable to communicate with him was so painful. She wanted to tell him Emily was pulling herself up on furniture and using it to walk a little. She was trying to teach Alice to read. Already she could recognize about twenty words and she knew the sound of every letter in the alphabet. It didn't feel right to be bringing two children up alone: they needed a daddy to have a balanced life. But Angus had insisted they were to sever all connection and she had to abide by that.

The estate agent in Bristol rang and said they'd received an offer of £22,000 for the house. She accepted this on the understanding the sale would go through quickly. She had rates to pay each month and it was eating up the money Angus had hidden for her.

Happily, she had one good thing in her life apart from her children, and that was Ralph. He came to see her often at weekends – last Saturday he'd taken her and the girls on a boat to Dartmouth. She knew now that he wasn't married, and that he was an accountant at a firm of solicitors in Paignton. It seemed he had inherited his beautiful house when his mother had died and he'd lived there ever since. He didn't question her about why she was in Totnes or about her children's father, and she had no intention of revealing anything until after the trial. For the first time in her life she wanted to confide in someone, but Ralph was a gentle, conservative man and she didn't want to frighten him off just yet. She was sure that once the trial began journalists would find photographs of her and slap them on the front page of their paper. Then Ralph would head for the hills and she wouldn't blame him. She was just glad to have his friendship and support now when she most needed it.

The saddest thing was that she really liked Ralph and wanted so much to keep him in her life. He was such a gentleman that he hadn't even attempted to kiss her yet – in fact it crossed her mind that he might be gay – but her previous life was enough to make even the most non-judgemental person shudder.

It was doubtful that anyone from the past would recognize her now if they passed her in the street. She'd copied the style of many women in Totnes. Sometimes she wound her hair up in a scarf and wore long dresses bought from charity shops, a fringed suede waistcoat over the top, lots of beads, flip-flops on her feet. She felt removed from her past life.

One Saturday Ralph suggested they went to the beach at Paignton as the weather was very warm – an Indian summer. Sally put on a swimsuit under her dress – she still couldn't swim, but it would be good to paddle with Alice and let Emily splash about.

People had commented to her that Paignton was very down-market, but the sandy beach was glorious and she felt those who had made such remarks were a bit up themselves. Maybe it *was* brash but that was part of the fun of many seaside places. Her thoughts went back to Barney and the day he'd taken her to the beach in Hastings. It seemed a lifetime ago now.

Ralph was so good with the children, building a sandcastle, holding Emily in his arms and taking her right into the sea, then jumping in the waves so she squealed with delight. Sally found herself looking at his lean, brown body and imagined peeling off the blue checked swimming shorts that fitted him so perfectly.

They had a lovely day. They went on the pier and let Alice play on the slot machines. They ate fish and chips. The children rode on several little round-abouts, and Ralph took Alice on a swing-boat and a small rollercoaster. Sally noted how tightly he held Alice on the rollercoaster, and wondered how a man who had never been married or had a child knew what little children needed.

The children were almost asleep when he dropped

them home. 'Come to Sunday lunch at my house tomorrow,' he said, as he carried in the buggy and the changing bag. 'It's time I cooked for you.'

Emily was in Sally's arms, leaning sleepily on her shoulder, and Alice was clutching a pink and white stuffed cat Ralph had won for her. 'That would be lovely,' she said. 'But haven't you got a more suitable fancy-free lady that you should be cooking for?'

He smiled his lovely wide smile, which made his cheeks crinkle, moved closer and kissed her lips lightly. 'You and your girls are the only people I want to cook for. I'll collect you at eleven thirty. Bring a change of clothes for the girls as they're likely to get messy in the garden.'

She could still feel the imprint of his lips on hers and looked at him speculatively for a moment or two. 'Will I need a change of clothes too?' she asked.

'Possibly,' he said, and laughed, a twinkle in his eyes.

She knew then that he was what she'd always needed and wanted. She hoped she and the girls could give him what he needed too. This time she wasn't going to mess it up.

26

Alice

Alice sat at her office desk, her head in her hands. Having Flynn down for just one night had been wonderful but over too quickly. She'd found it almost impossible to leave him and go to work the next day. But she had to organize a big wedding.

Just a few weeks ago she'd been excited about the challenge of this wedding, yet once she was there, she was constantly losing the plot, thinking she'd done things she hadn't, or going to sort things she'd already tackled. She was too professional to ignore that she wasn't giving her all to the job, and she needed to find a way to put things right.

Flynn said it was the same for him: he was losing concentration when he was playing and forgetting to contact people when he'd promised he would. He thought that having a two-week holiday together would sort out some of it, and might make clear what the next step should be. Should she work in London to be with him or he come to Bristol?

Alice was fairly certain there weren't the opportunities in Bristol that a musician like him needed. She could work in London easily yet she was loath to leave her flat and Clifton. The other consideration was the long drive from London to get back to Totnes. Setting all of that aside, how could they even discuss moving closer together when they hadn't had enough time to get to know each other?

The other troubling thing, of course, was the need to speak to Ralph. She knew that she had to clear things up for her own sanity. Ralph was a well-grounded, sensible man. He'd decide whether Emily needed to know anything or just an edited version.

One decision she'd come to about her mother's past was that she didn't need to reveal anything other than the bigamous marriage. Once that bombshell was dropped, she could move on to ask Ralph about when Sally had first come to Totnes and how she had met him. Somewhere along the line she was going to tell him and Emily about Sally's childhood as it made her need for security understandable. It also explained her love of secrecy.

The rest – Russian blackmailers, a disorderly house, setting fire to a theatre, the lies, deception and promiscuity – were just tales that didn't need to be told. She'd say that Barney had loved Fleur and painted her portrait. Angus had loved her too but wasn't strong enough to refuse her demands.

Alice just hoped she could pull this off and not give her father more grief. She had booked Monday as holiday next week. She would drive down to Totnes on Sunday, after she'd checked that the guest and function rooms used for the wedding on Saturday had been properly cleared and cleaned. It was common for family members to think they could stay at the hotel all day, and all too often the staff had to make clear that their time was up at twelve.

At nearly four o'clock on a wet Sunday afternoon, Alice's hands felt cold and clammy with nerves as she approached the turn-off for Totnes. Getting the wedding guests out of the hotel today had been an exercise in how to have a steel hand in a velvet glove. They were all behaving as if they were in their own home, with waiters and other staff to do their bidding. The bride and groom had left at dawn for a flight from Bristol airport to Naples, so Alice didn't even have them to appeal to: they could have asked their relatives and friends to leave.

It was draining, almost like rounding up sheep — they would get to the door, then remember something they'd left in the room. The floor of the main function room where the dancing had been was daubed with chocolate from the chocolate fountain and studded with half-eaten strawberries. It appeared someone had had a fight with the wedding cake: torn-off bits had been flung everywhere. Alice had to ask the staff to put all the wedding presents into a cupboard as none of the guests looked capable of packing and taking them home safely. The bride and groom could collect them after their honeymoon.

As she left, she asked herself why she even wanted such a stressful job, with ridiculous hours.

Ralph rang as she was driving. 'Just checking how long you'll be as I've put a chicken in the oven.'

'An hour tops,' she said. 'I thought I'd never get away and can't wait to reach you and relax.'

She wished she had been brave enough to ask Ralph to tell Emily not to come but she could hardly say, 'I need to talk to you about a sensitive matter without her being there.' That would only make him nervous. Now she just had to hope Emily was happy to be in her own home with her husband and children on a wet Sunday afternoon.

As always it was a delight to see Ralph. His face radiated kindness and sympathy because she'd had a tiring day, then a long drive. The dinner he'd been cooking was almost ready, and he poured a large gin and tonic to revive her. Looking around, she could see he was keeping on top of everything, cushions plumped on the sofa, coffee-table dust- and cups-free, no piles of newspapers on the floor. The kitchen was the same: work surfaces clear and wiped down, the black and white tiled floor spotless. She had no doubt he'd put a hot-water bottle in her old bed, even if it was still summer.

The dinner was beautifully cooked. He'd made gorgeous gravy and his vegetables were never mushy. He'd even produced a rice pudding. As they ate, he talked about the back garden and his plan to make a bigger terrace. 'When the grass is too wet to walk on, the terrace is never big enough for us all to sit on,' he said. 'I fancy a little balustrade around it too and growing some climbers onto it.'

Once Alice had established he wasn't intending to do the digging and laying of paving himself, she said she thought it a great idea. But she knew it was time to get on with what she'd come for. To delay was maybe to be lulled into putting it off.

She had just asked him if he remembered the slim dark-haired man who was at the church after Sally's funeral when Emily flung herself through the front door. 'Saw your car parked up and wondered why you were having a sneaky visit with Dad but didn't tell me.'

Alice's heart sank. Emily's face wore the spiteful expression she'd adopted when she'd thought Alice was her dad's favourite.

'Don't be silly, Emily. Alice has just made a flying visit. Sit down and stop being childish,' Ralph said.

'Oh, God, you were talking about me!' Emily exclaimed. 'He's told you about Mike's and my problems. Dad, I specifically asked you not to.'

'You haven't been mentioned,' Alice retorted. She'd almost forgotten how prickly her sister could be.

'If you must know, Alice was just asking about the slim dark-haired man at your mother's funeral.'

'The one you had lunch with the following day!' Emily narrowed her eyes in suspicion. 'You were weird about him too. You said he was boring. I didn't believe you. So, who was he?'

Alice was completely thrown. Emily enraged her when she put on the jealous-little-sister act, and she knew she wouldn't go until she'd picked off this particular scab. Alice was sick and tired of all this being on her shoulders too, trying to protect her father and sister from hurt, and almost wishing she'd never embarked on this hunt for family secrets.

'If you must know his name was Angus Tweedy and he claimed to be our father,' she snapped at Emily.

The moment the words left her mouth she wished there was a way of retracting them. But that wasn't possible. 'I wanted to talk this over with Dad quietly and calmly,' Alice added. 'Now your childish behaviour has blown everything out of the water.'

Emily stepped forward and slapped Alice's face hard. 'How dare you speak to me like that, you bitch? What is this? Your way of crucifying Dad when he's just lost his wife?'

Alice's face stung. She rose to her feet to hit Emily

back, but Ralph moved between them. 'Sit down, both of you!' he roared, which was uncharacteristic for him. 'Emily, I cannot believe you would be so nasty. I think I know why your sister wanted to talk to me in private about this man, and her motive for that would be to protect you and me. So, another word from you and I'll ask you to leave.'

It was clear to Alice then that Ralph knew at least part of this story.

'I'm so sorry, Dad. Did you know this man had married Mum bigamously?'

'Yes, I did. And I brought you two up as my own because he went to prison.'

Alice felt a weight lifted off her shoulders, but she shot a furtive glance at Emily. Her mouth was hanging open in shock and she was running her fingers distractedly through her hair.

'How could you do this to me?' Emily burst out. 'Just like that you tell me you aren't my father, and my whole life has been built on deception.'

'Don't be so dramatic,' Ralph said sharply. 'Just shut up and listen. It never occurred to me that the man I saw in the churchyard was him. But then I'd never met him. I only ever saw his picture in the papers, and it was some thirty years ago.'

'Excuse me, Dad, I certainly don't wish to reproach you with anything, but if you knew about this, why didn't you tell us?' Alice asked.

Ralph shrugged. 'When was I supposed to tell you? When you were seven and five, like a little fairy story at bedtime? When you were teenagers and flipped out about the simplest thing, like a blouse not being ironed? Before your weddings? That would've been a good time to make you miserable, wouldn't it?'

Alice could see the truth in that, and she looked at Emily, who was now crying.

'By the time you were old enough to understand, I'd long since forgotten you weren't my blood. To me you were both my girls whom I loved, and he wasn't ever coming back to claim you. You can say that was wrong of Sally and me, if you like, but you tell me what good it would have done to reveal it. You were loved and happy. Would you have wanted it any different?'

'No, Dad. I wouldn't have wanted to change any-thing about our childhood,' Alice said. 'But it did knock me for six meeting that man.'

'Angus,' her father prompted. 'You can use his name. It doesn't upset me.'

'Okay, I met Angus, and it was like the bottom fell out of my world. I was also scared about his motive for telling me at such a time.'

'He's obviously a psycho,' Emily butted in.

'He's not. He's a good man, if rather weak,' Alice said firmly. 'Dad, when did Mum tell you about him?'

'The day after his trial started,' he said. 'She called

me to her place first thing in the morning. I was about to leave for work but she said she had something important to tell me. She had several newspapers and there he was on the front page of two. She pointed to him. "That's my children's father and he's why I ran away from Bristol."'

'So, you've always known? I've been sweating over this for weeks, trying to find out more about Mum, to understand.'

'It's not hard to understand, darling,' he said gently. 'She'd shut her childhood out of her mind because it was so awful. She had to fight for everything because she felt inferior, made a lot of bad choices, and eventually met Angus and fell in love. But because of her past she didn't believe he would stay with her out of love. As you say, he was weak to go along with the marriage but he didn't do it to gain anything, only to give Sally security. When she told me about it, although I was shocked, I could see why he went along with it. Your mum could be a real force when she wanted something.'

'When did you meet Mum and where?' Emily asked, her voice cracking with emotion.

'I was in the front garden weeding one day when your mother went past pushing a buggy with Emily in it. You, Alice, were walking along my wall and I got up and spoke to you. You were very sweet – you jumped down into my garden and admired the flowers. You were only three, Emily going on for one. Sally and I chatted. She told me she'd just moved into a flat in Alexandra Terrace. The upshot of that was I volunteered to plumb in her washing-machine and we became friends.'

'I bet she had you lined up as the next sucker when she saw this house,' Emily said.

Ralph raised his eyebrows. 'You know, you can be very nasty, Emily. There's no need for that. We became firm friends, and I used to take the three of you out to places. I'd missed out on getting married and having children of my own, but until I met you two I didn't even know I wanted them. One day on the beach in Paignton I suddenly realized I was in love with all three of you. That was September, and Angus's trial for bigamy was in October in Bristol. Your mother didn't go as his solicitor said he didn't want her to take the stand. She wrote a statement, which I might add I read. She admitted that it was she who had instigated the marriage. Poor Angus got seven years, but his wife who lived in Monmouth stood by him in court, when she made a somewhat passionate appeal to the judge for clemency, and throughout his prison sentence. He has a son, your half-brother.'

'I suppose we're to meet them and play happy families,' Emily said.

'Stop that, Em,' Alice said wearily. 'You loved Mum

and Dad. You had a happy childhood. I've got a report in my bag about what our grandparents put Mum through. Read that and then tell me you've had it hard.'

She pulled out the Children's Department report and slapped it down in front of Emily. 'She went to work at sixteen as a mother's help. It looks to me very likely that the man she worked for raped her, and she ran away. Someone called Petula, whom I've met, befriended her, and took her to a theatrical digs. Later she was to become an actress and called herself Fleur Faraday. I met a man called Barney Marsh who ran a theatre in Hastings, fell in love with her when she was in a play there. He is now a respected artist, and painted her from memory. He gave me the portrait, which is beautiful.'

Alice stopped. She knew she'd said enough. 'How much of that did you know?' she asked Ralph.

He shook his head. 'None of it, Alice. It drove me mad that she was unable to confide in me. We went to Bristol once after we were married and I asked her to take us to where she lived with Angus. She said she couldn't remember the way there, or the address. Not once did she mention acting. She did say she worked at promotions, but even then she didn't say who for, what the products were. Why was that, do you think?'

'Afraid one disclosure would lead to more, perhaps.

I sensed from what I found out that she was like a deer, always on the alert for danger and poised to run. She never really learned to trust, except perhaps you, Dad. She certainly didn't trust Em and me. Remember when we were teenagers and went out on a Saturday night? She'd ask where we'd been and when we told her she'd accuse us of lying.'

Emily laughed. She'd opened the report but hadn't begun to read it. 'Gosh, yes, I'd forgotten that. I thought she was bonkers.'

'I'm going to wash up and make some tea,' Alice said. 'You go into the sitting room,' she said to her father, 'and you, Emily, read that report.'

An hour later, as the three of them drank tea and had a slice of cake, Emily finally spoke. 'I'm sorry I was so nasty about everything. After reading about what happened to Mum I've got no business to complain or to judge her. And, Dad, you might not be our biological father, but you're the only dad I want or need.'

'You never did say when you got married,' Alice said, 'and why did we never see pictures of the wedding?'

He disappeared out of the room, leaving the two girls puzzled. 'Don't say he's got the secretive bug now,' Emily said. 'One parent with that is enough.'

He was gone about fifteen minutes and returned carrying an album. 'The reason Sally hid this was because you two were bridesmaids,' he said, with a smile, and opened the first page of the album to show them getting out of the limousine with their mother. She looked beautiful in a pale peach long lace dress and the girls were in the same colour with garlands of flowers in their hair. Alice looked about four, Emily about two.

As the girls sat on the sofa together, turning the pages, they saw the wedding had taken place at the church in Totnes where they had buried their mother, and what a handsome couple Ralph and Sally had made. But they didn't recognize any of the fifteen or so guests.

'Why is that, Dad? Who are these people?' Emily asked.

'Well, my dears, it was thirty years ago. Some have popped off, some were work colleagues. Neither of us had any relatives, and your mum never contacted people from before she'd come to Totnes.'

'It's a shame she didn't keep in touch with Petula,' Alice said. 'She's fun and was really sad she'd lost touch with Mum. Her husband is a farmer near Arundel and their house is gorgeous. She took me to the gallery to meet Barney Marsh, which was when he gave me the portrait of Mum.'

Suddenly Alice was glad she'd done so much investigating. Some of it might have been distressing, and a lot she would never reveal to either Emily or Ralph. But she knew her mum now, and that was what she'd set out to do.

'Alice, did I dream it, or did you tell me you've met a rather nice man?' Ralph asked.

'You didn't dream it, Dad. He's called Flynn and he's a musician. In fact, I met him through Petula – he taught her son to play the piano. I really like him, and he feels the same about me.'

Emily, all earlier antagonism forgotten, now wanted to know more and Alice showed her a couple of pictures on her phone. 'He's gorgeous,' Emily agreed. 'Lucky you.'

'So, are you going to tell me what's wrong with you and Mike?' Alice asked her.

'I'm just bored with him,' Emily admitted. 'That makes me sound very shallow and I probably am. He's got no get-up-and-go, never wants an adventurous holiday, or to meet new people. I wish I knew what to do to shake him up!'

Ralph began to laugh.

'What is it, Dad?' Emily asked.

'I just thought if your mum was here, she'd be able to tell you a hundred ways to shake a man up.'

'Dad,' Emily reproved him, 'that's not funny.'

'Maybe not, darling, but *she* was. She used to make me laugh every day with wild ideas and projects. Her unpredictability was a tonic. So, take a leaf out of her book. Give Mike something to think about. Just don't go down the bigamy route.'

Epilogue

'Marry me?' Flynn said, as he and Alice approached the checkout in Waitrose. She turned to him in shocked surprise. There were about seven people in the queue behind him and the three nearest were all grinning.

'Why here and now?' she whispered, afraid he was making a spectacle of them.

Flynn just smiled and didn't attempt to lower his voice. 'I'm working on the principle that you won't want me to embarrass you by sobbing if you say no, or even arguing with you about it.'

'You wouldn't sob – you aren't the type,' she retorted, all at once unconcerned about their audience. 'You could've asked me on a moonlit night in Grasmere, or even dropped an engagement ring into my orange juice at breakfast. But you choose here as I put toilet rolls, bleach and light-bulbs on the conveyor-belt? You call that romantic?'

She wanted to laugh, as the people behind them were. But she held it back even when a man called, 'You tell him, love!' She transferred the rest of the shopping onto the conveyor-belt, keeping a straight face. One of the things she loved most about Flynn was his unpredictability. She could never second-guess him. He had razor-sharp wit, a creative mind and a wonderful sense of the ridiculous, too.

'Come on, love, put us all out of our misery!' another man shouted. 'Are you going to marry him or not?'

She half turned to face them. 'I think I probably will,' she replied. 'At least he chose Waitrose. I'd definitely have refused if it was Lidl.'

People began clapping, not just in their queue but the next one along too, and the cashiers were joining in.

Flynn and Alice were still laughing as they came out into the car park with their trolley of shopping.

'So that's a yes, then?' Flynn said, as they got to her car.

'Indeed it is,' she said, wrapped her arms round him and kissed him.

They had just come back from five blissful days in the Lake District. They had intended to go to Italy, but there were no flights available that suited them, and when Flynn said he'd always wanted to go to the Lakes, Alice was happy to go along with it.

Flynn picked the hotel, a luxurious one in Grasmere, and the room he booked overlooked the lake. All they wanted was time alone together. They spoke about fell-walking and hiring a boat but soon found they were so charmed with the beauty of Grasmere that they spent more time in the hotel garden looking at the mountain peaks reflected in the calm, still water of the lake.

Wandering along to a restaurant, taking a few gentle walks, eating ice cream sitting on the grass bank by the lake, and considering what they'd eat that evening was quite enough activity for them. Many people had told them it always rained in the Lakes, but it didn't: it was sunny and warm. On their last day they summoned up the courage to swim in the lake, which was heart-stoppingly cold, but they tingled all over when they got out.

Alice was able to tell Flynn the whole story about her mother, and in telling it she found the tension she'd suffered ever since the day she'd had lunch with Angus just vanished. It occurred to her she had had a lot in common with her mother: she didn't normally confide family matters or how she felt about anything to friends. Stuart was the only person to whom she had revealed stuff.

Flynn was a good listener. He took it all in, and any questions he had were relevant to him understanding better. He made no judgements. But, then, he didn't appear to have any problems revealing his feelings, or talking about family issues.

In the past Alice had never been entirely sure about any man in her life. There had always been 'but's – he's

357

a bit mean, or a show-off, insincere or boring. Flynn was none of those. In fact, each hour she spent with him she felt herself falling further in love with him and discovering new things to like as they bubbled to the surface.

One evening he'd asked to play the hotel piano. She'd never heard him play and his music delighted her and all of the other guests. He didn't play classical music, but well-known popular songs, and to some he even sang the words – Alice hadn't known he could sing. When he played the introduction to the Beatles' 'Something', he turned to look at her and, knowing it was intended for her, she welled up with joy.

On their penultimate day as they lay on the grass by the lake, Flynn propped himself on one elbow, looking down at her. 'I don't want to go back. I wish we could stay like this for ever,' he said.

She smiled and reached up to caress his face. She felt the same. They'd been making love all night, and the days of utter idleness were the best she'd ever known. She was afraid that once they returned to their jobs and different cities, the wonder of what they were feeling here would vanish.

'What are we going to do?' she asked. 'I mean, we both know we can't stay here. But being apart will be horrible.'

'What about if you got a job doing what you do

now but perhaps in the Reading area?' he suggested. 'I could carry on at the Barbican and commute. It's a straightforward drive from Reading to Totnes. Or you could catch the train.'

Clearly he'd been mulling over this idea. 'Hmm, that's a possibility. There's some great hotels in that area, better than the ones I work for now. And Reading is only half an hour to Paddington.'

'If we sold our flats we'd probably have enough for a really nice house too,' he said, tickling her nose with a blade of grass.

'Stop that – you'll make me sneeze.' She slapped away his hand.

She found it odd that her flat, which she'd once loved so much, no longer mattered much to her. Or her job. Sharing a life with Flynn was the most important thing to her now.

'Then I'd better come down to Totnes soon and meet your dad and Emily,' he said. 'Do you think they'll approve of me?'

'What is there not to approve of?' She laughed. 'I hope Emily has made up with Mike. He's a nice guy, and a great dad. The day I told them about Mum, Emily said she was going to try to explain to Mike how annoying he is. I know I'm no marriage guidance counsellor but I did think steaming in to inform someone of how annoying they are is hardly the way forward.'

'She's probably just as annoying.' Flynn grinned. 'I think in a relationship there will always be little things that bug you, but I read somewhere you have to consider each one and decide if it's a deal-breaker.'

'So what do I do that could be a deal-breaker?'

'I don't know,' he said, leaping to his feet. Holding out a hand, he pulled her up. 'But let's get a boat round the lake so I can think about it.'

The feel of the wind in their hair on that boat ride was exhilarating. But slowing down to get close to the shore on the opposite side of the lake and seeing deer under the shelter of the trees was wonderful. They saw a couple of kingfishers perched on logs ready to dive and catch a fish. And overhead a peregrine falcon hovered.

Alice realized it was years since she'd noticed the beauty and complexity of nature. She'd been too busy arranging weddings to consider what they stood for. But Fate or Destiny had given her a second chance to embrace love in all its guises, be that music, art, nature or love of Flynn, her family and friends.

As they got into her car in the Waitrose car park, Alice turned the key in the ignition. 'Well, now you've proposed and I've accepted, I think you'd better tell me what would be the deal-breaker you mentioned in the Lakes.'

He put on a very serious face. 'Well, if you become

a bridezilla that might do it. A musician I know told me his fiancée drove him to distraction going on and on about their wedding. Every day she'd have some new problem – the napkins weren't the same pink as the tablecloths, one of the bridesmaids had had her hair cut when she wanted them all to have the same style. He said he wanted to run away.'

'Is that a veiled hint you don't want any fuss for our wedding?'

'As that's what you do for a job I'm sure you could make it completely seamless. But I'd rather have just family and close friends.'

'I'd rather run away to Gretna Green with you.' She giggled. 'It's obscene how much money people waste on weddings. I think they completely lose sight of the vows they're intending to make. So I'm with you in just family and close friends. As we've both been divorced it can't be in church anyway. Some of the nicest weddings I've arranged have just been an intimate family lunch in a beautifully decorated private room.'

He leaned over and kissed her lingeringly. 'I love you, Alice. Whatever you want is fine with me. Wherever you want to live, that's fine too. Just as long as you want me there.'

She held his face between her hands. 'That goes for me too. You know, I think my mother must be smiling down at me. If I hadn't tracked Pet down,

I wouldn't have met you. I know Mum would have loved you. And Ralph will too.'

'My mum and brother will love you!' He grinned down at her. 'Mum always said I should find a bossy woman or I'd drift aimlessly.'

'So I'm bossy?'

'A bit, but that's not a deal-breaker.'

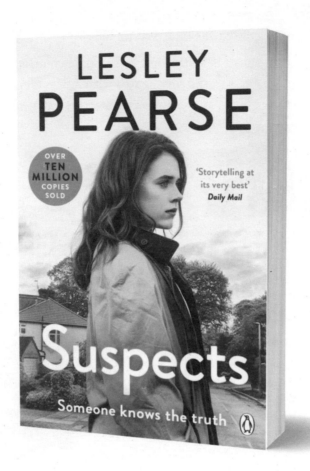

Suspects

When Nina and Conrad move into their first home
together, a young girl is found murdered nearby.
Soon, a spotlight is cast on all the neighbours,
each hiding their own dark and twisted secrets.

You'll Never See Me Again

When Betty escapes her marriage, she goes on the run, armed with a new identity. But she never imagined starting again would end in murder . . .

The House Across the Street

Katy must set out to uncover the truth about the mysterious house across the street. Even if that means risking her own life . . .

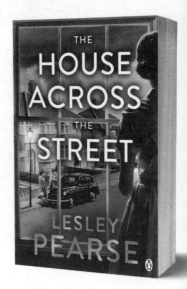

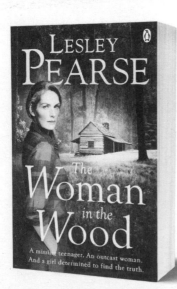

The Woman in the Wood

Fifteen-year-old twins Maisy and Duncan Mitcham have always had each other. Until one fateful day in the wood . . .

Dead to Me

Ruby and Verity become firm friends, despite coming from different worlds. However, fortunes are not set in stone and soon the girls find their situations reversed.

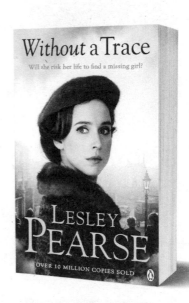

Without a Trace

On Coronation Day, 1953, Molly discovers that her friend is dead and her six-year-old daughter Petal has vanished. Molly is prepared to give up everything in finding Petal. But is she also risking her life?

Forgive Me

Eva's mother never told her the truth about her childhood. Now it is too late and she must retrace her mother's footsteps to look for answers. Will she ever discover the story of her birth?

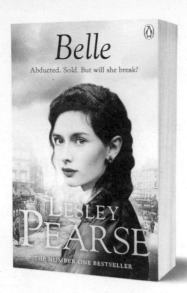

Belle

Belle book 1

London, 1910, and the beautiful and innocent Belle Reilly is cruelly snatched from her home and sold to a brothel in New Orleans where she begins her life as a courtesan. Can Belle ever find her way home?

The Promise

Belle book 2

When Belle's husband heads for the trenches of northern France, she volunteers as a Red Cross ambulance driver. There she is brought face to face with a man from her past who she'd never quite forgotten.

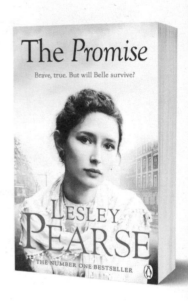

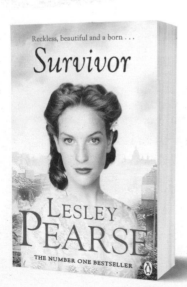

Survivor

Belle book 3

Eighteen-year-old Mari is defiant, selfish and has given up everything in favour of glamorous parties in the West End. But, without warning, the Blitz blows her new life apart. Can Mari learn from her mistakes before it's too late?

Stolen

A beautiful young woman is discovered half-drowned on a Sussex beach. Where has she come from? Why can't she remember who she is — or what happened?

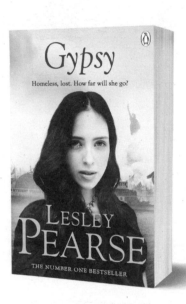

Gypsy

Liverpool, 1893, and after tragedy strikes the Bolton family, Beth and her brother Sam embark on a dangerous journey to find their fortune in America.

Faith

Scotland, 1995, and Laura Brannigan is in prison for a murder she claims she didn't commit.

Hope

Somerset, 1836, and baby Hope
is cast out from a world of privilege as proof of
her mother's adultery.

A Lesser Evil

Bristol, the 1960s, and young Fifi Brown
defies her parents to marry a man they
think is beneath her.

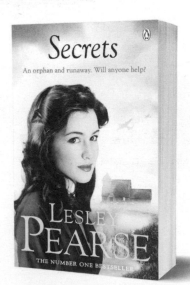

Secrets

Adele Talbot escapes a children's home to find
her grandmother — but soon her unhappy
mother is on her trail . . .

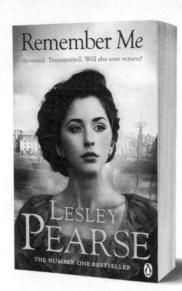

Remember Me

Mary Broad is transported to Australia as a convict and encounters both cruelty and passion. Can she make a life for herself so far from home?

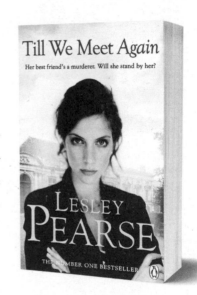

Till We Meet Again

Susan and Beth were childhood friends. Now Susan is accused of murder, and Beth finds she must defend her.

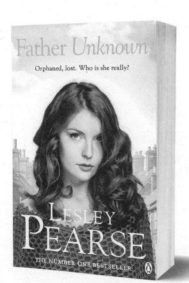

Father Unknown

Daisy Buchan is left a scrapbook with details about her real mother. But should she go and find her?

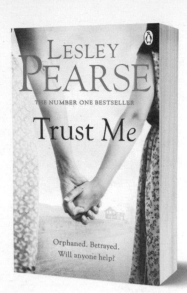

Trust Me

Dulcie Taylor and her sister are sent to an orphanage and then to Australia. Is their love strong enough to keep them together?

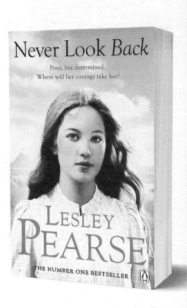

Never Look Back

An act of charity sends flower girl Matilda on a trip to the New World and a new life . . .

Charlie

Charlie helplessly watches her mother being senselessly attacked. What secrets have her parents kept from her?

Rosie

Rosie is a girl without a mother, with a past full of trouble. But could the man who ruined her family also save Rosie?

Camellia

Orphaned Camellia discovers that the past she has always been so sure of has been built on lies. Can she bear to uncover the truth about herself?

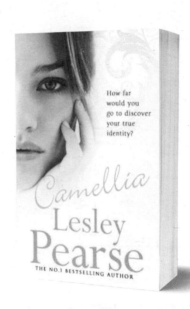

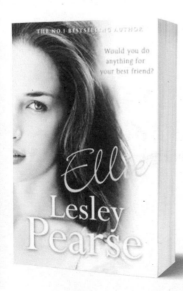

Ellie

Eastender Ellie and spoilt Bonny set off to make a living on the stage. Can their friendship survive sacrifice and ambition?

Charity

Charity Stratton's bleak life is changed for ever when her parents die in a fire. Alone and pregnant, she runs away to London . . .

Tara

Anne changes her name to Tara to forget her shocking past — but can she really become someone else?

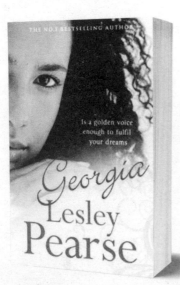

Georgia

Raped by her foster-father, fifteen-year-old Georgia runs away from home to the seedy back streets of Soho . . .